D J Edwards studied at Pembroke College, Oxford. He teaches English in a secondary school in Wandsworth.

Nuff Respect

D J Edwards

HEADLINE

First published in 1995
by HEADLINE BOOK PUBLISHING

First published in paperback in 1995
by HEADLINE BOOK PUBLISHING

10 9 8 7 6 5 4 3 2 1

ISBN 0 7472 4860 5

Typeset by CBS, Felixstowe, Suffolk

Printed and bound in Great Britain by
Cox & Wyman Ltd, Reading, Berks

HEADLINE BOOK PUBLISHING
A division of Hodder Headline PLC
338 Euston Road
London NW1 3BH

To Katy Staples

ACKNOWLEDGMENTS

I'd like to thank Nigel Pugh for his invaluable advice, also Helen Aitkins, Mike Cornick, Richard and Chris Easterbrook, Felicity Fox, Pauline Green, Shirley Hase, Nicola King, Helen Loughran, Jan McDonald, Winsome Moncrieffe, Charles Pinder and Julie Russell for their warm encouragement, and Angela Walters, Selwyn Marshall and Nigel Marshall for their lessons on Jamaican speech, and the sweetbread and flying fish.

AUTHOR'S NOTE

The story takes place in the autumn of 1989 and tries to capture the mood of that time. Readers who know South London will notice that I opened a branch of McDonald's in Brixton two years before the actual one, and I shifted the Southwark Institute of Adult Education to Stockwell.

1

The man called Roland

A lisping voice on the pirate station announced: 'Get fresh! Check out Fresh's Nightclub in Acre Lane, Brixton, for the best in soul, reggae, calypso, rare grooves and house. Tonight Ebony Enterprises, in association with the *Voice*, Britain's best black newspaper, present the seventh regional heat of Mr Superfresh, the ultimate contest for men. So, ladies, come and discover if your man is cool enough to face the heat.'

The bedroom floor was covered with soft snippings. Roland finished shaving Weston's neck. 'Mr Superfresh! Sound like a lavatory cleaner.'

'It give a positive image,' Weston replied. 'Ever heard of playing with words?'

'It still sound like a toilet.'

Weston studied his cut in a mirror, shook the towel into a cane waste-paper basket, and took a measure of TCB Dry Perm in one hand. 'It's a question of education. You need to be alerted to subtlety.'

Roland sat on Weston's bed and watched his younger brother's attempt to give his hair a slick-back sheen. 'You should have fixed the hair before the clothes. It's surely not cool to reach looking like a moulting rabbit.'

Weston bit on an Afro comb. 'Since when were you

the style expert, with your market anorak and Mr Plod boots? No, can I just say something? The hair is the finishing touch. It sways the judges.'

Roland stretched out. 'What I don't get is why these competitions are the business. People criticise women, so what are the brothers playing at?' He pulled an old teenage music annual from a neat pile of books beside the bed, and flicked through the once familiar pages. 'Hey! This was the time when Michael Jackson was black! Check the Afros!'

Weston screwed the lid back on the glass jar. 'Hair will always make a statement.'

'So what are you saying? Did Marcia put you up to this?'

'I consulted her. She encouraged me to enter.'

'I bet all the brothers say that. None will admit you crave attention for yourselves.'

'So what if I do? It's better than sitting night after night in your crusty flat. What's happened to you since Charmaine walk out? Nothing new. No clubs, no pubs, no blues. No grinding. No nothing.'

'Things take time.'

'But you're so visible. Everyone knows you. My colleagues tell me all the time, "I see your brother yesterday with his clipboard. He looks sad." Roland, you're becoming an oddity. People are talking.'

'Let them talk.'

'But you so serious and long-faced, you be joining Mother at church next.'

'About joining Mums at church! But at least she isn't posing.'

'No, but what's on her mind all the time? Death and worms and Judgement. You don't want to spend all your life with rotting carrots and cabbages. It's an embarrassment. You must plan.'

Roland slammed the annual shut. He had felt edgy all day. It had rained heavily for the first time in months, and there had been an argument with his supervisor over casual traders.

Weston was struggling with his tie. 'Help me with this.'

Roland drew himself up, and moved behind his brother. He pulled the silk bow tightly, then took a second glance at the mirror. When they had shared the bedroom, he remembered, the glass had featured Snoopy saying *'I hate Mondays'*. Surprisingly, Weston had not thrown the mirror out when he gained total domination, but he had obliterated the dog and message with masking tape and written out a motto which probably came from one of his business efficiency textbooks. *Short-term goals generate a sense of urgency*.

Roland mouthed the words. 'It's a pity you don't apply that,' he told Weston. 'You was supposed to be ready at seven.'

Weston went to the bathroom to trim his moustache in a better light, so Roland returned to the sitting room. Whenever he visited his mother's flat these days, he spent much of his time pacing like a caged animal. He always remembered the lectures his mother had given him and his brother. 'When I was your age, I had to carry bucket 'pon my head. We 'ave to feed chicken and cut sugar cane. We never used to gwon like you two.'

Mrs Stephens was snoozing in a red Dralon

3

armchair. At weekends she worked on the South Bank, slowly manoeuvring a giant polisher across the marble entrance halls of the headquarters of an international oil company. When the buses ran on time, she was at work by six in the morning.

Under a black and gold embroidered map of Jamaica the smooth-tongued host of a talent show pointed his finger from the 26-inch television. 'Folks, Opportunity is the name of the game. If it comes your way, don't knock it.'

Roland didn't think Opportunity would come by attending a male beauty contest with his brother. Off-screen it does not usually arrive heralded by lights or music. But after Weston's lecture, the phrase caught in Roland's consciousness like a burr. He knew it would run unwelcome through his mind all evening.

He had thought Opportunity was knocking when he moved in with Charmaine, but Weston soon discovered from his drinking mates that Charmaine was also being 'knocked off' by a heavyweight boxer from the Thomas A Becket pub on the Old Kent Road. That was why Roland had not knocked the living daylights out of the man.

He had also thought Opportunity was knocking when Lambeth Council appointed him as a market inspector – until he found that his days would be spent harmonising quarrels over 'knocked off' goods for sale. At first these disputes over videos and vegetables had been amusing, but he was growing weary of the desperation of sellers and customers obsessed with knock-down prices.

A blonde in a puffball dress butchered a number

4

from *Les Misérables* in a nasal tone. When she had finished the host asked: 'What do you hope for in life?' Roland kissed his teeth. They were about the only thing he did kiss these days.

Mrs Stephens heard nothing, not even the ballads, to which Weston sang along. There was a battle of sounds in the flat, and the soul music was winning. But Mrs Stephens was unconcerned. If Opportunity had wanted to knock for her, it would have had to raise an almighty alarm to rouse her. She had adopted the patterns of behaviour, particularly the sleeping habits, of the old, and though only forty-five, was usually in bed with her hot water bottle by half past nine, even in summer, her Bible open on the bedside table, the comforting words of which she mouthed noiselessly in the small hours when she woke.

A year or two ago she had resigned any hope of finding a man again, for life, for sex or love. She had not married the two men who had fathered her boys. Roland's father had stayed in Jamaica in 1966, when she came to England to live with her sister, and though she had adopted his surname and given it to her two sons, the family had lost touch with him. Weston's father Mr Langley, whom she met when she came to Stockwell, now spent the time between the mothers of his three children, among other women.

In the bedroom, Weston was brushing a pair of Oxford brogues. He continued sparring with Roland. 'You know, man, they didn't just dream up Superfresh. They did enough research to get that name. Branding, it's called. They even asked people in street markets.'

'If it's not a toilet cleaner it sound like some mashed-up yoghurt your dad might fetch from Sainsbury's.'

Weston spat at his shoes. 'The finale takes place up West. An event. The prize money is in thousands – a trip to Jamaica. Not just vouchers for hair products. *And* a trophy.'

'Oh uh.'

'It's an easy way of making money. You strut your stuff, flash your teeth, wiggle your butt, and you're rich.'

'If you're lucky.'

Roland regarded his brother's obsessive interest in this contest as a sign of the gulf which had developed between them since they had grown out of their teens. When Roland was a fifth-former, Weston had idolised and tried to emulate him. Instead of playing with other eleven-year-olds, Weston had won the notice of Roland's friends by his cheek and charm, and had joined in their football and basketball games. He had acted as a go-between in school love affairs. At the time Roland had found such devotion flattering and amusing, but recently it seemed precociousness was bearing strange fruit.

Weston's bedroom declared his new interests. Copies of *Ebony Man* and new black British style magazines were stacked in piles at measured intervals. Weights had been placed around the room like stepping stones. On a midi-system, compact discs of smooth-throated soul singers were arranged alphabetically: Freddie Jackson, Alexander O'Neill, Luther Vandross.

In his last years at school, Weston's friends had demanded: 'Are you a soul-head, or a rebel?' At that time at Stockwell Manor it was considered that if you were 'into' soul and not the deep pulse of reggae or the street sound of hip hop, you didn't know what time it was.

But Weston's musical interests reflected that he had recognised earlier than most what way England was moving, and he had applied to take a business course at Southwark College. His files of essays and lecture notes were still arranged on the bookshelves.

Roland mooched to the wardrobe and read another framed quotation: *Changing attitudes and work patterns requires time, determination and energy*. At present all he felt he had was time. So why was he wasting it with Weston? Perhaps it was the old teenage fear of being uninvited on a Saturday night and condemned to watch repeats of *Cagney and Lacey*.

When Weston considered himself ready, he glared at Roland's clothes. 'You might have made an effort, man. This is a class night. The posters say dress smart. You can't go in jeans – and that shirt look like it come years ago from some bargain stall.'

The polo shirt, it was true, had been one of a confiscated range shared among the inspectors. Roland had since renounced such share-outs, and ignored his workmates' taunts. If he was supposed to be upholding bye-laws, how could he play at the level of his opponents?

'I bet you even sew the little crocodile on yourself,' Weston jeered.

'No, Charmaine did.'

'There you are. Why she walk out on you? She want more than cheap fruit, trainers and shirts.'

Roland lifted one of Weston's weights. 'I don't need

clothes to show my worth,' he puffed. 'But don't panic. I've got my blazer and trousers in the car – Superfresh from the dry-cleaners. I'll fetch them.'

'Don't think we're using your car.'

'Do we need a car at all? Fresh's is half a mile down the road. We reach in ten minutes or we can bus it.'

'I left buses when I left school. Charlie's lent me his car.'

'It's just another Escort.'

'No, his is a metallic, ice-blue, sunroofed G-reg Cabriolet. Yours is a rusting P-reg held together by Blu-Tack.'

'We really need a sunroof this weather!'

'We need wheels.'

'Why?'

'Miracles can happen. You may score.'

'I can walk where I want.'

'We're not Boy Scouts. Anyway, I have to take other clothes. There are three changes.'

'What is this? Show Time at the Apollo?'

On the television, a Yorkshire vet was supervising a cow's difficult labour. It was almost Mrs Stephens' bedtime. Sunday was a heavy day. After cleaning, there was church at eleven, and again in the evening. It was the one day of the week when she too still took pride in her appearance.

Through her slumber, she sensed her sons were about to leave, so she roused herself to look them over. 'Sweet, eh? Where you a go? Bwoy, you a look stussed.' Roland had inherited his father's broad forehead and long loose limbs. He was also shy, but had a strength of character which surprised her.

Weston was stockier, more muscular, lighter-skinned and as aggressive as *his* father. In Mr Langley's time there had been many arguments and fights. At present he was suffering from a midlife crisis, and had taken up with an eighteen-year-old cashier from Sainsbury's. There had been a big row over this, and for the time being he was not around, though occasionally he left carrier bags of misshapen reduced goods on the doormat.

Such a withdrawal of erotic possibility had left Mrs Stephens with depression, which was not alleviated by readopting her Pentecostal faith. But she thanked God daily her sons were both in work. In their schooldays the image of them hanging around the liftshafts of the estate had haunted her, and fuelled her efforts to do well by them.

She stood up now to check Weston's jacket for fluff, but he dodged away. 'Why ya look so sweet, eh? You be careful.'

'Mother, I'm twenty.'

'Them club girls tink about one ting, you know. 'Member your Uncle Irwin and that woman from Grenada. In the end 'im died of a brain tumour.'

'Well, he didn't catch that from a woman, did he?' snapped Weston. He mouthed at Roland, 'Death and diseases.'

'The bwoy him rude and lack a fader,' sighed Mrs Stephens. 'What you two do to vex your mother. Watch what you get. Now, outta me sight.'

The thing to decide, Roland had already decided today in the early September rain, was what you really hoped for. A new job? A new car? A new girlfriend? A new hairstyle? He didn't think so. Unlike Weston, his happiness wouldn't be improved by shaving his head.

At school his contemplation had never been related to work, and at sixteen he had left with a dustheap of GCSEs which 'did not reflect his ability'. Nevertheless he had found a position in a bank. The glossy recruitment leaflets had made the job of clearing cheques and counting the payroll seem attractive. During the week Mrs Stephens had thrilled to see him going out of the flat wearing a suit, and to talk to the other dinner ladies about her son in a bank. But Roland had stayed clearing cheques for four years and had not been promoted. At twenty he left to work for the Council, where Opportunity knocked more equally.

He had said that by twenty-five he would be married, with a place to live, a job he enjoyed, a wife, a house and children. He liked the idea of the companionship and commitment which marriage offered, and it would have been a rare enough state in his family. When two years ago he had established himself in the flat with Charmaine and her two-year-old daughter, he had thought she was his special lady. As Weston shot the rapids of Brixton High Road in the borrowed car it struck Roland that all he had at twenty-five was Charmaine's rented flat – to which she might one day return and evict him.

Weston considered him an oddity because he had been on his own for a year now. Roland had heard on the grapevine that the women he had checked before Charmaine had all told their friends, 'He's a nice guy, but a dreamer.' The more he heard, the more determined he became not to change.

* * *

The bells of Lambeth Town Hall tolled nine. The television set had seemed to be speaking to him. If the bells had a message too, like – was it Dick Whittington? – their sound was muffled by the roar of the traffic, the speeding to pass through amber lights, and the revving of the engine to be first off at green at the traffic lights by St Matthew's Church. And that was just Weston in the Cabriolet.

'Is Marcia coming to see your triumph?' Roland asked.

'No.'

'Not supporting her man?'

'She doesn't need to be present physically. I know she's rooting for me.'

'Is Sherene coming?'

'Her is history. Off the scene.'

Roland smiled. Sherene had been Weston's girlfriend at college. As far as he could understand from the market gossip, Weston had switched to her sister Marcia three weeks ago when he had called at her granny's house in Tulse Hill, and Sherene had been working late at the office. Marcia had entertained Weston in Sherene's absence.

'She's just a hairdresser, yes?'

'It's an expanding market.'

'She should have shaved your head.'

'Too busy.'

'Hairdressing's a bit down-market after secretary, isn't it?'

'You're the one who's down the market. Marcia is developing a range of hair products for women of colour. She uses her initiative. Develops contacts. Makes the best of herself.'

11

Weston had grown up in a decade in which outward appearance was paramount. Style over content. Money over morality. He was still sensitive about revealing where he worked. He would never forget the bitter jibe of his schooldays: 'What do you say to a black man in England with a job?' 'Big Mac and fries, please.' For this reason he had never considered a Saturday job at the hamburger outlet. At that age, and as a counter assistant, it would have been too shaming. In his schooldays he had eventually found part-time work in Electric Avenue in a video shop, which had been a target for looters in the riots (or 'uprisings' as the dreads at school called them) in the early eighties.

He had thought long and hard about accepting his present job but he was a trainee manager and on his way to MANAGEMENT, and would not stay for ever with beef, buns, and gold stars.

The traffic lights checked Weston again beside the Town Hall. A dripping municipal noticeboard announced forthcoming events: a Youth Training Fair, the monthly meeting of the Fat Women's Support Group (this month: *Roly-Polys? The portrayal of fat women in light entertainment*), the 1989–90 session of evening classes, a sponsored bicycle ride for an Aids hospice, and a Job Club for Unwaged Claimants. Roland tried to note the details of the classes, but Weston sneered, and drew off just before the lights changed.

'What's the hurry?' Roland asked as Weston turned another sharp right into the 'sought-after' Georgian square and parked in front of a French restaurant ('one of those rare gems south of the river').

'I don't want to be standing still at twenty-five.'

'If you drive like this, you won't see twenty-five.'

'At least I'm living now.'

'That tells me where I stand.'

Though it had stopped raining two hours ago, as they walked back into Acre Lane, they were sheltered by Weston's golfing umbrella, which he had given Roland to hold.

A group of men and women was gathering outside Fresh's under similar umbrellas. The men wore butterfly collars and bow ties, the women tight-fitting skirts and high heels. It was a sartorial world apart from the hip-hop clothes of most of the black youth of London: padded jackets and enormous trainers with their complicated vocabulary of lace-tying. Weston greeted friends from school, college, clubs and shops, grabbing hands and slapping backs. They nodded to Roland. He wondered if Weston was right, if he made himself too much of an oddity, an outsider.

After five minutes of self-congratulation, Weston's friends moved away in a group. 'Laters.'

'Whappan?' asked Roland.

'They're off to eat.'

'McDonald's?'

'No. Owusu's.' This was an African restaurant which had recently opened in the High Road next to the tube station and Spud-U-Like.

'They'll miss the show.'

'No one will arrive till eleven. We're here for the rehearsal.'

Roland gave his brother a withering look.

A young woman wearing a black PVC mac and silver

shoes was leaning on a rail which would later separate drinkers and dancers. She tapped a clipboard with her gold Parker felt-tip and barked, 'You're late! Put your clothes in the wings and join the others on stage.'

Roland walked to the bar, bought a Red Stripe, then settled in a chair padded with green leather. Weston climbed the podium, and joined eleven other contestants on the stage.

The mac billowed into the middle of the dance floor. 'Gentlemen, brothers,' she shouted. 'Pay attention. You enter stage right, the side where Simeon is. Simeon, it's a shame about your leg. It's original, but plaster will hamper your style. You walk to the middle, and stand still. Are you listening, Albert?'

Albert was chewing.

'Then you walk to the front, pause again, walk to both sides, turn, walk upstage and exit left. Where Neville is at present. Simple, isn't it?'

In theory it was as undeviating a pattern as filing up for foot-washing in the church which Mrs Stephens attended. But the contestants were mostly confused as they attempted to realise the pattern. Some could perform the routine perfectly the first time, and others, like Weston, got the hang of it after watching others blunder. Simeon, with his walking stick, and one or two less encumbered others, seemed to have difficulty merely walking, let alone executing choreography.

The female employees of the club were scrutinising the men, and Roland, bored with the catwalk, looked them over. For a moment, he thought one of the bar staff was Charmaine, who still figured in his dreams. He had enjoyed looking at her, particularly when she was asleep and he could gaze at areas not usually praised in the soul or lovers' rock she had made him play: her ears, the back of her neck, her feet . . . or the fine soft down on her belly. He shivered. His mind was wandering in the subdued lighting. He downed his lager.

In the last run-through Weston grew more confident. His scowl turned to a smile, and after mock interviews, the rehearsal ended. He threw himself on a seat opposite Roland.

'Well, Mr Superfresh, how do you rate your chances?'

'No contest,' said Weston. 'Get me a drink.'

Roland bought him a juice. As he sat again, they were joined by a woman in a low-cut dress. Without asking, she took a sip of Weston's drink and repeated Roland's question.

Weston said nothing.

'Are you listening?' she asked fiercely, and took another sip.

Roland jumped in, 'You all right, Sherene? Long time, sister.'

'Am I your sister?' Sherene snapped. 'I don't think so. It's three weeks since I saw you. Not a long time. At your mother's. How is your sweet mother, Weston? Does she like her new daughter-in-law?'

Weston picked up his glass, and poured the remainder of the juice into the soil of a potted rubber plant.

'You know how mothers are,' said Roland.

'And brothers,' Sherene added savagely. 'Marcia told me to look out for you.'

Weston's eyes still avoided hers.

15

'We are sisters,' she continued. 'We do talk.'

'Where is Marcia?' asked Roland.

'Some beauty fair. In Nottingham, or some such nasty place. Ask your brother – he knows everything. It's a business opportunity.'

'If you've talked,' Weston began slowly, 'you know we regard this contest too as a business opportunity.'

'Your whole life's a damn dirty business.'

Roland coughed. 'Weston got the hang of the walk, didn't he?'

'He picks up things quickly. I'm sure Marcia's given him enough hints about the routine.'

'If you must know, we haven't discussed it.'

'I suppose that would be unprofessional.'

Roland was growing hot under his denim collar. 'Weston, you really styled that walk.'

'It's not the walk,' said Sherene. 'Any eight-year-old can walk.' She imitated a Cockney accent. 'It's the talk. The chat. The old verbal, know what I mean? What are you going to say, Weston? I hope you've improved your chat-up lines.'

'You should have watched *Blind Date*,' said Roland. 'Picked up some hints.'

'That's foolishness,' said Sherene. 'No, you're right, this is a business opportunity. Think back, Weston, to those marketing lectures we sat through when you couldn't keep your hands off me. All those notes in all those binders. Say something about business. Use those fine phrases you like copying out. Why should they be confined to your bedroom? Let everybody have the benefit. It'll show you're qualified, smart, educated. Women like that.' She began to move away. 'Thanks for the drink.'

'Even though she's saying it,' said Roland, 'it sound like good advice. But why is she saying it?'

'Family pride,' said Weston. 'She was my woman.'

Roland watched her totter to the other side of the dance floor. She was soon cuddling an overweight Bajan with gold chains whom he recognised as a supplier of sweet potatoes in the Granville Arcade. 'Her taste in men is improving.'

'I don't need her to style my words,' Weston said. 'I can speak for myself.'

Strictly speaking, this was not the first time Weston had been involved in a fashion show. In the fourth year at school, he had taken part in a show which had been organised, if that was the word, by the pupils themselves as part of an 'Enterprise Fortnight'. He learnt that the greatest reward does not always go to those who have worked the hardest. His group bought a job lot of Bob Marley T-shirts from a discount warehouse for 99p each, and made a profit through aggressive marketing techniques. Weston learnt that you can sometimes make money with little effort. Determination and strategy. Craft and guile. The two approaches often go together.

The teachers were furious. This was not the message they were trying to put over. The fashion show attracted criticism throughout the staffroom. 'It's selling them to the capitalist system.' 'It's encouraging them to preen and pout.' The teachers supervising the enterprise replied: 'It's their project. The students must have ownership of their idea.'

In the event the show had to be abandoned halfway through, as not enough teachers had been persuaded to give up an evening, and when Weston's friends and youths from other schools had tried to push in without a ticket, and a fight had taken place between staff and youth, the police had been called. The pupils involved in the show had also spent the ticket money they had collected on new outfits, before they had accounted for their takings.

At the time Mrs Stephens had demanded to know where Weston's new clothes had come from. ('Why you spend all this money and you know me no have a red cent to me name?') After hours of inquisition, she had removed the offending garments from his wardrobe, and taken them up to the school. The teachers had been embarrassed, as they were trying to forget the whole event, and they had not solved the problems of prematurely spent money and a disrupted evening. There had been an unsatisfactory scene between parent and Year Head.

Sounds were now being spun by two disc jockeys who ran a pirate station which operated intermittently from Roland's tower block. A pirate barber must have shaved their heads too, as the Aztec designs around their crowns showed more blood than skin. There was blood, too, spattered on their bandanas, and spouting from the lobes which held their earrings.

Insistent repeated phrases echoed round the walls: *'Fools in the house! Fools in the house!'* Roland wondered if they were sending a message to him and his brother. Weston looked preoccupied, so he moved across the still-vacant dance floor to the Gents. Beside the urinals was an enormous condom machine. For a moment, he hesitated. Then he slotted in some coins, and pulled out a drawer. Weston had told him that men were expected to carry them these days. It was a year now. This was a fact he would keep hidden from anyone who might be interested.

At half past midnight the organiser's mac was removed to reveal a silver dress. 'Welcome, brothers and sisters. The heat is on tonight. The men we have for you are hot, hot, hot. Later they may be persuaded to remove their clothes. Yes, I'm talking to you sisters out there and you brothers backstage. It's a night when the bulge in your pants can be matched by a bulge in your wallet. And this is serious money, brothers and sisters. The winners tonight will represent South London – the Brixton brothers, the Peckham posse, the Stockwell skankers –'

'The wankers of Wandsworth,' interrupted a drunk from the back, who was swiftly ejected.

'– in the national championship at the Hammersmith Palais on November sixth, when the whole country will see what it is to be young, gifted and black.'

'She just about qualifies for the last,' said Sherene, who had pushed her way through the crowd to stand next to Roland again.

The contestants first appeared in 'street wear'. From the style, it seemed the street was nearer Tunbridge Wells than Railton Road: wool jackets, corduroy trousers, Argyll socks, waistcoats and brogue shoes. Under the green spotlight some contestants had forgotten their hastily rehearsed steps, and to the compère's annoyance, ambled as the fancy took them. Others seduced the audience by running their tongues around their lips or rubbing their hands up their trousers. Weston scored approval by removing his jacket, flinging it carelessly over his shoulder and then swanking up the ten feet of extending red-carpet catwalk.

'He used to behave like that in school,' said Roland to Sherene. 'Never would wear his blazer.'

'He likes taking his clothes off,' said Sherene, 'but it's not worth the wait.'

'Weston Stephens,' said the compère. 'A trainee manager. He's twenty, and born under the sign of Taurus. He's quite a bull.'

The first section was followed by a coolly received fashion show by design students at Brixton College. Accompanied by drums and imitation bird noises, they displayed garments inspired by Africa. 'They don't come over,' said Roland.

'I've seen better on the mammas in your market,' said Sherene.

The evening dress section took the dream world into higher realms of fantasy. There are men in England who wear evening dress on a weekly basis, who frequent the opera, hunt balls, Henley, Glyndebourne . . . but few of them are black.

Neville was the first to be interviewed. In butterfly collar and bow tie, he said he would 'win or beat everybody up'. Colin, in a white suit, said his idea of a good night out was 'himself and three beautiful women'. Simeon, entering out of sequence with a gold-topped walking stick, said merely, 'I love you all.' Owen, whose surname was Licorish, said, 'I'm sweeter than any candy you could suck,' and added, 'I'm looking forward to hot and steamy nights on my bedspread.' This drew appreciative screams.

As Weston appeared, his friends and acquaintances cheered. 'His chest is forty inches,' said the compère, 'his waist is thirty-two, and his eyes dark brown. So tell us about yourself.'

'A cheat and a liar,' Sherene shouted excitedly.

'I'm into marketing,' Weston began. 'I'm here to create an image.'

'That's right,' Sherene screamed.

'Are you a man who's hard to please?' asked the compère, ignoring the heckling.

'No, I become hard to please my women.' Since this drew the loudest screams so far, Roland relaxed. But Weston continued, 'I want to achieve through hard work. I push myself onwards all the time.'

The Bajan sweet potato seller asked Sherene, 'What the bwoy say?'

Roland prayed Weston would not develop this vein.

'I evaluate emotional returns,' Weston declared, 'from my women. I have market penetration plans.'

'I put a set of licks in your clart!' yelled another drunk.

'Poser!' another man shouted.

'Batty man!'

'Boffin!'

'Chief!'

'Buppy!'

'Duppy!' yelled Sherene.

To regain the sudden burst bubble of popularity, Weston began to gabble from his Snoopy mirror. 'With determination and strategy, I can give my women time.'

'Get off!'

Some had been charmed by Weston's suddenly revealed vulnerability, but his words had lost him the popular vote. To have the gift of the gab as well as being good looking is excessive.

'Weston Stephens, ladies and gentlemen.'

As he left the stage to a few slow handclaps, Sherene yelled, 'Yes!'

Roland gave her a withering look.

She announced triumphantly, 'Strategy and determination,' and flounced back to the Bajan.

After an unfunny turn by a woman comedian the beachwear section provoked the loudest screams. This fantasy was the closest the evening came to the Caribbean. Realising he would soon have to face a crestfallen brother, Roland tried to blot that out by thinking of beaches he had visited. He could not remember going to a beach when he went to Jamaica for his grandmother's funeral. It would not have been seemly. Last week, though, he had tried to drive down to Brighton after work just to look at the sea, but the car overheated on the Purley bypass.

'Now guys,' said the compère, reappearing, 'here's the chance to prove that the only weights you lift are not just the shopping bags from Sainsbury's. Remember, sisters, this is a contest of personality. Bodies have nothing to do with it. It's how you put yourself across. And I know who I'd like to put myself across!'

There were deafening screams as Neville the wedge-top appeared in high-cut swimming trunks and flexed his muscles. Roland selected those who should never have entered: Colin, who had a serious hairdressing disaster – a curly wetlook perm which was melting under the spotlights; Owen, with a pot belly that during previous sections must have been held in by heroic breathing or a good corset; and Simeon, who appeared now with plastered leg, gold teeth, a gold walking-stick, and tigerskin swimming trunks.

Surprisingly, there were a few resurrected screams for Weston. Roland found it strange to see that the brother he had fathered and fetched from infants' school (an excuse to avoid detentions) could now be considered a sex symbol by anybody. He also found it hard to see why some men and women who had cheered Weston earlier were now booing, and vice versa. However, it remained clear that most of the audience considered him a show-off. Their favourite was Albert, a judo instructor with dreadlocks and a precarious jockstrap.

After a pause, and a fanfare on the sound system, the judges delivered their verdict. Weston was one of the 'magnificent seven' who hadn't made it. He was called back on to the stage and into the spotlight for a consoling round of applause.

Roland looked at his brother. His face was immobile, and he kept his dignity. Then he noticed that Sherene and the Bajan were beside him again.

'All those words. You knew that would set people against him.'

'He condemned himself.'

'Sweet, sweet,' echoed the Bajan.

Roland felt exhausted, drained. 'It was a dirty trick.' It was now half-past two on Sunday morning. He had been up since seven a.m. on Saturday. He looked at the dancers, now filling the floor under the mirror ball and the whirring fans, as the songs, in softer mood, spoke of the fulfilment of love. Fat chance, tonight. Yawns are not the language of passion.

Why had his discontent come to a head in this nightclub, of all places? Because he had been affected by Weston's urgency and ambition? Because he still felt a brotherly protection towards Weston, and was bitter because he no longer wanted his care? Because he felt old, as the ages of the heat winners were announced – eighteen, twenty, twenty, twenty-one, and twenty-two? Because he felt sickened by the pursuit of glamour? Because he was smitten by unrequited and undirected lust? Because the nightclub shouted that life should not be all hard work, that he should not be on his own, and that the pursuit of happiness is allowed?

Weston was beside him now with his bags. 'Too bad,' Roland said. 'You did your best.'

'Don't patronise.'

'We should have realised she was up to no good.'

'Sherene had nothing to do with it,' Weston replied impatiently. 'Brixton's a backwater. It can't recognise class.'

'At least you tried.'

'I should have entered up West. I said that all along.'

Roland yawned.

'I've made contacts. I'm going to develop a business plan for those African fashions. Somebody needs to focus their image.'

Roland could remember a time when Weston would have beaten up anyone who called him an African.

These days he was irrepressible. 'The Council has a business advice department,' he said wearily. 'They could help.'

Weston ignored him. Why, Roland thought, did he bother?

He couldn't stop yawning. Some day he must develop his own plan and focus his image, but right now he needed to go to bed. 'Come on, I'm going to kiss the pillow.'

'No, man, the dance floor.'

'No way. See you around. I'm dussin'.'

2

Lorna's revelation

Miss Robinson was envious of Lorna's bronzed oval face. She consulted the file. Twenty-seven, it said. She would have placed Lorna younger. The eyes – green, sparkling, alert – contradicted her rigid stance. With her tan, Miss Robinson thought, Lorna should highlight those eyes with the shadow now on sale at larger branches.

'How long have you been with us now?'

'About five minutes.'

'Don't be clever. I think you know what I mean. Your time at Marks?'

Lorna could see her neatly completed application form, and the self-assessment sheets she had ticked a month ago. She was being asked questions when the answers were already known, but she knew why. It was a ritual to be performed with forced enthusiasm on each side.

Once a year employees at all Marks & Spencer stores are summoned by a Personnel Officer. What has been pleasing is praised – the ability, as the staff manual details, *to work effectively within an established discipline*. What has not been so pleasing – dallying in the toilets after break, too much chat with colleagues at checkouts – is also discussed, over

27

a cup of coffee and a digestive biscuit.

But this informal teatime routine does not mask discipline. *Too little resilience under pressure*, the manual warns, *is not acceptable*. Neither is *straining against prescribed behaviour*. It detracts, Miss Robinson reminds employees, from career advancement.

For the interviews at the Brixton office, Miss Robinson had chosen a dark suit and blouse with complicated ribbons. Lorna thought it looked like a fussily tied Christmas present. She could sense that Miss Robinson was feeling fussily tied, as she herself had all day.

'Lorna, you've scored yourself six out of ten for job satisfaction. Have you enjoyed your first year here?'

'Most of the time.'

Brixton is not Miss Robinson's favourite store: it seems content in its status as a food outlet, and the staff lack dreams of career advancement. Apart from supervisors like Lorna they are mostly part-timers: mothers and grandmothers whose incentives are the staff discount and free hairdressing facilities.

'We must agree on a score here. What haven't you enjoyed in your work?'

'The routine. The sameness. I feel part of a machine.'

Irritated by Lorna's truthfulness, Miss Robinson glanced through the window at the traffic in the High Street, slowed by the drizzling rain. Pedestrians were ignoring the red lights at the crossings. Dodging in and out of the speeding cars, they worked effectively against established discipline.

Lorna saw Miss Robinson scowl. As the day had worn on, her stomach had felt increasingly tighter. That evening she had another self-appointed interview to which she had yet to summon her parents. She hoped to show resilience under pressure, and to work against their established discipline.

The digestive biscuit lay untouched on a plate decorated with fieldmice – a tableware range which had been reduced in price soon after its introduction in selected branches, and then discontinued, and distributed for staff use.

'You've had a chequered career, haven't you, Lorna?'

'You could say that.'

Lorna had sensed Miss Robinson was stalling. She had to give her the standard twenty minutes. 'I wouldn't call it a career. I always wanted to work in a store, but I started a youth programme in hairdressing. Then, when I found I was allergic to the chemicals, I worked for a while in a typing pool.'

'And you didn't leave for promotion?'

'I got restless.'

Though restlessness is a common enough condition among young women in London, where illusory offers of alternative jobs beckon through the doors of employment agencies, or from the pages of free magazines distributed at stations, it does not mix easily with clearly thought out career aims.

'You went to Selfridges? Which department?'

'I started in cosmetics, but got moved.' Out of her teens, Lorna had put on weight. She was soon considered no longer svelte enough to promote Nina Ricci or Estée Lauder under the harsh revealing lights of a prominent selling position. 'I did stints in the Food Hall, Carpets, Haberdashery, Stationery, and Leather Goods.'

'It all seems unfocused.' Some stores, reflected Miss

Robinson, had a cavalier approach to career development and to using the people resource cost-effectively. 'And then you came to Marks, and took a drop in salary. Why was that?'

'Brixton's closer to home.'

'You're still living at home?'

Twenty-seven, and still at home. It was a raw nerve, and growing rawer. Lorna asserted herself. 'Isn't this getting off the point?'

'Lorna, whatever you may think, we do not treat people as machines.' Miss Robinson consulted her file again. 'You started with us as a sales assistant, but we soon made you a supervisor.' She continued mechanically, 'You have commercial awareness. We were pleased with your suggestion about the re-siting of the sandwich bar. You're good with people. You mostly treat staff and customers with respect. But you could go further.'

'What do you mean?'

'I can't recommend you for further promotion with so little on paper. CSE Grade 3 in Needlework isn't much use to anyone.'

'It is if you want to run up a pair of curtains.'

'I know you don't talk to customers like that.'

'I'm not that stupid.'

'I know you're not. But you're not making the most of yourself.'

For the first time Lorna looked at Miss Robinson with genuine interest.

'Try to improve your qualifications,' the Personnel Officer urged. 'English would be the most useful.'

'I was good at English at school, but I missed the exam.'

'Why not try an evening class?'

It sounded like the advice for finding a gentleman companion offered in her mother's magazines – what Mrs Duggan called her 'weekly books'.

In the years before the frozen chickens and cook-chill meals had ousted the skirts and jumpers, when Lorna was seven, as a treat she had been taken to the Brixton Marks by her grandmother. Lorna had stared at the new pennies in their change. Granny had said the store had a direct delivery every day from the Royal Mint.

Lorna had shown commercial awareness early, and shops had become her favourite game. Two years older than her sister Diane, she had enjoyed bossing her from the counter of an old cardboard box which had packaged the family's first freezer. Those golden pennies Granny had given them to play with seemed like those in the pot at the end of the rainbow in the books which she sought comfort in when she tired of Diane's whining protests, and declared it was early closing.

Lying in the bedroom in the Victorian terrace which the Luftwaffe had missed, and which the council had always been on the verge of pulling down or renovating, Lorna had dreamed that one day she would work in a shop. First it had been Woolworths, because of the toys, then any big store in Oxford Street. The West End is only a bus ride from Camberwell, and from her early teens until she was able to lie herself into a Saturday job, she had spent the last day of the week walking up and down that littered, crowded, magnetic street.

She had relished it all: finding out what was new, catching glimpses of pop stars in HMV, even the men flogging fake Gucci jewellery from suitcases on the pavement, and the squatter shops with their cheap scarves, T-shirts and Marilyn Monroe posters. There was always a sense of possibility. After all, at the outbreak of the war her granny had seen an African prince there – Prince Monolulu, displaying a gas mask under his tribal feathers. She had often told as well of the time when Selfridges had a roof garden and tea was served on lawns in the sky. It sounded more elegant than a burger in McDonald's.

The street whispered, *spend, spend, spend.* Lorna knew from the age of seven that although you couldn't take it with you, money was very important. Mr Duggan had worked for the Post Office since leaving the Navy, and an early start each day had given him time to earn on the side decorating or re-wiring when the neighbours started buying their houses and calling them 'properties'.

Mrs Duggan worked as a cleaner at the depot of Southwark Refuse Collectors and through example and anecdote had taught Lorna that wealth can come from the unlikeliest sources. The cleaners, like the dustmen, searched through rubbish for treasures, and her brother had connections with the Borough Road antique market, where before dawn on Fridays torches shine on valuable or not-so-valuable goods wrapped in newspaper.

Between them, her parents had saved enough to afford first the caravan at Dungeness, then the bigger-berthed model at Lydd-on-Sea, and they were now buying a bungalow at the same place. They were looking forward to being on holiday permanently.

Lorna had considered what she was to tell her parents during her Club 18-30 holiday in Benidorm. In mid-August, with her gin and tonics and Piña Coladas, on the balcony and by the poolside, she had plumbed the depths of her anxieties. What would happen to her at thirty if she still had the unfulfilled dreams and desires of an eighteen-year-old?

This summer she had already felt patronised by the girls from Marks who had gone with her: Louise, who was twenty-one, with two children whom her mother had looked after for the fortnight since Kevin, their father, claimed he would be spending all the daylight hours on a building site at Canary Wharf; and Tracey, who was twenty-two and awaiting her second divorce. Louise had told her that children leave you knackered, and Tracey that all men are worthless: 'All of them, Lorn. You're better off without them.' Lorna wished she had enough experience to agree.

The three women had spent nights in the bedrooms of the male holidaymakers, but they were mostly loutish lads who after too many bottles of San Miguel were too drunk to perform any acts more erotic than wetting their boxer shorts or knocking themselves out against bedroom doors as they tried to pull condoms on wilting erections. Despite their worst intentions, Lorna and her friends were too reserved or too old to attract the more libidinous Spanish waiters.

For most of the time the three women had discussed their lifestyles, as *Cosmopolitan* had taught them their situations must be called. They gave each other support and for one shining fortnight stood apart from their lives. Under the Spanish heat they had resolved they could bear things which in England had seemed unbearable, or that they could at least act to change them.

Lorna had a fear of wasting her life which she could not express to the others. One of her problems, she decided, was that she was not yet saddled with husband or children or even boyfriend, only her parents. In theory she had an infinity of choices. But what choices?

As for men, she sometimes felt that nothing could equal her fantasies. As she moved around the store, directing which food had passed its sell-by date, she looked at the men shopping for food, or imagined herself in tender situations with the delivery men, and the Saturday boys stacking the shelves.

Waking from her reverie, she was called to mitigate a dispute between two customers over the last free-range chicken in the chilled cabinets.

On the 45 bus back to Camberwell Green, Lorna pulled a copy of *Cosmopolitan* from her tapestry bag. *'Is love woman's whole existence?'* asked a feature writer. Lorna knew it was not, but had always craved that it should be.

She turned the pages, and began reading an article about how unlikely it is that single women in their thirties will ever get married. She thought of her parents. Fred and Rose Duggan had been an anomaly in their families. They had not married until January 1963 when Fred was thirty-five and Rose thirty-three. 'At least you was legitimate when you was born,' Lorna's granny, Rose's mum, had said. Being born on the right side of the blankets had been very important to Granny. She had been scathing about the unmarried state of the 'coloured' mothers who were moving into their street. In her last years, she had spent much of her time muttering about how 'they' had 'changed' the neighbourhood.

When she arrived home that night her mother was watching *Blind Date* in the front room. Three cocky young men were delivering chat-up lines. Not moving her eyes from the screen as Lorna came in, Rose asked, 'Did you fetch any of that posh bread, Lorna?'

'They only had the ones with sesame seeds.'

Her father was upstairs in the bath listening to a phone-in about air traffic control strikes. Above the inarticulate comments of Brian from Bromley, he yelled downstairs: 'Did you get a spotted dick?'

'No, I didn't,' cried Lorna, removing her mac.

On his one visit to the store, Fred had been amused to see that suet and currant puddings were now packaged and sold individually. He had never forgotten it.

Contented now that his daughter was home, he sank back into the bath and started singing verses from some half-remembered hymn. He had fitted the bathroom when he was forty, and could never regard a long soak in a centrally heated room as anything but a luxury.

Her mother tittered at the crude responses of the television screen. She did not laugh, however, at the exchange between Lorna and her father. Their shared vulgarity was a bond from which she felt excluded.

When her father banged on the ceiling, Lorna went

upstairs and began rubbing Lifebuoy across the broad
frame of his back. At five foot four and fourteen stone,
he was overweight. Since the heart attacks, the Post
Office had put him on light supervisory duties. 'Like
licking stamps,' Lorna's brother-in-law Barry had
jested. Lorna had tried to smile, but her father's
precarious health worried her. He was due for
retirement in a few months. How would he take her
news?

At half-past seven they sat down to tea beside the 24-
inch television.
    'If opportunity comes your way . . .'
    'I'd knock his stupid block off,' said Fred. 'Turn
that rubbish off, Lorna.'
    'That girl I like may be on,' said Rose. 'She might
sing that song.'
    Fred shook salad cream over his prawns, lettuce,
cucumber and tomatoes, and filling his mouth, asked
Lorna, 'Was you going out?'
    'Baby-sitting for Diane.'
    Fred thought that with two kiddies Diane should
stop at home more. Rose agreed. After all, they had
two videos now. 'Where they going?'
    'Some pub up the Old Kent Road. Barry has to fix
some deal.'
    'They can go pubbing but they can't be bothered to
come round here,' moaned Rose. It rankled. Diane
and Barry lived in a flat in a privatised, refurbished
council estate near the Surrey Docks. As Barry had
been a council tenant, they had been given a cheap
deal. Rose found it hard to accept that the en-suite
bathroom, the fully fitted kitchen, the ceramic hobs,

the underground parking and the river views had all come so effortlessly.

'How are they expecting you to get there?'

'Barry's picking me up. About nine.'

'You watch his driving,' said her mother.

'They rely on your good will,' said her father. 'It's too bloody convenient. How much are they paying you?'

'I don't do it for money. I like to see Jason and Natasha.'

'Then you're bloody daft. You let people take advantage.'

'So do you, Fred,' said Rose. 'You should be out yourself, Lorn. Dancing.' She spoke as if London was still graced with glittering ballrooms.

'I've gone off discos since Benidorm.'

'Well – a show, then. Or a walk in the park. These light evenings won't last. Make the most of them.'

Lorna wondered when her mother had last gone for an evening walk in the park. As she did not want to buy crack or be knocked over by skate-boarders, it seemed a daft suggestion.

'She can't go out if she's bloody stuck in her sister's place all the time, can she?' grumbled her father.

Lorna changed to a subject nearer her agenda. 'You think I should go out more?'

'Yes, you work hard enough,' said Fred.

'So what about when you move?'

'What do you mean?'

Lorna repeated herself. 'What about when you move to Lydd?'

'There's loads of places to go out. The drinking club. Dymchurch, Rye – you know. You don't need me to tell you.'

'No, you don't need to tell me.'

'You do like it there, don't you?' her father asked.

Lydd-on-Sea is locked in a fifties time-warp, a preserved cover from *The People's Friend*, but Lorna did like it: the openness of the sky above the Channel, the shingle and pebble beaches, the stretches of sand. 'Yes, I like it.'

'What's the problem, then?' asked her father.

'We don't even know if we've got the bungalow yet,' said Rose.

'It's empty. You have the money. There should be no problems.'

'I don't know if I'll be able to leave this house,' said Rose.

'Make up your bloody mind,' said Fred.

'I've made up my mind, Dad,' said Lorna, breathing deeply.

'Have some prawns,' said Rose. 'You know, I've come to the conclusion that Marks' prawns aren't as good as Tubby Isaac's.'

'You have some more, Mum,' said Fred.

'I've come to a conclusion, too,' said Lorna. 'I think I'll stay here.'

'Yes,' said Fred. 'Phone up and tell Diane you're not well. It's a nasty evening.'

'I don't think you've recovered from that holiday yet,' said Rose.

'It would be best to stop in,' said Fred.

'I'm not talking about tonight.'

'You're not doing it again tomorrow, are you?' asked Fred.

'When you move to Lydd,' said Lorna slowly, 'I'm going to stay in London.'

'Well, you might not have worked out your notice. You can move down when we've got things sorted out. Diane can come and stay here for a change.'

'She'll bring the kids,' said her mother.

'We'll need someone to see things are tied up this end,' said Fred.

'I'm going to stay.'

'Yes, you said.'

'I'm not going to come to live at Lydd. I don't want to live at Lydd.'

'Well, where else shall we go?' asked her father, puzzled.

'You've always liked Lydd,' said Rose.

Lorna SPELT IT OUT. 'When you move to Lydd, I'm going to stay up here in London, live and work up here. Not for just a week or two. I'm not giving up my job here.'

'You don't like your job!'

'It's not just the job. I want to live up here.' Her mouth was dry. 'More things are possible. There's more going on.'

'There are things going on in Lydd,' said Fred.

'I'm staying up here.'

'You're not moving in with your sister?' asked Rose suspiciously. 'I bet Diane's put you up to this. She's got that spare bedroom. I bet this is her idea. Very useful for them, having you there all the time.'

'I'm not moving in with Diane.'

'You can't stay here,' said Fred. 'The council won't let you. We told them you was coming.' He was beginning to see that Lorna was serious. 'So what will you do?'

'The council might have to house me.'

'You're not moving into some flat on your own,' Fred continued. 'You're too old. Why do you want to do this now? Why didn't you say before?'

'I never wanted to before. I've always loved . . . It's been . . .'

'So what's happened?' asked her mother. 'It's not some bloke, is it? I bet it's some bloke.'

'Is it some bloke, love?' asked her father.

'You're not in trouble, are you?' snapped her mother.

'Of course not.'

'That bloke from Selfridges hasn't turned up again, has he?' asked her mother.

Lorna was aghast. 'Martin? I haven't seen him for years.'

'You can't live here on your own.' Fred returned to his earlier protest. 'The council won't let you.'

'It's what the coloureds do,' sniffed Rose. 'Pass the rentbook from one to another.'

'I don't know what I'll do.'

'Well, you want to bloody think,' Fred shouted. His Saturday evening routine had been disturbed.

'I *have* thought!' Lorna shouted back.

'Don't go raising your voice,' yelled Rose. 'It's those two you went to Spain with, isn't it? They put you up to this. You're not moving in with that Tracey. You're not living on that estate. And that other one's been married twice already.'

According to the stations of independence outlined in *Cosmopolitan*, Lorna should have asserted her will years ago. But the situations of the readers are not always the same as Fleet Street writers. With Lorna's habit of avoiding difficult decisions, economic necessity, too intense love for her parents, established comfort, and the daily struggle of existence, it had taken years for her will to triumph. But she could not bury herself in Lydd. Her parents would come to rely on her more as they grew older, and she would rely on them.

It may be that Lorna felt herself more necessary than she really was. Her parents were creatures of habit, as all who have reached three score must be, and had accepted that Lorna had cast herself as an unmarried, dutiful daughter. Considering their own *curricula vitae*, this was strange.

Both their childhoods had been engulfed by the war and left them nervous and insecure. They had been evacuated to the country in 1939, Fred from Bermondsey when he was thirteen, and Rose from Walworth when she was ten. They had both returned to London after Dunkirk when their mothers felt it was better to face the bombs with their children, and 'if you was 'it, you all went together'. Later that year Fred's house had been hit, and he was the only person in the rubble who survived. His father died in a torpedo raid in 1943. The next year Fred joined the Navy, and landed at Sword Beach in Normandy. It had been enough to put him off ever going abroad again, though he had relented later and taken Rose and Lorna twice to the Spanish Costas. He had not been happy when Lorna started going to Benidorm without them.

'When your family has considered you set in your ways,' the article Lorna had read on the bus had run, *'a late marriage will be regarded as surprising.'* Rose's family and Fred's cousins had regarded their late

marriage and later children as very surprising.

Her parents had always treated Lorna as precious and as an adult companion, though they were more relaxed with Diane, who was born two years later. Lorna's teachers had accounted for her combination of maturity and insecurity as due to having 'older parents'. Since Diane had married at eighteen, Fred and Rose had done their best at Christmases and weddings and christenings to shield Lorna from comments that it was about time she settled down, and in their own conversation they still talked about 'when Lorn gets married', rather than, as Lorna felt increasingly these days, and as the magazine article warned, 'If'.

At twenty-seven, Lorna wondered how many of her friends and relations were already placing her on the shelf. Unmarried. No children. Still living at home. Not a career girl. No steady man. The big three-oh looming. Did this really worry her? Or was it other people who made her worried? As the article had said, was her happiness and status only defined by her relationships with other people?

Lorna's volte-face had shocked Fred and Rose but they were not tyrants. As they washed up, they acknowledged that they were talking about something more significant than their usual Saturday evening grumbles. 'It is quiet in Lydd,' reflected Rose. 'There's not much going on.'

Every day for the last month Fred had wondered how much he would miss his workmates, the bargains in the Walworth Road, and his allotment in Herne Hill. Now it seemed he would have to add his elder daughter to the list. He snapped at Rose, 'You bloody well want to move there.'

'It's always me who has to take the blame, isn't it?'

When Lorna came down from her bath at nine, Barry and Diane were there. They told her that her baby-sitting services were no longer required. Barry's mum had turned up at the Surrey Docks after some hanky-panky on Barry's dad's part, and she was looking after Jason and Natasha. 'Come for a drink, anyway,' offered Barry. Diane looked daggers at her husband. Lorna, however, thought it would be politic to leave her parents alone.

'Lipsticks' was on the Old Kent Road, opposite the Thomas A Beckett. In the early 1980s it had been The Dun Cow, a tatty pub with pool-tables and an out-of-date jukebox, but then the brewery designers had blanked out the windows like a Black Maria.

Barry parked the GTI on the main road, leapt out, and ushered the women inside. Diane tottered in red high heels; Lorna followed in flat shoes. 'Who are you meeting?' she asked, as Barry held the secret door open.

'Some bloke what's fixing a contract for some warehouses.' He placed two Malibus and pineapple and some dry roasted peanuts on the glass table, then disappeared into the gloom.

The sisters sank into a leather settee. As children they had never shared the same interests, and Diane, always praised as a particularly pretty girl, had put most of her energy into her appearance. Intelligence equal to Lorna's had secured her the job with the Abbey National, and at seventeen she had met Barry through the grille when he came to pay in his earnings. She had secured these when they married.

The vicious ultra-violet light made the drinkers seem ghoulish. As there were mirrors everywhere, it was hard to tell what was real, and what was reflected. As she studied her image, Diane stubbed out her menthol cigarette in a pot holding a plastic weeping fig.

'Why not use the ashtray?' said Lorna, but Diane sipped her Malibu and ignored the suggestion. She worked hard at appearing superior, fulfilled and distant with her sister.

Lorna knew Diane would not initiate small talk, so she took a helping of peanuts. All the taste had been dry-roasted away. Marks would never have sold them. She coughed. 'I told Mum and Dad tonight I'm not moving to Lydd with them.'

'You what?'

'I'm not moving to Lydd. I'm staying in London.'

'Where you going to live, then?'

Don't worry, Lorna thought. Your designer flat will not be invaded. 'I'll sort something out,' she said aloud.

'You can't afford a mortgage.'

'I've got some savings.'

'You spend it like water. You've just been on holiday again, and you're always buying things for Jason and Natasha.'

'I'll work something out.'

'What's this bungalow like, anyway?'

Diane's interest in her predicament was minimal, but Lorna noted she was prepared to ask about property. 'You can see the sea if you stand on a chair in the kitchen.'

'I bet the roof leaks and the wiring's faulty.'

'Couldn't Barry look at it for them?'

'He can't afford the time.'

'Dad would really appreciate it.'

'Can't he do it himself?'

Lorna sighed and looked around. The harsh music was making communication, let alone conversation, difficult. There were a few survivors from the pub's pre-designer days, older than her father, sitting with their walking-sticks and deaf dogs, bewildered by the strobe lights and soul music.

'Why you staying?' Diane asked unexpectedly. 'Is it some bloke?'

Lorna nearly choked on her ice. She couldn't begin to explain.

'You're a dark horse.' Her sister stared at her.

Lorna tried another handful of peanuts. 'I had my annual review today. She told me to do an evening class.'

'Whatever for?'

'English, something like that.'

'You've got a job already. Why bother?'

'It might help with promotion. And I like writing. I kept my diary in Spain.'

'You must have had time on your hands.'

'I think I'll go. Just to see if I can do it.'

Filling in catalogue forms was the limit of Diane's off-duty writing. 'Do what? You can write already, can't you? And read?'

'Study.'

'They hold those classes in right dumps. And the people they get are weird.'

* * *

45

At eleven Barry directed them to the car and drove to the redeveloping streets between London Bridge and Waterloo. He drew up outside Southwark Cathedral, near the vegetable market. Rotting cabbages, lettuces, cucumbers, abandoned crates, and the dim lighting made the pavement precarious. Barry led the confused sisters past that week's rediscovered Elizabethan theatre, with, even at this hour, its posse of actors protesting in well-modulated tones, into a street of closely packed warehouses. 'There you go,' he said.

'What?' snapped Diane, from under her umbrella.

'Where your housekeeping comes from.'

'You've dragged us to this stinky street to show us where you're going to work?' Diane moaned.

'Yuppie flats,' said Barry. 'First they're gutted. Then we fix the wiring.'

'Barry, it's nippy,' said Diane.

'Let's look at the river,' he said, ignoring her.

'Where the hell's that?' Diane had never shared Lorna's passion for riding around on buses, and was ignorant of her city's geography.

Barry led them out of the darkness, past a recently dug out marina and a golden concrete riverside pub. 'They had brothels round here, you know,' he said.

'Trust you to know that,' said Lorna.

'My feet are soaking,' whined Diane.

'Look at the river.'

'I've looked.'

It hurt Diane that Barry was more excited by old history and new money than the prospect of taking her home. As they stood on the jetty, she saw only the rat-infested mud, and shivered at the water into which a disco boat had sunk last month.

Barry savoured the private moment of darkness. The lights on the north bank, the decorated cranes, represented the life he was attaining: cash in hand, a good-looking wife, good kids, and a home fit for a toff. It was hard work, but he could keep going. The building society would hardly repossess the flat, since Diane was so thick with the Branch Manager.

In Spain Lorna had tried to think pious thoughts in the churches on the day trip to the hinterland. Now she tried to think poetic thoughts as the river lapped by, but her mind was too buffeted by conflicting hopes and worries. She could not even compose the secret verses she tried to commit to her daily diary.

She felt relieved that she had finally spoken to her parents. But why was change always so painful? She wondered if the change in her circumstances would also change her routine and her luck.

As the river was muddied, so were her thoughts. She needed to work out a version which soothed her. You could do that . . . through thinking and writing.

3

Adult Learners

'Enough respect,' chirped the DJ, 'goes out to Albert of Clapham, the new South London Mr Superfresh. And big up to Angela, Selwyn and Nigel of Battersea. This upcoming rare groove is wicked . . .'

From his bed, Roland found the ringing phone under piles of newspapers. 'Yo.'

'Roland, the keys.'

'What keys?'

'Charlie's keys.'

'Charlie's keys?'

'The keys to his car. In your jacket pocket. I gave them you for safety.'

'Is it?'

'And my wallet. You walked off with both.'

'What about yourself? Did you walk any lucky lady home?'

'I don't walk women home.'

'So no bups?'

'I don't shop around. Roland, Charlie needs his keys. I need my wallet.'

'Where you phoning from?'

'The Manager's office.'

'I thought you was Manager.'

'Second Assistant Manager.'

'Low down the scale.'

'About low down the scale!' Weston snapped. 'Roland, Charlie's screwing. He needs the keys five minutes ago. There's a match at Clapham Common and the team strip is in the boot. And he has a band rehearsal in Dalston straight afterward.'

Charlie was the manager of an aspiring band called Fear Eats the Soul which Sherene had sung in.

Roland rubbed his eyelids. 'Doesn't he have any spare keys?'

'Not that he can find. Except for his band, he's like you. Dysfunctional.'

'Do you dis everyone?'

Weston was losing all patience. He should not have been making a personal call from the Manager's office. He should have been orchestrating the cheerful response of his employees to customers' demands, and checking they were recommending this month's blackcurrant and apple pie.

Roland returned to dozing. He had fallen into bed at three, and though he had not been disturbed by the all-night blues which had taken place in a flat along the landing, he craved more sleep. He let the phone drop by the side of the bed. One of his ruling passions was to order life reasonably, but this did not include his bedroom. Trousers fell where they were removed. Socks and shoes became separated from their partners. Pullovers and shirts had become an accustomed extra layer to the carpet.

After Charmaine walked out, his mother had arrived from time to time to tidy, but though his flat was only on the next estate, she soon tired of this self-

imposed additional chore and Roland's blank response
when she asked: 'Chah, why you no settle down? You
need a woman to look after you, cos you cayn look
after fe yourself.' Weston, too, was critical, when he
visited. He came to avoid his mother's sermons, but
usually stayed to deliver one of his own.

Amid the piles of clothes, the same questions
surfaced every morning when Roland woke. Could he
have stopped Charmaine walking out? Why did
Weston now feel he could lecture him? Why was it
difficult to relax in Stockwell? Why did his moods
range widely?

The urge to answer questions had manifested itself
in the purchase of piles of books, hardback and
paperback, from the market and the boot fair at the
Oval.

Not many boys in Roland's class had taken to books
as they had to basketball, football or dominoes. The
only novel which had made any impression on him at
school had been *Of Mice And Men*, but since then he
had stumbled on science fiction and fantasy, in which
moral problems and alternative modes of existence
are explored through Time Hawks, lost princesses,
and burnt-out desert planets.

Roland had also recently bought some of the
remaindered stock of a black bookshop, which had
flowered briefly under the concrete tripods of Brixton
Leisure Centre until it was replaced through market
forces by a business selling imported American trainers
at £90 a pair.

This year he had alternated books on meditation,
spiritualism, UFOs and self-help with biographies of
black leaders. He made no notes, presented no essays,

nor had any system, but he had begun to make connections. Marcus Garvey had taught him that a man without knowledge of his history is a tree without a root, like the saplings which the council planted optimistically on his estate from time to time.

When in recent, bolder years he had questioned his mother about her history, all he could glean was that she had come to England, according to her, with one cardigan and a bar of soap. She was equally taciturn about his father. All that remained were the two photographs of a tall man in a wide striped suit and a panama hat.

From Malcolm X he had learnt that you should liberate yourself by any means necessary, but sometimes he felt, as today, that his liberation in these last years had not gone much beyond the daily struggle to emerge from the bedcovers.

The phone rang again. He picked it up, yelled, 'Soon come!' and threw aside the duvet. When he was half-dressed, he picked up a copy of *The Voice* from the dressing table and skimmed over articles on why black children need black families, stories on misjudged inquest verdicts, news from the Caribbean, to the small advertisements. He had circled a number of the Lonely Hearts in this edition, but he did this every week, and had yet to reply.

Next to a box announcing a charity dance in aid of sickle cell research was a block about evening classes in Lambeth. This time he noted the details. Weston had persuaded him to start weight-training with him twice a week, but he lacked the commitment. It was his mind he wanted to develop, not his muscles.

* * *

Mrs Stephens, done with polishing, was at home preparing for the service. As she removed the plastic cover from her two-piece, she looked, as she always did on Sundays before church, at the framed photographs of her sons at various stages of growing up. Roland and Weston had attended Sunday school when they were small, and each week learnt the Golden Text to recite to the whole class.

During the week they had suffered the taunt of 'church boys', but they had progressed to the adult congregation. They stopped attending when they realised that the few men there under forty were aspiring pastors or the musicians. They had never been fully baptised. Mrs Stephens prayed for them daily to return to the fold.

She herself drew strength and pride from the unchanging Sunday services which made the muggings, burglaries, neglect and disappointments bearable. She knew she was made in God's image. She knew that in church she was not despised or rejected.

She adjusted her large blue and white hat, and thought of the Sunday mornings of her childhood. Before church her father would take his donkey and his mule to the sea to give them a swim. She was not allowed to go with them: that was a privilege reserved for her brothers.

Roland squeezed into an orange plastic seat next to a plastic trashcan under a healthy plastic Tradescantia. He recalled his first ever time at McDonald's, when he had picked up Weston from a more affluent classmate's ninth birthday party. It was in the West End, one of the first of the chain to be opened. The children had sat in a roped-off area with paper visors and toy trumpets. Weston had stared about him with his eyes wide, beaming as he sucked the straw in his lumpy chocolate milkshake.

Weston was not grinning now as he showed a tramp to the door. The grey-haired old man shuffled out cussing. When his brother joined him, Roland said, 'You should have let him stay. Given him a coffee – on the house.'

'He stank. Must have been drinking all night – cheap British sherry or meths. We don't need that kind of customer.'

'But you're not some flash hotel. You're a burger joint.'

'It's the principle. There are many other fast-food outlets opening. We don't want to lose out.'

'He was hungry. He's human. You're always mouthing off about human resources.'

'How's he a resource?'

'You told me,' said Roland, warming to his theme, 'that as Deputy Assistant Sheriff, or whatever, you're the public face of the store.'

'The public don't pay to eat with tramps.' Weston moved away to reprimand a schoolgirl part-timer who was supposed to have been on duty at eleven.

When he rejoined him, Roland asked, 'And why's she leaving so soon?'

'Unreliable. I've dismissed her.'

Roland chewed a muffin thoughtfully. 'You don't get black tramps, do you?'

'Not in Brixton, no.'

'But,' Roland continued, 'you do in Kingston.'

Weston's eyebrows rose. 'Kingston?'

'Kingston, Jamaica. I've heard your dad mention them.'

Weston looked at his brother coldly. Mr Langley was not to be spoken of. If he saw his father outside the betting shop, in the market, or drinking in The Atlantic public house, he blanked him.

'You never listen to what he says,' said Roland.

'He'll tell you what you want to hear.' Mr Langley had claimed that when he had first come to England as an ex-serviceman, he had lived in an air-raid shelter in Clapham.

Roland sank back into the bucket seat and glanced around the restaurant. Every table was littered with paper bags, napkins, plastic boxes and spoons. Waitresses were moving around collecting the packaging. He felt that if he sat there long enough he, too, would be picked up and binned. He knew that Weston saw horizons beyond the buns and burgers, but wondered how he could tolerate the streamlined routine.

'I'm going on a course tomorrow,' Weston announced. 'Personnel practices.'

'I'm starting a course, too.'

'What course?'

'Well, I'm going to enrol.'

'What for?'

'Evening school.'

'Car maintenance? It would be cheaper to ditch the car.'

'English.'

'English?'

'Reading. Writing. You know – improve my skills.'

'English at evening class.' Weston spoke as someone whose college diploma, he never tired of repeating, entitled him to apply for a degree. 'Well, I didn't check you for a scholar. But you won't learn anything in English. Try Business Studies.'

'I don't want facts. I want reasons.'

Weston barked at the assistants as he returned to the counter. 'Let's see some action here!' At Roland's stage of life, he thought, his brother should not be spending his evenings in some rundown school.

When Lorna returned home on Monday evening, her mother had gone three doors along the street to watch a video of a neighbour's son's wedding. Fred had just returned on his bike from the allotment with a clutch of beetroot, which he was washing under the tap. As Lorna stood beside him and filled the kettle for a cup of tea, his eyes avoided hers. He did not wish to argue about last Saturday. He knew that on some matters his daughter could not be dissuaded, but the fact that she had not first confided in him alone still hurt.

'I enrolled for that class, Dad,' Lorna said, plugging in the kettle.

The purple malleable skin of the vegetable suddenly required all her father's attention. The earthy smell filled the kitchenette, and mingled with the smoke from a cigarette burning undrawn on the windowsill. 'Oh,' he murmured.

'It was packed.'

'Great place for dossers.'

'They put me in the top class.'

'So they should have.'

'I had to fill in another form.'

'What time do these classes end?'

'About nine.'

'I suppose you'll want me to fetch you, when they put the clocks back.'

Lorna knew her father would be there at half past eight, fidgeting in the entrance hall, or running the engine of his car. 'It's just off the main road.' Why was it so difficult just to thank him? 'There are people about.'

'That's what I mean. Don't wear that belcher you fetched from Benidorm.'

'That's for evenings out.'

'So what's this then?'

'More like work. That woman at work said I should do it.'

'You're always mouthing off about her.'

'No, I want to do it.'

'Then will they give you more dosh?'

'That's not the point.'

'They get blood from you.'

Rose was discontented when she came in. The wedding had been a top hat affair, in a country church near Chelmsford, not a register office, like Diane's. She and Fred had spent too much of their savings on the reception at the Berni on Denmark Hill. Everyone had said it was lovely, but it had been spoilt by Barry's father getting drunk and smashing several champagne glasses. They had footed the bill for those, too. At the Chelmsford wedding, the sit-down buffet had consisted of Coronation Chicken, and flan with kiwi fruit. She sighed. 'The church did look lovely on the video.'

'I don't see the point of marrying in church just because it looks better on a video,' said Lorna.

'It's something to show your children.'

'A birth certificate can prove they're not bastards.'

'There's no need to be unnecessary.'

'I wouldn't have a video,' Lorna declared, squashing her mother's hopes. 'It's like nothing is real nowadays unless you video it. Tracey had to cut the cake five times at her last reception because the film stuck.'

'A video's the only way she can remember what bloke she was marrying,' grunted Fred.

'It's a waste of money,' Lorna continued.

'It's a souvenir,' said Rose.

'What's wrong with memories?' asked Lorna.

'Memories fade,' said Rose, sadly. 'Videos don't. That's why Di likes to video the kiddies.'

'If they ever sit still long enough,' said Fred.

'They're growing,' said Rose. 'They'll be grown up before we know where we are. They might as well live in Spain.'

'You only get worked up when they do come round.'

'And what do you do to help me?'

'Barry did talk about moving to Spain for good,' said Lorna, 'but Diane said she'd miss the shops.'

'There's a Marks in Gibraltar,' said Rose. 'I remember you saying. You know, your gran would turn in her grave if she knew how little she fetches them kids round. We saw your gran every day.'

'That's because she lived here,' Fred said.

'I've been to enrol for that class, Mum.'

'What will you have to do?' asked her father.

'Read some books. Write some bits.'

'I remember those bits you used to write when you

was little,' said Rose. 'Telling the teachers what colour wallpaper we had and everything. If you ask me, they had a cheek asking.'

'Yes, Mum.'

'Yo, long boy.'

Roland turned round. A week later, at five o'clock on Monday afternoon, a young woman in an executive suit was standing in a queue of customers by a fruit and vegetable stall in Electric Avenue. Roland tried to avert his eyes. He could not be seen snubbing people in public who, for whatever reason, wished to talk to him.

Sherene was carrying a blue and white Marks & Spencer plastic bag, from which were spilling packets of ready prepared lasagne. Roland caught the escaping pasta, but looked at Sherene coldly. Handing her the packets, he asked, 'What, no soul food?'

'The day Marks sell rice and peas, that day you'll know England is an integrated country.' She spoke loud enough to entertain the queue. Squeezing a mango, she continued, 'How's Mr Superfresh?'

'You made sure he didn't win.'

'But is he distressed?'

'Ask Marcia. She must see him more than I do.'

'Marcia and me don't exactly see eye to eye just now. More like eye for an eye.' She laughed at her own joke.

'They say sisters will scratch one another's eyes out.'

'And brothers bind together, is that it?'

'If possible.'

Sherene had reached the head of the queue. The

stallholder put the fruit in a paper bag. 'Here you are, darling. Take extra for your granny.'

Turning to go, Sherene fixed Roland with her eyes. 'I hear you're turning scholar.'

'News travels fast.'

'I heard it on the grapevine.'

'Well, the grapevine can't have much to talk about.'

'Granny favours you brothers. She likes to know your business.'

'I can't think why.'

'So what you learning?'

'English, it was to be. But not now.'

'What happen?'

'I went on Friday to enrol, but they was full. They said I should write a specimen page. Then they might consider me.' Roland wondered why he was telling this to Sherene and the fruit and veg queue. The truth was that, in his self-imposed solitary state, he would sometimes announce his closest secrets to anyone who passed the time of day.

'Sound like taking urine to the doctors. A piece of piss.' Sherene cackled again. 'So you've written this specimen?'

'No. Couldn't be bothered.' He had resigned himself to believing that the evening classes would join that pile of life's might-have-beens which accumulates and oppresses.

Sherene looked stern. 'How you know they're not just putting you down? They take one look and think you cayn study. They don't know you, Roland. You could write a killer essay.'

Roland looked surprised. 'Weston took your advice and ended up in the shit.' People stopped calculating their required provisions, and gave their full attention to the row. 'So what's your angle on this? To humiliate me too?'

'I don't get you brothers,' said Sherene, gathering her bags. 'One is full of shit and does everything. The other takes shit and does nothing.'

Roland could call himself lazy, but his mental development was not tittle-tattle for the Walters sisters and their granny. He gave the stallholder a warning that his pitch was extending beyond the legal limit.

That evening, he found a yellowing pad of A4 and a biro which worked and didn't leak. He tried to write, to say, as he had been directed, what his education had been so far. At work he had to keep records, write contravention warnings, complete witness statements, but he could not remember when he last wrote anything more personal than a birthday card. As with all skills unused, he had become rusty. He sat on the sofa, with the curtains open, the lights of Parliament, that powerhouse of words, in the distance, and penned a few lines. But try as he might he could not put his thoughts into words that satisfied him. Over and over again he ripped out sheets and screwed them into balls. He remembered lessons in school where he had done the same thing, but from boredom, not frustration.

Slowly sentences formed. Somehow, he accumulated the suggested number of words. Once he had counted them, he read his piece through.

When I think about it now, all I remember is that my education did not do me much good. My first school was Effra Road. The first book I could remember is Shadow the Sheepdog. *It had a blue cover. After I read it I wanted a collie dog for a long time. My big school was Stockwell Park. I was in 1L at first. Mr Evans was my form tutor. In the first year my best lesson was woodwork. In the fourth year my best lesson was English. We had discussions and read* Of Mice And Men. *I reckon I started learning when I left school. That is why I want to go night school now . . .'*

It would do. After a search in drawers which revealed a mislaid calculator and leather gloves, and the condoms he had bought at Fresh's, he found a buff envelope, and addressed it. He might receive no answer, but pride was restored. They could not say he had not tried.

On Friday came a reply. Due to the unprecedented demand for exam work, another teacher had been engaged, and Mr Stephens' written English had been judged of a standard competent enough to join the first class next Wednesday.

'Well, isn't that dandy?' Roland said to himself as he shaved, cursing his razor bumps.

In 1932 the London County Council had blessed Stockwell with a health centre, built in white concrete in the streamlined shape of a liner. The purpose was to provide a family club with sporting and quiet activities – at the time a radical proposal. The building had sailed through the bombings and, as the need for lice inspections and tuberculosis decreased, it had been transformed into a centre for adult education. In the simpler 1950s, carpentry, dog obedience, cake decoration and car maintenance had been the most popular courses. By the late 1980s there was a more substantial menu including steel-pan tuning, archery for people with disabilities, women's assertiveness training, clowning and juggling, Asian sweet-making, preparing for your own death, desk-top publishing, family trampolining, bilingual car maintenance, judo, lesbian history, post-Colonial literature, and mixed volleyball.

Roland hoped he had found the right room. Except in reverie, he had not been in a classroom for nine years. He still felt diminished by the desks and chairs. In his memories he had conjured up only the good times, not the constant possibility of humiliation, though at school it had been mostly the teachers who had been humiliated.

He sat down at an empty desk near the back (old habits die hard) and wished he had brought something to read until the teacher arrived. The latest planet saga. The *Daily Mirror*. His letter from the Institute. Anything, to pass the time and fill the silence. He had come straight from work, after a bag of chips in McDonald's. Now that he was sitting it seemed a long time until nine o'clock.

The people who were filling the classroom were eyeing him and each other shiftily. He noted there were twice as many women as men, and that their ages ranged from teenagers to the pensionable. Two sulky schoolgirls seemed to have been dragged along by their mothers. A serious-looking young woman had placed a large new dictionary on her desk in the front row. A young man wearing a crucifix was reading *Brighton Rock*.

Though Roland had not given the matter any

thought, some students had wondered what the teacher would be like. The schoolgirls wanted a good-looking hunk who would not draw attention to their mothers. A car mechanic, returning for a third year, wanted a teacher who would mark his work promptly and not lose it. Some of the West Indian women wanted a disciplinarian.

The teacher who bore the burden of these expectations seemed flustered to find the classroom open and occupied. He dropped a pile of hot papers on to his desk, and announced, 'The photocopier would keep jamming.'

There was no smile of sympathy or recognition from the class. His students were suspending feedback. In the second row, Lorna wondered why the photocopying had not been organised beforehand. She was used to properly prepared presentations. And despite her best intentions, she was wondering whether any of the men in the class seemed particularly attractive. No one had struck her immediately. At first glance, she did not think much of the teacher. He was a tousle-haired man of about thirty, with thick glasses, curly brown hair, and what seemed to be a nervous grin.

'Nice to see you all here so promptly,' he said, out of breath.

He was searching now in the desk for a stick of chalk. He found a stubby remnant the size of a wad of chewing gum, and printed his name on the blackboard. 'My name's Rob Poundsford, your teacher for this course. You can call me Rob. Later, you must tell me your names or the name you prefer to be called by.'

The class made no comment.

'You will have various reasons,' he continued, 'for enrolling to study English. Some of you because you like reading, and want to read more. Some of you because you like writing, and want to write more. Some may want a qualification which shows what you can do.' His eyes scanned the listeners' blank faces. There was no ripple of assent.

Removing his denim jacket and sending biros tumbling to the floor, Rob continued with his opening remarks which he had hastily rehearsed during the car journey from East Dulwich. 'Language is a tool.' The schoolgirls looked at each other and giggled. 'How we use it affects our lives.' This set the girls off worse. 'Often we don't know what we think about something until we have spoken about it or written it.'

The students were concentrating on the man, not the words. Unconsciously Lorna warmed to his voice, which was educated Cockney, and had a mellow tone. She liked the jacket and jeans, which were stonewashed, from Top Man, she thought, though Marks had just introduced a similar range, and the baggy white shirt with discreet embroidery was new this autumn in the *Next* catalogue. There was a ring on his wedding finger. He didn't seem the type to have videoed his wedding.

After he had explained the examination system, Rob announced that they would be looking at the 'process of reading'. Suddenly for Roland the football he was missing on the television seemed much more attractive.

'Do we have comprehension?' the mechanic asked.

'Yes,' said Rob, 'but I hope comprehension – that is,

understanding dawning – is what happens every time we read. Whenever we read we try to make sense.'

The dictionary owner shifted uneasily. By this time in the lesson she would have hoped to have been parsing sentences, looking for one of the nine types of adverbial clause. At her school in Guyana she had been praised for this skill and her neat handwriting.

Sensing unease, Rob passed round the photocopies. Some had come out blank or with illegible patches. It took some minutes for all the class to have the required sheets. They were not used to dealing with cascades of paper, and much fell to the floor. After scrambling under the desks, Rob said, 'You should have three pages each. The first, on blue, is from a James Bond book.'

The dictionary owner looked unhappier. She had not come out in her second-best church clothes to read trash.

'The second extract, on green, is from *David Copperfield*.' This cheered her a little. Charles Dickens was English Literature.

'The third is from *The Diary of Adrian Mole*.' The looks of discomfort and incomprehension increased. Lorna thought she really was wasting her time and money. Was this man just a trendy like the teachers she had avoided in her last year? Roland was intrigued. There must be some reason for this stupidness.

Rob read the first passage, about James Bond meeting a glamorous female spy. When he had finished, he said, 'Now, that's about a man gaping at a woman. As you read it, what difference does your sex make?'

'I didn't read it. You did,' said a man at the back.

'I wouldn't ever read it,' said one of the mothers.

'No,' said Rob, 'perhaps not normally. But for the purposes of this exercise, consider your sex. Does our sex make any difference to our reactions?'

'I'd rather see the film,' said the mechanic, ignoring the question.

'I never watch those films,' said a second mother.

'But,' said Rob, 'isn't that the point? Men feel attracted to the idea of Bond. It's a male fantasy. Women can't see the point. Isn't our response to Fleming's writing different depending on our sex? If we're men, heterosexual men, don't we fantasise with Fleming? Women, on the other hand, find it distasteful.'

'How do you know what we think?' asked the second mother.

'It's a rather obvious point,' said the Catholic, who was hoping to enter a seminary.

'The film does it better,' said the mechanic.

'So,' said Rob, determined to make his point, 'our judgement of a text depends on our sex. Yes?' Though there was no agreement, he printed the word SEX on the board in large letters. One or two students shifted in their seats. Lorna could not tell if this was because the seats were uncomfortable, which they were, or because, like her, they were unsure of the drift.

'Next, if we can look at the passage from *David Copperfield*. This is where an old sea captain, after a long search, finds his daughter. She has been seduced by a gentleman, who has since abandoned her.'

'Is everything we read going to be like this?' asked the intending priest.

'No,' said Rob. 'Is there anyone who would like to

read the passage to us?' There was not, so he read it himself.

In the grammatical structure of Dickens' narrative, the subordinate clauses decorated the main ideas like the tracery of Victorian ironwork. The dictionary owner's brain was working overtime. Lorna remembered having seen a made-for-television film with Susan Hampshire. On the whole, though, she thought Catherine Cookson did such stories better.

When he had finished, Rob asked, 'Now, how is our reaction different from the Victorians'?'

'We know more,' said Lorna quietly. Unintentionally, she had spoken aloud.

'Sorry. What did you say?'

Lorna coughed. 'We know more about these things.'

'Good,' said Rob. 'Now what do you mean by that?'

People turned or leaned forward to look. Lorna gulped. 'Seductions. Broken families. Daughters who disappoint their fathers.' She wished she had kept quiet, and blushed.

'Good,' said Rob. 'So our attitude to the text depends on our historical viewpoint?'

'That's not what she said,' said the Catholic. 'She said we know more about the seamier side of life nowadays.'

'You see it on the telly,' said the mechanic.

Regardless, Rob continued, 'It depends,' and he wrote the word TIME on the board. 'How much time has elapsed since the piece was written. *David Copperfield* means something different to us after one hundred and fifty years. *Hamlet* can't mean the same to us as it did to the Elizabethans. Someone once said you need a new interpretation every three weeks.'

'Excuse me, that's not what I said,' Lorna interrupted, embarrassed but concerned that she should be reported properly. 'I didn't say nothing about time and history.'

'Sorry,' said Rob. 'What's your name?'

'Lorna Duggan.'

'What did you mean then, Lorna?'

'Well, it depends if you know anything – about what's being written about. I mean, if you do, well, the story must mean, sort of, more to you than if you don't.'

'That's good.' Blown off course, but encouraged by a thoughtful response, Rob added KNOWLEDGE OF SUBJECT on the board.

Before setting out, Lorna had determined she would keep quiet. She had wanted to size up the others before she opened her mouth. When she had spoken the women had glared, and the men had stared. She hoped they would not put her down as pushy. She vowed to say no more that evening.

Roland, who had looked up when Lorna spoke, was still puzzling over the Dickens. The vocabulary and structure tonight seemed a stumbling block.

'The third piece presents more of a problem,' continued Rob, conscious that he was not taking everybody with him. 'It's from *The Diary of Adrian Mole*. Would anybody like, perhaps, to read this last piece?' Nobody did, so he read Adrian's jottings about the break-up of his parents' marriage.

Lorna remembered it had been serialised in one of her mother's magazines. Roland thought it was stupid. When Rob had finished, the man at the back said, 'That was on the telly, too.'

'It's only pretending to be about Adrian,' said Rob. 'That's the AUTHOR'S INTENTION. That's what the author wants – to make us think it's a genuine diary. It was actually written by a thirty-nine-year-old woman, writing as the character. If we didn't know that, how could we tell it wasn't written by a thirteen-year-old boy?'

'They don't write diaries,' said the mechanic.

Rob couldn't elicit the answer he wanted, that the writing was too knowing, that it showed more a mother's concern than an adolescent's, but it was nearly time for a break, so he changed tack. 'Does it change how we feel about a text, if we know about the author? If we knew Shakespeare was a child molester, would it make us think differently about his plays?'

Roland and Lorna couldn't say that it had ever concerned them deeply, but they were content to see KNOWLEDGE OF AUTHOR added to the list of variables. Lorna wrote down the words in a notebook with a pretty flower design on the cover, which had been reduced in the January sales.

Roland had not brought any paper. Searching his pockets, he discovered his MoT certificate inside his jacket and wondered if copying down Rob's words on the back would render it invalid.

After ten minutes more of what he hoped was discussion, but in reality was more him twisting what the students said into the answers he had determined, Rob added, AGE, CLASS and RACE to his list.

Lorna copied the last words dutifully. Roland was still trying to work out the connection between the words. He decided to memorise them, anyway, to pass the time.

Rob concluded his thesis: 'So you see, how you judge something may be the result of varying factors.'

'Does that mean that nothing we say about writing is right or wrong?' asked the prospective seminarian.

'In one sense, yes.'

'Well, that's no good, is it?'

'I think it's time for a break now,' said Rob. 'Back at ten past eight. The canteen is by the office.'

Structuralism had stalked through Rob's English course at Warwick University, and now weakly informed his teaching. Roland had thought that reading offered answers, certainties. If so many things had to be taken into account before you could say anything, he was confused. Lorna thought it was worse than the considerations which had to be made when she was re-ordering different types of quiche for the chill cabinets. At least there she had to obey strict regulations. As far as literature was concerned, Roland and Lorna did not yet have enough respect for their own judgements. Others who had not been following had been so fazed sitting in desks, handling photocopies, paying attention for an hour, and worrying lest they should be asked to comment or read out loud, that Rob could have read from *Thomson's Directory* and they would not have noticed.

In the second half, to reinforce his points, Rob asked the students who had returned to work in pairs. He gave them passages from various publications, and asked them to comment, remembering the headings on the board. The dictionary owner had a recipe book, the seminarian the Highway Code, Lorna a Pronuptia catalogue, and Roland a car maintenance manual. Was the teacher trying to tell him something?

'Pretend you're a visitor from outer space,' said Rob, 'who can speak English but knows nothing of our customs. Given that you're a Martian or from Venus, what would need explaining?'

Some of the class, had they still been capable of thinking, might have decided that pretending was not necessary. This was too much. Trashy paperbacks. Different kinds of rubbish. No stories, poems, questions, comprehensions. Working in pairs. Pretending you're a Martian. Rob had not estimated how traumatic it was for some to return to education. They were shy enough about attempting the task, without being asked to share it with a stranger and act as if they were a five-year-old. Some sat rigid with the shock, wishing they had escaped when there was an opportunity.

But some light shone through the gloom. The dictionary owner enjoyed looking up 'succulent' and 'endive'. The prospective seminarian, on his own particular planet, found a similarity between the Highway Code and the Ten Commandments. On the paper he was given Roland pointed out that the car maintenance manual assumed knowledge of the subject. Lorna was unable to think of anything to say about her catalogue, although she decided that none of the wedding dresses would be her choice.

'Next week,' Rob announced, drawing the lesson to a close, 'we'll see why some writing is called literature and why most of what you've been looking at just now isn't.'

For homework they were given a passage from *Great Expectations*. As he saw more Dickens, Roland's heart sank. He didn't know if he would bother to return next week.

Lorna had a headache. She wondered if her expectations would be fulfilled. Rob seemed a nice man, but he went too fast, and didn't always listen, and if you couldn't arrive at the truth about anything, she wasn't going to be too happy.

When she wrote her diary that night, she tried to describe each of the men in the class, and found herself thinking particularly of that black man's liquid eyes.

Fred's telephone calls to the solicitor's had eventually laid open that he and Rose could expect to be in the bungalow by Christmas. He would have phoned every day, until Lorna warned him what they might charge for conversation.

It was like her to be concerned. Something must be sorted out for her. The problem kept him awake at nights. Rose kept saying, 'She'll change her mind,' but Fred recognised that what he hoped would be paradise – well, nice – for him and Rose might be purgatory for his elder daughter. He could understand that she might feel threatened by a feeling that things would always go on the same. Though in his teens, thanks to the war, he had experienced enough upheaval to last a lifetime, in his late twenties and early thirties before he met Rose, Fred had begun to feel a similar panic, a sense of time passing.

How could he help Lorna? He must not try too hard; that would hurt her. What he hoped for most was a man who would come along and look after her as tenderly as he had done, though he knew that in his eyes no one would ever be good enough for her. He couldn't magic a bloke out of the blue, but he hoped she would meet someone eventually, marry and have children. She was good with kids.

Where could she live? She couldn't stay in the house. The rumour was that the council was re-allocating these terraces to black families. He was pleased that Tracey hadn't been mentioned so much lately. He didn't want Lorna moving into the estates near the Elephant, and if the council rehoused her on her own, that's where they'd put her. He had heard from his workmates tales of what went on up there: muggings, youngsters buying crackerjack, or whatever they called it, postmen being attacked if they didn't deliver Giros on the expected day. Share with Tracey, and she'd end up pregnant, or worse.

Nor did he want his daughter in a bedsit. He didn't know much about them – indeed, he'd never been in one, though he knew that some of the surviving Victorian houses on his rounds were divided into them, but from reading the *Express* and listening to phone-ins, he associated them with loose living and loneliness.

While Rose snored, night after night in September he lay awake. The men at work said, 'Your Lorna'll meet a bloke sooner or later. She'll be getting desperate soon – she can't afford to be choosy. It's working in that shop what's done it. Made her snotty.'

So which was worse? For Lorna to marry in haste, or to wait? Unmarried at twenty-seven, in Camberwell, where most people had got married, or even divorced, before they were twenty-one . . . Lorna was an oddity. He felt a fierce protection towards her which seemed

to be increasing as he grew older. He wished he could
say the same for Rose and Diane, but there was little
about them which surprised him any more. He hoped
things would be different with Rose in Lydd, where a
change of routine might shake them both into
behaving better to one another. He envied her, that
she could sleep so soundly. But then, these days she
did the harder graft.

That night, Rose sipped her Horlicks and read the
problem pages of the women's magazines she swopped
with neighbours down the street. She put aside her
worries about her own family and impending change,
and fell asleep deciding what advice she would give to
a woman who had discovered her husband dressing in
her underwear.

On the third Saturday in September, it was Diane's
twenty-fifth birthday. Barry was taking her to the
Docklands Arena for this year's final concert by the
Rolling Stones, with laser beams and fireworks. Lorna
had agreed to mind the children. She made it a
condition, though, that Diane and Barry call round
for tea in Camberwell first. She had bought a Marks
iced cake with flowers and bows.

At six the doorbell rang. It played *The Isle of Capri*,
one of its repertoire of tunes, slowly, as if its battery
were fading. 'Where are the kids?' Lorna asked,
opening the door to *Danny Boy*.

'With Barry's mum,' said Diane, looking past her
sister. 'She's taken them to the London Dungeon.'

'We was supposed to be all together.'

'Don't go on like an old auntie, Lorna.'

'We haven't seen them for weeks.'

'They're not showpieces.'

'We'll call round tomorrow,' said Barry, hanging up his sheepskin.

'See that you do. They'll be furious.'

'You mean you are.'

When those who could eat anything had finished, Barry asked, 'Sorted yourself out yet, Lorna?'

'I'm not moving in with you.'

'I was talking to Frank along the road,' said Fred.

Lorna wondered what this had to do with anything.

'You know, Dave's just got married,' her father continued.

'Lovely wedding,' said Rose. 'I saw the video. Beautiful reception. No trouble.'

'Anyway,' said Fred, 'Frank said now Dave's gone he's got the spare room. So I said what would he say if I said Lorn might be interested.'

Lorna looked at her father, surprised and hurt.

'I know, love,' said Fred. 'You've been so busy with your late nights.'

'It would be nice to be consulted.'

'He'd said he'd rather you had it than some African.'

'Lorna could help Myra with the housework,' Rose chipped in.

'Can we stop talking about what I could and couldn't do?' asked Lorna. 'I mean, it is Di's birthday. What did Jason and Tasha give you?'

'It's a shame we can't ask them,' said Rose pointedly.

'Jason bought me a bottle of Dioressence and Natasha a Spandau Ballet CD.'

'That was nice.'

'They don't know yet.'

'Will you stop their pocket money?'

'No,' laughed Barry. 'Stop their building society accounts, more like.'

Rose winced. They had more money than was good for them. She ran on nervously, 'You'll get your present after tea, Di. It's just something from Marks. I wasn't sure if you was a size ten or twelve these days, with your diets, but you can always change it if it doesn't fit. That's the beauty of that shop.'

Suddenly, Lorna felt tears welling up inside. Everyone should have been happy. She remembered birthday teas from her childhood with Diane's dolls and miniature tea sets. In those days she could say exactly what came into her mind and people would smile and laugh.

She was stunned that her father had aired her problems and a solution at this tea time. Why did he have to talk about her to everyone? Why hadn't he spoken to her about it before, discussed it in her bedroom, sitting on the end of her bed, asked her what she thought?

Frank and Myra, for God's sake. How could her father think of disposing of her to neighbours whom she hardly knew to pass the time of day? The voluntary spies in the street would be watching her continually, to see how she 'coped' with being on her own. Wherever she ended up, it would have to be away from Station Road.

It occurred to Roland that if he abandoned the evening class, Weston would gloat and crow once more about his own studies. When he finally sat down to read his

homework passage, the night before the class, he
found he had no paper to write the answers on. He
had no cash to buy a pad from the newsagents by the
tube station which sold everything, so he walked to
his mother's.

He had just missed Mr Langley, who had delivered
a Sainsbury's peace offering: lagers, unsweetened
mandarins, sweetcorn with peppers and red kidney
beans. He had been frostily received by Mrs Stephens
and Weston, not invited to eat, and had left, reclaiming
the lagers.

Weston was preparing callaloo soup. 'You want
food?' he asked Roland, chopping spinach leaves.

'Please,' said Roland.

As schoolchildren Roland and Weston had eaten
the same meal twice daily, once at dinnertime with
their 'free dinner' tickets, the fifth-former avoiding
the eager admiring eyes of the first-former, and again
at teatime, when they ate whatever dishes Mrs
Stephens, as dinner lady at the school, had been
slipped by the head cook. ('You take it, love, we all
have a bit. It's the least we can do with what they
pay.')

Weston had said disgustedly at the time that the
Stephens family had the 'most white' diet of any black
family in Stockwell. Soul food: blackeye peas, ackee,
saltfish, breadfruit, okra, yams and sweet potatoes,
the chief goods of Brixton's market, had been strictly
for Sundays. The rest of the time it had been cheese
pie, bubble and squeak, chocolate pudding, and Arctic
roll. Even so, Roland and Weston had eaten hungrily.
Mrs Stephens still said of them, 'The bwoys eat me
up. They can yammi. Them yam too much.'

Roland watched now as Weston rolled some chicken breasts in spiced flour. Hoping to avoid inquisition on his studies, he asked, 'Marcia all right?'

'She's at work.'

Mrs Stephens was sitting at the kitchen table flattening and folding plastic bags. 'I tell him tell her come cut my hair, but he cayn remember. Not fancy enough for she.'

'Marcia will only cut at the salon,' Weston said. 'Her scissors, combs and chemicals are there. I said I'd get Roland to drive you there after work, but you won't budge.'

'Me 'ave to go to work hevery day. Me don't have a husband to help me cope.' Mrs Stephens looked at the tins. 'What use they to anyone? Him tink he can sweet-talk me by bringing mashed-up tins.'

Not wishing to hear any more about his father, Weston asked Roland, 'How are the lessons?'

Roland breathed in. 'OK. The teacher's a bit weird. D'you have any paper? I've been given some homework.'

'You shouldn't leave assignments until the last minute,' nagged Weston. 'Get a routine. Get organised.'

'People work differently.'

'Not if they want to succeed. You need a timetable.'

Roland knew about Weston's timetables. Some years ago he had one of the first Filofaxes to be seen in Brixton. Now he had an electronic machine into which he could punch everything important. Roland had often felt like punching him with it. 'You'd have been happy as an android, wouldn't you?' he said.

'Organisation is everything,' quoted the B.Tec National Diploma in Business and Finance.

'A bwoy dohn need fe go boasify himself to mek him look smart,' said Mrs Stephens. 'Man look at de outside, but God look at de 'eart.' She finished putting the tins away, and moved into the living room to read a Church publication.

'So are there any sorts in this class?' asked Weston.

'You said I must take it serious,' said Roland. 'I'm there for the teaching.'

'Yes, but those classes are ripe for pick-ups.'

'A few mammas. Some English girls. But they mostly keep their heads down.' He thought of the girl with auburn hair who had spoken up for herself.

'Early days,' said Weston.

'I saw Sherene in the market a while ago.' Roland did not see why Weston should have the monopoly on irritation and superiority.

'What does she say?'

'Nothing much.'

'Good.'

'Does Marcia behave like her?'

'They're not alike.'

'How come Marcia's never here?'

'She's a businesswoman. She works late.'

'Doesn't that leave you on your own?'

'I don't need to be with my woman to know she's mine.' Weston often sounded as if he were a lyric writer for a mushy soul singer.

'How you know she's not giving others the eye?'

'Move from me,' said Weston. 'You lose women like you lose everything else.'

Mrs Stephens reappeared and saw the furious expression on Roland's face. She muttered to herself, 'W'appen? Wha you a fight fa? You're both brothers.

Wha you a hargue fa? Me say you a go get whey you a look fa.'

They ate in silence. Weston had also made dumplings to accompany the chicken. His father had showed him how when he was a child, before things became bitter. Now, when his father did earn money, if not from gambling or tailoring, it was by selling dumplings from a van at carnivals and reggae sunsplashes.

Mrs Stephens always maintained that dumplings were all Weston's father could cook. As she poked the chicken, she began to moan, 'You ask him fe cook rice im no know.'

Roland tried to tell her about the English class, but Mrs Stephens could not understand why Roland had not finished with school years ago. 'We bring you over he fe heducate you, and learn fe speak better. Why you a go school, a fe your age?'

After the meal Roland was given five sheets of A4 and dismissed quickly, as the next 'window' in Weston's schedule was weight-lifting. Roland thought his brother's schedule was suspect if it involved working out so soon after eating his tea.

Ten minutes later, back home, Roland worked out with his homework assignment. It was about a country boy who had been educated to be a gentleman, and then was embarrassed when his sister's husband, a blacksmith, came to see him in town. It sounded like Weston when his dad was around. Roland's mental muscles were not as weak as he feared, but the jerk chicken kept repeating.

Lorna had completed her Dickens homework on the

Sunday evening. This had not taken her back to her schooldays, because she had seldom done any then. Barry and Diane had called round with the children in the afternoon as promised, but not until five, and they had to leave again at seven. Her parents had not yet agreed whether this was a slight or had shown enough respect. As Natasha had broken one of the best tea cups, from a service bought by Rose's mother, and Jason had whinged about his abandoned Transformers, their going had been mostly a relief. Rose and Fred had then had the whole evening to discuss how much they had been snubbed.

Lorna had found the reading and writing more agreeable than listening to this post mortem or watching *Highway*. It had taken her mind off less academic questions that were plaguing her.

Some of what the teacher had preached on that first evening had sunk in. After completing the comprehension, not wanting to go downstairs, she had written out Rob's list again.

She had begun by printing SEX clearly. What difference did being a woman make, not to reading, but to living? If she were a man, she asked herself, would people worry so much about her being on her own, or tell her what to do?

When she had written AGE and HISTORICAL, she decided at first that she was better off living in the 1980s than in Dickens' time. As far as she could remember from the film of *Great Expectations*, the women had all finished jilted, burnt, or hit over the head. On second thoughts, Walworth was not too dissimilar nowadays.

She had finished her Marks' Swiss Mountain bar

and had thought of her first sexual encounter, with Paul, in a flat on the estate where Tracey now lived. That first evening, when she had gone to a party on the fifteenth floor, a television set had fallen past her ears as she looked hesitantly over the balcony of a dark walkway. She remembered the flying television and the subsequent crash more clearly than the fumbling deflowering on the heavily patterned carpet.

She thought again of Martin, the shopwalker from Selfridges, who had been twice her age when she was twenty. He had been willing to leave his wife and children for her, but she came to the conclusion that she did not love him enough to be the cause of so much suffering. She had enjoyed feeling noble but it had been the distress in her father's eyes when she had told him Martin's age which had mostly checked her ardour. She had never revealed the wife and three children. Sometimes the truth had to be doctored.

She had wondered whether Rob's list would help to arrive at the truth of anything she read. She had never needed such a guide before to enjoy a book. The historical romances she favoured gave you a good story you could lose yourself in whilst eating chocolate. She had decided, though, that such books wouldn't interest you as much if you were a man, and wondered what kind of books that black man read.

The atmosphere at the second class was less reverential than the week before. Some students were more cheerful, some surlier. Last week they had been children on their first day of school, likely to be picked on, unsure of each other. Today they were more comfortable.

The dictionary owner had acquired a Thesaurus in which she could look up, pore over, inspect and examine unfamiliar words. The seminarian sat in the front row with a *Dennis the Menace* folder given him by a younger brother who could not understand why anyone would want to be a priest. The garage mechanic was reading the *Angling Times*.

As Rob faced the class, a man at the back said, 'We're not doing what we did last week again, are we?'

'You had me lost,' said another.

'The point of last week,' said Rob, trying to sound calm, 'was that when you read you have to ask questions.'

'Do we have to do that in the exam?' The man in the back row changed his fire.

'The exam is different. They ask the questions.'

'So why did you start with this other stuff?'

'Look, there's more to studying than just taking exams.'

'That may be true for you,' the man grumbled. 'You've got your qualification. We've nothing yet. You're supposed to be helping us.'

Around the room there was a ripple of support. 'We're here to get good grades,' said one mother's daughter. She felt that if she attended each week, she should be awarded a pass as an act of grace.

'Are we starting proper work this week?' asked another.

Some smiled at the teacher-baiting, but the silent majority wondered why Rob didn't just tell them to be quiet. The arrival of several latecomers, including Lorna, who had been caught in a traffic jam, created a diversion. Roland watched her slide into a seat. When they had settled, Rob asked, 'Did you enjoy the Dickens?'

'Why does the blacksmith talk funny?' asked a bluff Irishwoman.

'Dickens was trying to show his country speech,' said Rob. 'It's always difficult to represent how people speak. It's only ever approximate. You have the same problem if you try Cockney, Scottish, Irish, or West Indian.'

'Excuse me,' said a Jamaican nurse, 'why is West Indian a problem?'

'Did Dickens do West Indian?'

To Lorna it seemed she had not missed much by being late. The trouble with discussions like this was that they could waste whole lessons. It had been an ideal way in school to avoid work. Now she was paying for education, she was fussier.

'Perhaps we should look at the story,' she said in her politest tone. 'Can you go through it with us? Tell us what answers might be expected.' As she turned to shift her chair, she noticed that the black man was watching her again.

'Yes, well, that's what we're getting on to,' said Rob.

After they had read the homework passage, and discussed answers, Rob continued: 'Right, this class is called English Language but, as today, we're often going to be studying what is called English Literature. I'd like to start by asking you what you understand by Literature.'

'Can't you just tell us?' asked the man at the back.

'So what is literature?' Rob repeated. In Lorna's

childhood her gran had used the word to describe the booklets that came with a new fridge or television. When something went wrong with a piece of equipment, she would ask, 'Where's the literature?' Lorna had usually moved the fading brochures from the kitchen cupboards when she had been playing with the colanders and saucepans.

'So who decides what is literature?' asked the Irishwoman impatiently.

Slowly, Rob compiled a list of literary forms – novel, play, poem – and steered the class to a proposal that it could specifically mean works of the imagination. 'So why are some writers of literature considered greater than others?'

''Cos some toff has decided,' grinned the mechanic. He had decided to play the class clown, though he was digesting every word as fast as fish gobbling bait.

'So are bestsellers at airports literature?' Rob continued.

'To some people,' said Lorna, becoming irritated, 'what you're saying might sound snobby.'

Roland was impressed. As he had noted, this young woman seemed sure of herself. There was sense in what she said. But was she also one of those pushy women who wouldn't let a man have his say?

Rob put the idea that writers were like football teams, with some always in the First Division. Lorna thought only a man would think like that.

At the break more disciples gathered round Rob than the week before. Sean, the seminarian, wanted to continue his discussion on Graham Greene. Yvonne, the owner of the dictionary and thesaurus, wanted to know what other books could be recommended.

Cynthia, the Jamaican nurse, asked how many black writers were in the First Division. Claudette, one of the schoolgirls, asked Rob if he were married.

In the second half Rob read the opening of *Great Expectations*, where Pip is alone in a misty graveyard late on Christmas Eve. He read with a passion and shyness which suited the passage. Then he announced that the homework was to describe a familiar place at a particular time of day and year so that it would be made clear to someone who had not seen it. He gathered possible ideas in spidery writing on the board: Caribbean beaches, an airport, a fishing lake, a church, a food store, a football ground, a market.

By chance Rob took the market as an example and showed that one way of gathering ideas for writing was by grouping them under the five senses.

Though he preferred to sit back, Roland could not avoid supplying some details of what might be on sale and how shoppers might behave. 'One thing is that people bring different things for carrying stuff away,' he found himself saying, gulping as he began to speak. 'I mean bags. Some bring old plastic bags. Others get brown paper ones from the stallholders, but they're not strong and often split. Some have proper shopping bags – mostly women – in straw or material. Some have rucksacks.' His voice wavered. 'It all depends.'

Lorna was surprised. Not only did he have soulful eyes, but here was a man who knew about the habits of shoppers. She must get to talk to him.

4

Feminine itching

'We may not have a candlestick-maker,' a notice above
the entrance to the Granville Arcade in Brixton market
has announced for years, 'but we do have butchers,
bakers, grocers, greengrocers, fashion shops,
household goods, cotton and bedspreads, shoes,
cosmetics, pictures, lamps, fabric, records, pet shops,
dairies, hardware, florists, a sewing machine shop,
an adoption centre, cafés, children's wear,
hairdressers, wigs and ladies' clothes.'

Despite this cornucopia, when she arrived in
England Mrs Stephens had missed more than anything
the open village markets back home – the fruit piled
high under palm trees to shield it from the strong,
clear sunshine: mangoes, pineapples, custard apples,
ripe bananas and juicy lemons. She had missed the
smells, too: of cinnamon, cloves, ginger, nutmeg,
pepper and beeswax. Her mouth still watered at the
never forgotten but unavailable taste of water coconuts
and mountain honeycombs. She pined for the wet
flapping of snapper fish as they were wrapped in
newspaper, and the rough feel of whelks' shells. In
her dreams she heard the clucking of chickens and
the cries of the vendors: 'Buy a quarter no' gal.'

Columbus Joe, who had come over on the *Windrush*,

had set up a stall in Brixton market in 1948. Some said that he had discovered Brixton for Jamaicans. Whatever the truth, the market had adapted slowly and uncertainly to West Indian immigration, and in the 1950s you had to look hard to find familiar comforting food there. By the 1960s choice had improved, but Mrs Stephens swore the food never looked as good or tasted the same as back home.

Recently, shopping on the way home from school, she has begun to feel crushed by the structures the market shelters under: the curving shops in Electric Avenue, the arches and entrances of the overhead railway, the crumbling arcades, the multi-storey car park, the glowering Leisure Centre. Roland has offered to shop for her, and deliver on his way home, but though he is paid to prevent crooked dealing, she does not trust him to pick the best and not be cheated with rotting produce from the back of the stalls.

A bird as weary as Mrs Stephens, flying over Brixton on a late September migration, accustomed to the symmetry of country town squares, would find its market lay-out confusing. From the air it would be a Chinese character, a dash to the left (Station Road), a curving line to the middle (Electric Avenue and Popes Road), and several small bold strokes (the arcades and other isolated patches of trading).

The Station Road section is half-road and half-coppice of silver bollards and black lampposts. The first stall here usually has flowers and fully grown rubber and cheese plants. It is another legend that on the same site in the early 1960s, marijuana plants were sold as innocent indoor decoration, but sadly for those seeking a piece of *sensi* these days, this is no longer the case. Outside a pattie shop which boasts *You've had the rest, now try the best,* all summer long an elderly Jamaican in carpet slippers has been shuffling to the reggae from two giant speakers.

A stallholder opposite, with gold teeth, and tracksuit and sunglasses in all weathers, who sells tapes and used to play his music too, has forsworn to do battle with his system. These September days, when it is not raining, he spends more time at the white plastic tables outside an Italian delicatessen than on his feet. Despite the smell of cappuccino and Parma ham, he does not forget that he is in SW9, not Sorrento.

The dancing carpet slippers are watched by the white *Guardian* readers in The Jacaranda Tree, a café which its customers believe strives hard to sell food and drink the production of which has involved no exploitation of man, beast or plant. On leaving the café one student says to another, 'The market is so vibrant,' but pulls her leather satchel closer to her body.

Towards the end of the road, beyond the hot-dog stand, beyond the egg stall, opposite the protractor-shaped lock-up entrances where, under the arches, the traders store their rubber-wheeled medieval carts, the market offers the lowest quality bric-à-brac and the most worn-out clothes. Those who are desperate enough to search through these piles for warm clothes or school trousers ignore the trans-vestites who buy felt hats which they hope will appear fetching in the subdued disco lighting of The Fridge.

Witness against such abominations is made from time to time. There are stalls that offer bibles and Christian literature. Avoiding the hawkers of *Militant* and *Marxism Today* on Saturday mornings, church groups sing and preach in Atlantic Road. Members of Mrs Stephens' church have begged her to join them, but she has a distaste for standing among the outer leaves of cauliflowers and discarded Windward Island banana boxes.

When she can afford it, Mrs Stephens buys from under the red and white awnings of Murrays Meat Market on the main road where, at the end of the days, joints are auctioned downwards. Lorna's granny, who liked a change of shops, would bus down to Brixton for the fun, but Rose has never been keen on the place, and always sticks to East Lane.

When she does have a fancy for fish, Mrs Stephens buys her favourite snappers these days at a fishmongers on Seventh Avenue. Next door is a Wig Bazaar where, impervious of the smell, in the days when she cared about such things, she used to examine half-knots and yah-yahs. Now she only frequents that Avenue for cheap birthday cards, Jamaican sorrel and the shop which specialises in WX and outsize clothes.

The Saturday before the third class, Roland remembered the essay, and, as the teacher had suggested, he began to jot words down on his clipboard. He needed a quick eye in his job, but usually his observations were blinkered: he was trained to note overpitching, blocked gangways, dud weights and dangerous toys. Looking at the familiar as if for the first time, he noticed an 'a' missing in the illuminated sign advertising Market Row, and the skylights revealing peeling red and white paint.

He saw a number of youths, aged about fifteen or sixteen, walking sulkily behind their mothers, pulling their shopping trollies for them. Such boys, he knew, loudmouths in the playground, and flash before teachers, still fear maternal discipline. He spotted ILEA clothing vouchers being exchanged for Acid House sweatshirts, but decided that was not his problem. He averted his eyes as well as he walked past the parlour where Charmaine would have her fibreglass nails fitted.

As he stood and scribbled, he sensed that one of the traders, displaying Bob Marley and *Free Nelson Mandela* T-shirts, thought he was noting some irregularity. 'Yeh, man, all t'iefed,' the stallholder laughed. 'From some warehouse down Streatham. Jimmy's already booked me.'

As Roland smiled in return, he noticed a young woman assessing a rail of blouses. She was selecting one or two with their hangers, and measuring them against her body, testing, as women do, if the colours clashed with her shining hair. It was the girl with the chat from the evening class, Lorna Something.

He wondered if she would acknowledge him in the market. He was used to being ignored. Several girls from his class at school, whom ten years ago he had cussed and teased, now towed their children round the market, but blanked him.

Under her arm Lorna, too, was carrying a clipboard, paper and pen. She had a way of standing, Roland thought, which showed she was used to being looked at. Did she, then, work in the market in some way? Was she conducting a survey?

Suddenly she noticed him and came over

immediately. 'Hello, Roland! What are you doing here?'

'Work. I work here.'

'Really? What as?'

'Market inspector.'

'Oh – so you should find this homework easy.'

'I don't know about that.'

'I didn't know they had them.'

'What?'

'Market inspectors.'

'Somebody has to control this lot.'

'I suppose you're right.'

'So you're making notes, too?'

'The teacher said we should, didn't he? I had to pick up something from work, so I thought I'd come here, have a fresh look. I don't usually shop here. So that's what I'm doing.' Her voice trailed off.

'So how you doing?'

'It's hard to know where to start. All that "senses" business he went on about is supposed to make things easier, but I think it just confuses you more.'

'So you work near here?'

'Yes. At Marks'.'

This was a surprise. Roland had thought that their assistants would be snobby. He was about to ask if she had time for a coffee when he saw a stallholder beckoning. 'I'd better let you get on.'

'Yes,' said Lorna. 'See you Wednesday. Goodbye, Roland.'

She had noted his name immediately Rob had asked, and repeated it to herself at home. She thought it sounded exotic – Spanish, perhaps – but not daft, like Jason or Natasha.

She looked at what she had written. She often bought things on the main road, but rarely ventured into the interior, and didn't know where things were. A lot of the fruit and veg were new to her and as for most of the clothes, they were of poor quality and roughly made. Marks' would have rejected all of them. Their inspectors were much more fussy.

She replaced the top on her biro and made her way back to the main road, glowing that Roland had remembered her name.

When she arrived home, Diane and her father were in the kitchen.

'Don't bloody come it, Di,' her father was saying. 'Every bloody Saturday. She never gets out.'

'She's out now, isn't she?'

'Evenings, I mean.'

'She doesn't mind. Gives her something to do.'

'She won't be doing it when we've moved, you know.'

'Why not? She claims she's stopping here.'

'I'll fetch her down at weekends, if necessary.'

'Well, you'll have to write the work schedule,' said Lorna, entering the kitchen.

'Been out?' Diane asked, hoping to deflect her father.

'Brixton market.'

'That's a right dump.'

'All that foreign food,' her father said.

'You think spaghetti hoops are foreign,' said Lorna.

'Did you keep a tight hold on your bag?'

'No, I was mugged twice and I've just staggered home.'

'Don't be clever. Did you fetch anything?'

'Nothing special.'

'You weren't working today.'

'No, I went to make notes. I've got to write about markets.'

'Why do they always make you do such stupid things?' asked Diane. 'Why don't they set you business letters? That would be more useful.'

'Lorna's always loved scribbling. You never have.'

'Well, she's Scorpio,' said Diane. 'A water sign. Good with words – or supposed to be.' She looked at Lorna as if she privately doubted the evidence of astrology. 'Me, I'm good with figures. That's being a Virgo.'

'Scorpio. Virgo. Load of balls,' snorted her father. 'I'm bloody Pluto.'

On the third evening, Rob told the class that through one of the generous handouts of the dying ILEA he had been given ten tickets to a Shakespeare play in a fortnight's time, and during the break he wanted to know who would like to go.

When he had answered twenty questions about where the play was, what time it started, what time it ended, what bus went there, could you buy drinks, could you smoke, Rob moved the lesson on. He asked the class to suggest combinations of characters and places to write about. Sean suggested a monk shopping in Mister Byrite. He claimed to have once seen Cardinal Hume looking sadly at some denim shirts in the Army & Navy sale. Lorna, who had arrived late, suggested a peasant girl from Tyneside sent on service to a country house. 'Obviously very close to your own experience,' said Rob, who was becoming more acerbic each week, as he and the class relaxed.

Roland had thought of a time traveller setting foot on a desert planet, but was glad he had not voiced his suggestion. He was also considering why he had been so concerned that Lorna might be absent.

As an example, Rob read a piece from Hardy. A woman appeared stark and distant against the Wessex landscape.

'It's majestic, isn't it?' said Sean.

'He uses long words, don't he?' observed Albert, the man at the back.

Rob was about to say that Hardy had educated himself by extensive reading, that he was obsessed by his lack of formal education, that he tried to make up for it by using multi-syllable words, but remembering his class, said instead, 'He thought you shouldn't judge people by appearance.'

'We all do, though,' said Sean, piously. He enjoyed Rob's sermons, and was waiting for him to take the names of those interested in the play.

As the weather grew chillier and *Dallas* more inviting, the class dwindled to a solid core. Rob's group methods, regarded at first with suspicion and distrust, had by the fourth week made the survivors talk to people they would normally never have addressed.

Lorna was beginning to relish the twenty-minute break more than the lessons. It made a change, she wrote in her diary, to be with people who did not talk entirely about mortgages, or redecorating bedrooms, or driving tests, or weddings. Cynthia, for example, the Jamaican auxiliary nurse, told her that she hoped the GCSE would gain her a place on the State Registered course.

Lorna marvelled at the schoolgirls with their mothers – Gloria with Laverne, and Esther with Claudette. At the girls' age she would never have submitted to an evening class, and her mother would have been out of her depth with Rob's torrents of hard words.

The mothers came to ensure that their daughters did as well as they could, as they could not trust them to work at school. Their adolescent sulkiness was wearing off. Gloria wanted Laverne to be a lawyer, and Esther wanted Claudette to be a doctor. Lorna thought that *LA Law* and *The Cosby Show* had much to answer for.

Yvonne, who owned the dictionary and Thesaurus, had lent Lorna a novel about Guyana, which kept mentioning strange fruit and trees, but made a change from Catherine Cookson. She wondered if Roland's childhood had been similar.

Albert, the sixty-five-year-old Trinidadian bus conductor, had come to Stockwell in his late teens. He could remember the trams and trolley-buses which used to run along the Walworth Road, which Lorna's gran had talked about. Darren, the car mechanic, had arrived late tonight in his overalls. He had a cheeky grin, but it was Roland who had the nicest smile. And he didn't seem to wear a ring . . .

During the break, while Rob was monopolised by Sean, Lorna sat at a table overlooking the centre's swimming pool with Darren, Cynthia and Roland. The topic was Shakespeare.

'Back home,' said Cynthia, 'we had this teacher.

She believed everybody should take turn to read out loud. So whatever we read, it was round the class, a line at a time. We read *The Merchant of Venice* out loud, but not in parts. One line at a time. It was madness.'

'We had some video of *Macbeth*,' Darren remembered, 'with enough witches. All in the nude. This MacBeth's wife was nude, too. She comes on walking in her sleep, in the buff.'

'We did some *Romeo and Juliet* once,' Roland told them. 'None of the boys would read, so the teacher was Romeo. The girl reading Juliet couldn't handle it.'

'We read *Macbeth* too,' Lorna said shyly, 'or rather, bits of it. Then we had to do a newspaper front page about his death, and so on. I remember I spent more time on all the adverts for shops I stuck round the borders than the story.' Everybody smiled politely, including Roland.

Lorna felt relaxed. It was nice to be with blokes whose immediate interest was not to get your knickers off, but all the same, she wondered if Roland would be interested in more than stories about Shakespeare. Had he put his name down for the play?

'I enjoyed what you wrote about markets,' said Rob, after the break. 'It's not easy to be original on such a subject. Listen to some gems. Claudette, you said that dried-up apples are "like skin pitted with spots". But there's no y in "acne". Beryl, your list of vegetables was full, but you were supposed to be writing a description, not a shopping list. Roland, you said that the skin of an orange is "like the surface of an undiscovered planet". Good – but there's only one t in 'planet'. Actually, all of you, can you just listen, just because you're writing about greengrocers, you don't have to spell like them. But thank you, Roland, you made me see the market afresh. Finally, Sean, I don't think that with this title the examiners will want an account of futures trading in the City. You're being too clever. Stick to Golden Delicious, not Golden Handshakes.'

Now that the class had mastered the complexities of description, and learnt a few new spellings, Rob moved on to argument. Roland learnt that within the definition of English coursework folders, 'argument' was not what he heard most of the time in his poorly soundproofed flat or whenever he met Weston, but the exploration of ideas. 'Considering a subject,' said Rob, 'you have to look at many factors – historical, social, psychological, physiological, personal, physical, economic, religious.' Yvonne's fingers worked overtime.

Rob asked the class for a topic. Most were dumbfounded, but Laverne offered 'abortion'. Her mother gave her a look. Laverne had already written an essay on this at school for Child Development, and hoped to avoid further work.

Rob sighed. Every year a girl student would suggest this topic. Although in his laziness he might host the discussion, he knew that abortion, like drugs, homosexuality, or even his old chestnut, surrogate motherhood, was a subject which most could only write about powerfully if it became important to them through circumstances.

He wrote his headings on the board and they took

them one by one. Albert talked about back-street abortionists who had been exposed years back in the *People*. Sean would have liked to explain the church's position, but was not allowed. Lorna said she thought men were in a weak position to mouth off about the subject. Roland kept quiet. He never, Lorna thought, talked just for the sake of it.

The homework was to take a topic about which they felt passionate and to air their views. Lorna breathed deeply. She could sense which way her passion was running.

Rose rarely met Lorna from work, but when she heard the Christmas lines were being put out, and she had to go to Brixton anyway for her teeth, she made an exception. Trixie at work had put her on to a new dentist near the police station.

As she followed Lorna round the shelves, she kept dabbing the corner of her frozen mouth with her handkerchief, for fear that she was dribbling. Even without this handicap, conversation with Lorna these days rarely developed into dialogue. She filtered criticism. Like the mucky stuff that came out of London taps, she could do without it.

Lorna was transferring boxes of glass baubles from a wire cage to the shelves. 'Mum, you'd better not stand talking all night. The manager will have a go at me. Go and look round the food. See what's new.'

'Can't I see the other bits round the back?'

'You know it's not allowed.'

'You must be keeping the best back.'

'Mum, I don't finish till seven. Go and look at the reduced stuff.'

'I was before I spotted you. It's mostly old bras with no boxes, gone yellow and grubby round the hooks.'

'Mum, I have to finish this.'

Rose picked up a bottle. 'Foaming bath oil. Why they make this stuff beats me. It's all right for a while, then it goes flat and leaves you goose pimply. Who wants to sit in cold bubbles? Not to mention,' she whispered, 'the feminine itching you get from all this stuff.'

'Mum, Dad asked me to fetch some chocolate digestives.'

Though she often ate a packet alone at a sitting, Rose was jealous of Fred's negotiated treats. Her mouth was swollen, and her top lip overhung the bottom one, but from the side of her aching face she spat, 'Biscuits are bad for his teeth.'

Lorna replied, 'How was the dentist?' then realised she had granted dispensation for a further flow of words.

'I had two fillings. Didn't hurt much. Nice surgery – very clean. I've got another appointment next week.'

'Blimey, you must be keen.'

'Quite a nice bloke. Nicely spoken. Coloured, but educated.'

Lorna blushed. Would her interest in Roland remain a pleasant fantasy? She would have to shake herself out of it, or act upon it. 'Mum, they might run out of those biscuits. They're our most popular line, after frozen chickens and tights.'

Though her mother did not sanction the purchase, she was never one to be deprived of buying anything, so she moved swiftly towards the biscuits. Lorna was spared a description of the dentist's double-breasted suit, and the furnishings of his surgery.

Usually Rose liked to have her Christmas presents bought and wrapped by Guy Fawkes' Night. That way she could enjoy the run-up to the big day: the lights, the trees, the Salvation Army carols on Camberwell Green, the parties at the depot and the Post Office. But this year the cloud of moving disturbed her anticipated pleasure. Where would they be? Where would home be? When would Fred retire? What would he be like, around her all day long? Were they wise to move to the seaside at all? In the end it had been her idea. She had heard enough about couples who moved to the South Coast, and the husband dropped dead the minute he smelt the sea. At least the air would not be new to Fred. They had been going to Lydd since after the war, when the barbed wire was still on the beaches. Now there was new wire, but that was to stop you straying too near the power station. On Christmas Day this year would they be walking on the beach and then returning to their own bungalow?

As she shuffled forward in the checkout queue, inertly picking up bars of chocolate and bags of popcorn, she thought about what she had to say to Lorna. The journey home together would be a rare opportunity to speak. Lorna did not appear to have given her future much thought. These evening classes seemed to have made her even more tired and grumpy than usual. She spent all her spare time scribbling in her bedroom. What was she going to do? Fred still favoured her moving in with Frank and Myra. Because it was not her idea, Rose was not keen. Trixie at work, recently widowed, had spare rooms in her house off East Street. Trixie could do with the money, and since at nine of an evening she either went out to the pub, or to bed, Lorna could have much more the run of the place than at Frank's.

Rose had determined to use the walk to the stop, the wait, and the ride on the bus, to urge her claim. She would be putting Lorna in good hands, doing Trixie a favour, and getting one over on Fred. When it came to speak, though, her mind was as numb as her mouth, so during the walk she rehearsed her case. When two buses had come along, too full to accept passengers, she began. 'I'm not looking forward to Christmas this year.'

'Why not?'

'Everything will be at sixes and sevens. I like to have things done properly.'

'I'll come to Lydd. Christmas by the sea will be nice.'

'It won't be like it's always been.'

'It'll be different.'

They boarded a third bus and had to stand towards the back. As the bus lurched round corners, Rose glared at the several young children, out on their own, who occupied seats and were spilling Coke and Scampi crisps over themselves and other passengers. It was not an ideal place for an emotional mother with a sore face to wring an agreement from a tired daughter.

Lorna had seen Trixie knock back large measures of gin and tonic at Christmas parties and perform the hokey-cokey, the Lambeth Walk and the Birdie Song. 'I don't get you,' she told her mother, and the eight-year-olds chomping their crisps. 'You don't want me to move in with Frank and Myra, who are dead quiet, but you're quite ready to let me share with some old lush.'

'Trixie's a good laugh.'

'She's just buried her husband. She probably hits the bottle more than ever now.'

'You should be grateful people are concerned. You don't seem to be.'

In the neutral public space of the bus, uncomfortable and observed, Lorna felt bolder than she could be at home, where the rooms reminded her not only of childhood joys, but of tantrums and humiliation. She told her mother, 'You're scared I'll move in with my mates, so you and Dad go round seeing if you can palm me off with anyone you know who has a spare room. It's my problem. I'll sort it out.'

Rose was irritated and disappointed. Lorna had not given her suggestion proper consideration. Her own ideas for finding accommodation were flimsy. She'd end up in Railton House, the Salvation Army hostel, or in a cardboard box.

Lorna was panicking quietly to herself, but she could not let either parent see. Her mother would gloat, her father be distraught. The appearance of sloth was necessary. When action was required, she would act. As her thoughts turned to Roland again, she realised he worked for a council, Lambeth it must be, not Southwark, but it was a council. He might be able to suggest something.

When Fred returned from work that afternoon, there had been a letter waiting from the solicitor. It seemed action might be nearer than they all imagined. The contract was ready to sign. 'They should have sent it Recorded,' grumbled Fred. 'I can't think what they're playing at. Look what they put on it – second-class, one of them franking things. Posted Tuesday.'

'I thought people only used second-class if they didn't care if things got there or not,' said Lorna. 'Like writing a postcard from Spain to someone you don't like.'

'Don't be clever,' said Fred.

'Ignore her,' said Rose. 'She's been in a funny mood all evening. Let me look at this letter.' For a minute she squinted at the type and the attached sheets. 'You have to sign something, don't you?'

'Of course I bloody have to sign something,' said Fred. 'That's why they sent it.'

'Don't sign till you've read it properly,' Rose fussed. 'Remember what happened to Den and Irene and that time-share in Alicante. They ended up forking out hundreds.'

'I'll ask Frank to have a look.'

'I don't want the neighbours knowing all our business.'

'You was always in and out of their house until you took against them.'

'We got some digestives,' said Lorna.

Fred waved the letter. 'I'll fetch it back myself. I'm not trusting this to the boys in the van.'

'You should know,' said Rose.

Argue for what you feel passionate about, Rob had said. When Roland considered it, he only felt passionate about loneliness. He was beginning to realise that whatever subject he scribbled on, his words were about himself.

The class and the company were becoming necessary. In the week he approached Wednesday evenings with the least inertia. Otherwise he did not go out. Last week Steve had phoned about playing a match for the bank team, but on Sunday morning bed compelled him more than the pitches of Clapham Common. For weeks he had not joined mates at the pub, and he no longer knew the consensus on women, Arsenal, cars, the poll tax, bands, the government, bomb attacks, train crashes and sports gear.

Charmaine's leaving had bruised him more than he'd realised. The hurt was deep and still surfacing. He sometimes felt he would live the life of a hermit forever, with no prospect of improvement – a Michael Jackson alone with no chimpanzee, or a Luther Vandross, closeted with no wardrobes of suits.

And yet, though he was mistrustful, there were women as well as words at the class; neither seemed as easy to pick up as Weston had suggested, however. The nurse attracted him, though there was something stiff and matronly in her manner, but mostly it was Lorna, the girl from Marks, who interested him.

Tonight he had declined to join his brother and Marcia at the opening of a rum and cocktail bar behind M & S, but Weston had allowed Roland to meet him after work for a swim. Weston used the Leisure Centre more for its hot showers and preening space than for the exercise.

In the men's changing area there was a posse of boys, too young to beg for work in the market, who were testing the locker doors for forgotten ten-pence pieces. Roland could remember doing the same at their age at Clapham Manor Baths. The money he found was spent on chewing gum and football stickers; Weston had placed *his* coins in a savings tin.

Roland could not locate Weston in the showers or by the handbasins (*Notice: these are NOT urinals*). He must have already gone through the footbath to the pool. Roland removed his market suit and pulled on his trunks, an old pair bleached by chlorine, with the netting in the gusset shrunken by launderettes.

After the outside chill, the pool's warmth was welcoming. It encouraged lazing at the ends. Notwithstanding, there was a maelstrom in the middle which forced slower swimmers to the sides. Roland recognised his brother's strokes.

As he approached the shallow end, Roland slid into his lane, but Weston chose not to notice him, executed a swift turn, and kicked him in the teeth.

A Rastafarian in Hawaiian shorts was also ploughing ahead. Weston could not be cut up by a dread, particularly one with the handicap of weighty locks, so a contest developed. At the end of two lengths, the Rasta came to a rest, and shook his mane. Weston, however, continued his display.

Roland pushed off himself. His breaststroke awoke muscles he generally ignored. After three lengths, he perched himself at the deep end, and facing away from the water, stared through the sheet windows to the railway line. After a while, Weston surfaced beside him.

'Going for gold?' Roland asked.

'I don't come here to play.'

'Sorry, I forgot. Everything is serious,' said Roland. For a minute, feet on the ledge, they balanced in the water, eyeing the female swimmers. Roland thought he glimpsed Sherene, of all people, at the other end. Why did he have women on his mind all the time now? He thought he'd chosen to be a scholar. He must be imagining things.

When he finished his survey, Weston said, 'In my bedroom there are piles of your old books. Can you take them away tonight? When you finish your swim.'

'What's the rush?'

'They're crowding my space.'

'They've been there for years.'

'I have to rationalise my possessions.'

'Talk English. You're sorting out old rubbish. I'll pick them up when I've time.' He rubbed the chlorine from his eyes. Was it Sherene in the lime-green swimsuit? His mind would be producing that nurse and Lorna next. He noticed that Weston was sulking. 'How's Mum?'

'How should I know?'

'What's she up to?'

'Out.'

'Where?'

'Some tent on Peckham Rye.'

'What?'

'Some gospel meeting.'

'Still preaching, is she?'

'Not to me she isn't.'

'Whenever I show up I get a lecture.'

'Only because you let her.'

'And you don't?'

'No, I don't.'

Roland knew that Weston found his mother an embarrassment, a constant irritant, a reminder of who he was. He climbed out, sat on the poolside, dangled his feet in the water and changed the subject. 'On Monday we're going to see some Shakespeare play.'

Weston had no opinion on Shakespeare, but asked, 'What's this week's essay on?'

'An argument. I'm going to write about sport.'

'Well, come round and collect your football annuals. Good reference material.'

Roland had not been hallucinating. Sherene suddenly popped up between them. She must have swum underwater, approaching like a submarine. She looked at Roland's trunks, 'Now on anyone else,' she said, 'those would look stupid, but on you . . .'

Sherene's one-piece emphasised her cleavage. With her wide eyes and glossy hair, which seemed to shake off water, she was a beauty. Roland had to remind himself that she was also devious.

'And you still have the little Speedo number, Weston,' she continued. 'Still, size isn't everything.'

Weston blanked her.

'I didn't know you came swimming,' said Roland.

'As your brother would say,' said Sherene, 'life is a sport.'

'Did Marcia say where I was?' Weston asked suspiciously.

'I know you,' said Sherene. 'You may have changed your girl but you won't change your habits.'

'This is a large pool,' said Weston. 'Take your nonsense elsewhere.' He launched into a fiercer crawl.

Sherene struck out after him, but Weston was soon halfway down the pool. Roland dived in and caught up with Sherene. Catching her breath, she told him,

'Your hair needs attention. I could trim it. Marcia's teaching me.'

'No, thanks.'

'Are you going to this new bar tonight?'

'No way.'

Swallowing a mouthful of water and spluttering, Sherene replied, 'Well, I've heard the adverts – "The Tropical Bar, where trend meets class". But if Weston goes, it's more trash meets rass.'

Roland dipped below the water. On surfacing again, he asked, 'You going then?'

'If Clinton can get away.'

'Will they accept market traders?'

'It's attitude,' Sherene replied, struggling to maintain balance, motion and spite. She reached the narrow end. 'Belief. Weston says it's the inner person that matters.'

'In that case why go to these places to show off?' asked Roland, resting.

'Oh, get a life, Roland. You have to stay conscious of what's happening.'

Roland knew Sherene wanted to stay conscious of what was happening with Weston and Marcia. 'Who says it all happens in trendy bars?'

Sherene looked into his irritated eyes. 'Still too busy to relax, Roland? Still hard at your studies? Not found a soul mate yet? Some thin-lipped red-skin girl you read poetry with at the Tate Library?'

'It's not a pick-up joint. I go to learn.'

'Weston always combined both.' Hearing his name, Weston came to rest in mid-stroke. Sherene looked at him. 'Weston, you're too restless, even in the water. Be like Roland. Mellower.' She sensed she had scored a hit. No one had ever cussed Weston's swimming before. It was time to retire. 'Weston, I'll join you for a cocktail later. Roland, it's a shame you don't go out. Remember, as your brother would say, "life isn't a spectator sport". Don't spend all your life on the sidelines. I'll check you later.' She swam away sinuously.

Roland asked his brother, 'If we drowned her, would the attendants ever notice?'

But Weston had overrun his schedule. He leapt from the pool and headed towards the showers. Under the steaming water, he said, 'You encourage her. She'll never achieve anything. She's too unfocused.'

As they parted by the steps, Roland said, 'Don't spend all your hard-earned wealth tonight. You know how they boost the prices in those places.'

'I'll be buying drinks for useful contacts,' said Weston. 'Sometimes you have to speculate.'

5

Going to a show

'You're lucky, going to a show,' said Rose. She poured hot water into a stainless steel pot, twenty seconds after the kettle had boiled.

Lorna sighed, as she ironed her chosen blouse. In the kitchenette, it was a squeeze for the ironing board, her mother, and herself. 'It's not a show,' she corrected.

'What is it, then?'

'A play.'

'Well, play, then. What's this play called?'

'*Twelfth Night*.'

'Sounds Christmassy. Who's in it?'

'I don't know.'

'No stars?'

'Not that I know of. It's Shakespeare.'

'Chancing your luck, aren't you?'

'What if I am? Nothing ventured.'

Rose squeezed the tea bag with a spoon. 'One's enough when there's just two of us. Your dad always puts two in. It's a waste.'

'At least he uses boiling water,' said Lorna, squirting cold droplets from a plant-mister on to the blouse.

Perched on the kitchen stool, Rose dunked a digestive. She did not particularly like the biscuits,

113

but Fred was not going to eat them all. 'Where is it you're going?'

'The Barbican.'

Rose looked blank. London north of the river was alien territory.

'The City. Near Moorgate.'

'Oh. Your dad got us lost up there once. On the way back from that wedding in Walthamstow. You'd never think he once had to find places for a living. Funny place for a show.'

'There's offices and banks up there,' said Lorna. 'It'll be handy for them. And there are shops now. Big names.'

'I expect it's all yuppies.' Rose sipped her tea. 'Who else is going?'

'Just some of the class.'

'Is he married, this teacher?'

'He's got a wedding ring.'

'That don't mean a thing these days.' Rose put her hand to the side of her face. The tea hurt her teeth. 'Is your dad meeting you?'

'It'll be all right. It's a group. The others live up the road.'

'Don't take a lift, Lorn. Phone your dad if you get stuck.'

'Did he sign that contract? Diane said it looked iffy.'

Rose was pleased that Lorna was behind in the latest developments, but resentful she had not been consulted either. 'Don't ask me what your dad or sister do or don't do,' she moaned. 'I'm the last to be told. I'm only the one who will have to see to everything, pack everything up before we go.'

'While you're packing,' said Lorna, 'you could get rid of some stuff. Take it to a boot fair.'

'You'll be having some of our bits, so don't go telling me to flog everything off,' said Rose, pouring a second cup of lukewarm tea. 'Sometimes you have it too easy.'

The buses favoured Lorna, and having it too easy, she arrived at Brixton tube station at half past five. The arrangement had been to meet at six. None of the class was there. A man with a staff and a conch shell offered to tell her fortune, but she smiled politely, and moved slowly along the parade.

She looked in a shoe shop displaying the latest trainers, with pump action, transparent soles, and protruding tongues. She moved to the next window and studied the slingbacks for some minutes. Then in the glass she recognised the reflection of a longed-for figure.

Roland was standing near the road. How long had he been there? Had he been watching her? Could he have come early especially, hoping she might be there? Or was her fancy running away with her? She wondered if he would move over when he saw she had spotted him. He had always been friendly before when they met in the market, and at the class, but could it be anything else? He had been in public then, or in a group. Now, if he joined her, they might have to wait together for at least five minutes. Would he come over?

He was talking severely to a trader selling prints of jazz singers and the rooftops of Paris. Was he warning the man about byelaws? Was he, like a policeman, always responsible, even when not on duty? He was

not in his market clothes, but wearing a dark blazer
and a white shirt. As far as she could judge from this
distance, it seemed neat and crisp. Who did his ironing,
she wondered? Did he still live at home with his
parents, or did he live alone? Or did he have a girlfriend
on whom he dumped his washing? Was he married?

She saw that he had seen her quizzing him and
watched him excuse himself amicably (and rapidly?)
from the print-seller. He cut a passage through the
crowd rushing from the station, came over, and asked,
'How you doing?'

'OK, thank you,' Lorna replied. 'I'm early. I was
looking at the shops.'

'Sizing up the opposition?'

'Well, let's just say I don't think Marks need worry.'

'You need cash to shop at your place,' Roland
replied.

'You need cash to shop anywhere.' Lorna took in
his brown eyes again. *Was* he married? 'Now those
trainers are what I call pricey,' she gushed, indicating
the shoe shop where a group of youths was now
studying the latest refinements.

'The whole business is a con,' said Roland. 'Making
people want the right name tags. People get so fussed
over names.'

'My sister's little boy has to have all the right gear
or he gets cussed at school.' She checked herself. He
would not want to know all her family details yet.
Cosmopolitan said that men found it a turn-off. What
could she say about Shakespeare?

Roland replied, 'My brother has to have all the
right gear too, and he's twenty.'

'Well, let's hope he'll grow out of it,' she said.

He smiled, but it seemed more from politeness than amusement. Did he think her too pushy? She thought of what she could say to move the conversation away from families and remembered something she had read in the *South London Press* last week. 'Most of the muggings round here are to get money for trainers, apparently. Some kids will have a go at anyone to get money. They're so desperate.'

Roland looked at her with an unfathomable expression. Of course, she had put her foot in it. Why had she brought up muggings and trainers? He would think she had mentioned them just because he was black, and think she was making some point. Her mouth always ran away with her. It was true, though, the reason. The article had said that just as many white kids were involved as black, but she couldn't very well say that now. Now she couldn't even look him in the eye.

Gloria and Esther joined them, dressed in their Sunday best. They had not been able to persuade their daughters to take up Rob's offer of tickets. The girls had been despatched to an aunt with instructions to complete their homework, and not to be allowed to hire a video. Albert arrived next, in a flared suit which came out on posh occasions. He had also brought a duffel bag containing a thermos and a Tupperware box with chicken sandwiches inside. Yvonne had the *Collected Works of Shakespeare* in sight-destroying print which she had snapped up that weekend in a W.H. Smith sale. Sean stood engrossed in the *Evening Standard* and the Enya cassette on his Walkman. Darren arrived from the

same bus as Cynthia, and Roland moved towards
them.

Lorna noted Roland's going. He must have thought
she was getting at him. She cursed all these people
who had interrupted her chance to talk more to him,
but mostly she blamed herself.

Rob was last, arriving at a quarter past six. Only
Sean listened sympathetically to his tale of parking
his car. The others were politely cool. Lorna had
never had patience with Rob's lateness – it did not
show enough respect – and she was now in no mood to
be tolerant. When he asked if anyone had worked out
the quickest route to the Barbican, she sensed his
casual attitude again, and any remaining lighthearted-
ness evaporated. The evening was spoilt. She had
blown it with Roland. They would arrive late, and she
didn't fancy sitting through a load of old-fashioned
gabble. She might as well make her excuses and leave.

After the change at Victoria to the Circle Line, Lorna
was squashed next to Albert's thermos. He would
have shared a sandwich, but these were not conditions
for a picnic. Albert told her about his wife who had
gone back to Trinidad ten years ago, and never
returned. Lorna looked sympathetic, and shouted, 'It
can't be easy,' but her mind was at the other end of
the carriage. Even in the crush, under Sean's high-
pitched giggle she could hear Roland's deep laugh.
Something was amusing him. She craned her neck to
look. He seemed to be having more fun than she was.
Could she move down the carriage? Would Roland
share the joke with her?

At Moorgate the City of London had painted a yellow line to lead pedestrians along the high walkways to the Barbican Theatre. It reminded Lorna of the one she had followed in hospital after her father's heart attack. One false step there to another colour and you found yourself awaiting treatment in the Gastro-urology Department.

Like children who have vowed not to step on pavement cracks, the group started to walk carefully along the line. Rob steamed ahead with Sean, Darren and Albert. Gloria and Esther, whose ankles were swelling, were in the rear with Yvonne and Lorna. Lorna noted with concern that Roland was now some yards in front, chatting animatedly with Cynthia. She followed them anxiously with her eyes. Surely he was not the type to take offence without reason? She hadn't intended any. But what was he talking about so eagerly now?

As they advanced through the maze, to quench her chattering mind, she gazed up at the balconies of the grey concrete towers. In silhouette, they reminded her of the serrated edges of a cheesegrater. Had all this writing and reading gone to her head? She would put it, anyway, in her diary. Was it a simile or a metaphor? What did it matter? She would note it down. But mostly she would write out her conversation with Roland, their *short* conversation, and decide what she really thought. Was he still talking with that Cynthia? That was the trouble with nurses, they were trained in listening.

Trying to put aside her disappointment, she looked at the flats more closely. 'They don't go in for nets, do they?' she said to Gloria.

'They may be well off round here,' said Gloria, 'but concrete's concrete.'

'They go all mucky after a while,' said Lorna. 'It's the rain. Yet they cost a bomb to rent. My brother-in-law did some wiring up here once. There's a waiting list to get in.'

'On our estate,' said Gloria, 'there's a waiting list to get out.'

'I wouldn't move here,' said Esther. Despite the glimpse of St Paul's, this wasn't the London of bright buildings she had pictured in her childhood Jamaican dreams.

Lorna saw that the men were now all together, ahead of them. Even Cynthia had now hung back. Had she too said something out of place? Or had she and Roland arranged to meet later? Would he run her home? She had to find out.

The men were laughing again. Lorna hoped the evening was not going to develop into a boys' night out. They had come across an illuminated stretch of water with revolving fountains, and all stopped to stare down. As the women joined them, Sean repeated, 'Yes, it does look like a sewage works.' Lorna wondered if the whole class had caught the disease of searching for far-fetched comparisons, and watched to see if Roland found this amusing.

The line led them through a small door and then abandoned them. When Lorna had been to see *Cats* and *Phantom of the Opera* with Tracey and Louise there had been glossy photos in the foyers, like the displays Marks put up to show the newest lines and teach you what to team with what. Here there were a few arty posters, but no enlargements of people in the play. They only knew they were somewhere important by the static electricity from the golden handrails and the posh carpets.

Inside, their laughter and conversation subsided. To find the main foyer, they had to take a lift to a lower level, and try as she might, Lorna could not squeeze next to Roland. She was a little ashamed. A week ago she had been telling herself it was good to debate points with people when you went out, rather than assessing men, so why was she suddenly so concerned that she might be stuck all evening with Gloria and Esther?

She knew now she would be miserable if she had to spend the evening near anyone else but Roland. Even though her shop training and her love for her father made her compassionate with all sixty-year-olds, she did not see herself as a listening ear for Albert in his loneliness. She did not respect Rob enough to consider him as anything but a teacher, and anyway, he was married. Sean irritated her by his pushiness, and Darren was a laugh, but really, just a poor imitation of Diane's Barry. No, it was Roland she wanted. Roland, who had spoken few words to her, but who seemed modest, quiet, thoughtful, hiding a sadness she wanted to share or help get rid of, but who also seemed to have strength of character and could evidently be a laugh. She had thought so much about him, and not only about his personality. She needed to know if he was 'attached', as her mother would say. If she managed to have a proper talk with him, would he open up? She would have a quiet word with Rob.

Though she was impressed by the foyer's height and space, it had a confusing number of bars, toilets, ticket desks, stairs, trollies and shuffling queues. She looked at the people sitting on leather seats reading the programme reverently, drinking lager from bottles with old-fashioned stoppers, or listening to students scraping away on violins. Hoping to draw Roland into conversation again, she said loudly, 'It's funny they allow buskers.'

'Will they buzz off if we chuck them enough money?' asked Darren, wincing.

'This,' said Rob, waving his arms, 'you have to understand, is a modern cathedral. Culture is now our god.'

'It's more like Gatwick,' said Lorna. She caught Roland smiling at her remark. Had she been over-sensitive? Perhaps there was hope! She noticed, and noticed that she noticed, that most of the bar staff and the people selling teas and coffees were black. Also, come to think of it, apart from their group, there didn't seem to be many black people going to the show. One or two couples, done up smart, and a few teenagers, in those floppy clothes they liked, probably from a school party, but that was it. She wondered if that was why some of the old biddies were giving their party dirty looks. But it might have been because Albert had brought out his thermos.

Despite her worries, they had made good time, and there were fifteen minutes before the play started. She felt like a coffee herself, but was shocked by the prices – almost as much for a cup as for a whole jar in Marks. Gloria and Esther suggested an expedition to the Ladies, so they would know where it was in an emergency. Lorna invited Cynthia to accompany them. In the toilet Gloria admired the gold taps and mirrors, but Cynthia said the pans needed cleaning. Esther said that when you looked closely, the whole building inside was just painted concrete. 'No different to our flats.'

'How much the tickets?' Albert was asking as they rejoined the group. Roland had been buttonholed by Sean.

'The ILEA paid,' said Rob. 'I said we're studying Shakespeare.'

'And are we?'

'We are tonight.'

'What's it about then, this play?' Rob had told them the week before, but Albert needed reminding.

'People who make fools of themselves for love.'

'Easy,' said Albert, looking at Lorna. 'You don't need to tell me. When opportunity come, take your chance.'

Lorna moved back a few paces. She had tried to read *Twelfth Night* last week. In the first scene alone one character had used so many similes and metaphors that she had given up and decided to see if it made more sense on the stage.

Made bold by desire and trying to betray no calculation, she asked Rob, as casually as she could manage, 'Shall I give out the tickets? I know how you hate organising these little things.'

'Might as well give it to an expert,' said Rob. He pulled a crumpled envelope from the top pocket of his jacket, and handed it to her.

Lorna sorted out the numbers on the tickets and with an innocent smile asked the group in general, 'You don't mind where you sit?'

Detaching himself from Sean, Roland said, 'I want

non-smoking. Near the emergency doors.'

Who was he trying to impress with his second-hand joke? Cynthia? The whole party? Lorna had been the first to compare the place to an airport. He had looked her in the eyes as he spoke. Was he letting her know that at least he found her amusing? She felt a little more comfortable.

She allocated herself A9, Roland A10, and Cynthia A11, so that he would not suspect anything, and she could see if she had a serious rival.

'Wow!' said Sean, as Lorna handed him a ticket. 'Row A in the stalls!'

'Reserve your exclamation of delight,' warned Rob, 'until you're inside.'

The seats were in the front row, but the stage floor was at eye-level. Lorna reckoned that watching the play they would be like toddlers gazing up at adults. But though the view was restricted, the seating order was perfect. She could keep her eye on Cynthia, and she had Roland where she wanted him.

The party found their seats and sat down, making the level of noise which is the prerogative of any large group. It reminded Roland of the shouting of casual traders in the mornings before pitches were allocated. One or two ticket-holders stared ungenerously, as if they were intruders, and Roland thought their prejudices must be confirmed when Darren opened a spraying can of Coke and a packet of cheese and onion crisps.

Rob muttered something to Darren about it not being a video, and their reactions affecting the performance. Roland said not to worry, he had brought his football rattle in his jacket. He was beginning to realise that Rob was much more conventional than he wished to appear, and enjoyed teasing him.

He was in a lighthearted mood. He had tried to fathom Cynthia. She had not been at all open, and it had not bothered him. Neither was he irritated by Sean's endless chat. And, most promisingly, Lorna had manoeuvred herself next to him. He was waiting for her next move.

Sean had bought a programme at £1.50. When report of the price reached Roland in a vocal Chinese whisper, he replied that last year at Wembley he had paid £4 for a Michael Jackson souvenir booklet. And, he added, he didn't even get to keep it.

Why not? thought Lorna. She wondered if, ten years ago, he had spent hours practising the dance steps in *Thriller*, as she had. Michael Jackson had been her idol but her father had never allowed her to pin any posters of him on her bedroom walls. Who had he gone with to the concert?

Cynthia stopped staring around the auditorium and asked Roland if he went to many concerts. Lorna's ears pricked up. Was she playing the same game?

'No,' Roland sighed. 'I seem to have given up lately.'

Why? thought Lorna. Had something significant happened in his life? She would have gnawed at these questions but it was her turn for the programme which Sean was passing round with Gloria's box of Berry fruits. It contained a compilation of writings, drawings and photographs of prisons.

'One of the characters gets locked away in darkness,' Rob explained.

'I thought you said it was a comedy,' commented Albert, vainly offering round his sandwiches.

'Remember it's not the same play for us as it was for Shakespeare's audience,' Rob said.

The performance began with a wind band in tuxedos playing melancholy jazz. Roland could sense the two women on either side of him, Cynthia shifting uneasily, and Lorna pretending to be studying the stage.

'Did they have saxophones then?' asked Gloria loudly.

'Well, they've got the clothes wrong,' said Yvonne, who had found her place in the *Collected Works* and was prepared to follow the play like a sermon's text and prompt if necessary.

Rob passed a message to Darren that he really should save the rest of his crisps for the interval and silently hoped that Albert would stop exclaiming out loud whenever a new character came on the stage.

Unfortunately the front row suffered the harshest effects of the dry ice used in the second scene to suggest a storm at sea. It billowed in a cloud around their heads and obliterated all vision. Roland started coughing, but through the mist could see that Lorna was studying him more than the stage.

The Shakespearean sailors kicked dust into their faces and sprays of grit landed on Lorna's freshly ironed blouse. No wonder, she thought grimly, they give these tickets away. It would have helped if they had at least swept the stage before they began.

Her nostrils were quivering like a rabbit. She could smell Roland's aftershave. It wasn't overpowering, but spicy, with a hint of the ocean. During the mist, her leg had touched his. Quickly but reluctantly she had shifted back but the warmth remained.

When the mist cleared, and metal frames had stopped revolving and flying up and down, the set looked like a giant freezer basket. Lorna felt as if she were floating herself, into uncertain territory.

Yet as far as the play was going, was she in for a heavy evening? She feared she would not understand and that Roland might notice. She willed herself to concentrate. She didn't want him to think she was a fidget. At first, the twentieth-century costumes were disconcerting. She supposed it was cheaper for them than the doublet and hose and those massive dresses you read about in historical romances.

Some of the actors were black, which was a surprise. Lorna recognised two of them from *The Bill* and *Brookside*. The best was Feste who sang his songs to a Calypso beat. The shipwreck seemed to have taken place in the Caribbean. That was why the fat knight and his mates got drunk on Malibu. She couldn't remember anything like that in Jean Plaidy.

Gradually, despite herself, as well as noting Roland's reactions, she became interested in the conflicts in the play: the Duke, who went on about the idea of being in love but never did anything about it; the Countess, who was in that coffee advert, falling for the girl dressed up as a boy; the girl falling for her master, who thought she was a bloke; and the head servant, who like Miss Robinson thought he had the right to boss everyone about, taking a shine to the Countess.

It was a lot more like real life than *Macbeth*. She

could sense that Roland was following closely. She must show she was similarly enthralled.

No one in the party was fidgeting. Darren's crisps lay uneaten on his lap. Yvonne had not found it necessary to follow the text with her finger. Sean had stopped echoing the ostentatious laughter of the other know-alls in the audience. Albert was on the edge of his seat. Whenever characters made declarations of love, he responded with an audible 'Oh dear!', and when the head servant was being spied on, he shouted, 'Behind you!'

These remarks drew tuts of disapproval from the permed hairdos and grey suits. Rob decided that they were like the responses of the groundlings in Shakespeare's time, and so were acceptable.

Roland thought he could tell that the actors were amused and pleased too, as far as any actors' faces ever show what they're thinking, and not what they're pretending to think. He registered how Lorna responded to it: the love scenes and complicated plotting and Albert's additions. He thought he knew what she was thinking, and pretending to think. With her sitting beside him, he knew he felt both pleased and agitated. He had forgotten what it was like to be next to someone whose reactions interest you. He could also hear Cynthia sighing. He wondered if she would prove a problem. He chuckled at the prospect of such a problem.

Lorna recorded his chuckle in her memory for playback later. Whenever she thought he would not notice, she glanced at him, and tried to work out what he was thinking. She caught his eyes three times and her hand brushed his when she picked up her stray handkerchief. She noticed too that he looked at Cynthia once or twice, but this did not distress her unduly.

It was hard work, taking in his reactions and the play, and after an hour and a half her senses were doing overtime. By the interval, she was exhausted.

At the bar she stiffened when Roland asked Cynthia what she was drinking. An orange juice. Lorna debated in her mind if any particular drink would make a better impression when Roland asked her, as he surely must. Meanwhile he was pressing Cynthia, 'All that partying on stage hasn't given you a taste for something stronger?'

Had he seen the prices? Lorna thought.

'Just the juice,' said Cynthia sharply.

Lorna judged that whatever the cost Roland was taken with the idea of matching drinks to the production. Like her, he was having an evening out, and wanted to celebrate being somewhere stylish. When he did ask her (thank God!) she replied, 'Malibu and pineapple, if that's all right.'

Roland grinned. Had she matched his notion?

When the drinks arrived, Cynthia removed her juice, and inspected the glass. Taking the Malibu, Lorna said, 'Thanks very much.' Trying to sound bubbly, she continued, 'It's good, the play, isn't it?'

'It's all right,' said Cynthia.

'It's like church,' said Roland, 'when you first go. You have the feeling most people know what's going on, and you have to learn.'

Was he a church man, thought Lorna, and drinking rum?

'The music's wrong,' said Cynthia. 'It's not what you expect in Shakespeare.'

'I disagree,' said Roland. 'It suits the holiday mood.'

'It's not much of a holiday for some, though, is it?' said Lorna, excitedly. 'They're all getting very worked up. And some of what's happening is vicious.'

'That's true,' said Roland.

'On the other hand,' Lorna continued, encouraged, 'perhaps you're right. It is a bit like holidays. I went to Benidorm this summer, and it was a nightmare. Everybody chasing everybody else and a lot of cheating.' She paused. The Mediterranean was shallow and calm compared with the uncertain waters of questioning into which she now dared to move. 'Did you go away, Cynthia?'

'No. I was studying. I can't afford holidays.'

Lorna breathed deeply. 'And what about you, Roland?'

'No, I didn't.'

She noted the answer. Not: 'I went with my mates,' or 'We didn't go anywhere this year,' but 'No, I didn't.' He wasn't married, and probably wasn't attached! The file she was compiling was filling up satisfactorily.

In the second half the drink made Roland even more relaxed and optimistic. The play showed that you couldn't have love without some pain. As his mother had said all the time when he was small, 'If you want good, your nose has to run.'

The clown sang to a slow pan beat about it raining every day. Roland thought he would adopt it as an anthem for the market. With any luck it would be raining again when they reached Brixton. Would

Lorna accept a lift? He visualised his car still parked (he hoped) by Kwiksave in the market. Would she think it a rust-bucket?

The clown's song was so sweetly sad that Lorna regretted it when the production ended with an up-tempo dance during which the actors encouraged the audience to clap along. Albert stood up and waved his thermos in one hand and his sandwich container in the other. Lorna wondered if she would have the chance to talk to Roland again before they reached Brixton.

After the change at Victoria, the party found a carriage with seats facing one another. They were in celebratory mood. They had survived. They were equal to the hairdos and suits who thought only they were good enough for Shakespeare. They were theatre-goers! Even the token madman in their carriage (a schizophrenic drunk who asked Sean ten times if he were Cliff Richard) could not dispel their sense of triumph.

Esther told Rob that the play had been 'most unusual'. Albert was drunk with euphoria, not rum. 'We have shared this evening together,' he preached. 'It's taken us away from dull grey Englan'.'

At Brixton station Darren disappeared quickly. Albert ran puffing for a bus, shouting goodbyes and thanks. Rob asked if anyone wanted a lift in his direction. Sean and Yvonne accepted. Roland said he had his car too, that he was only going up the road to Stockwell, but if that would be of any use to anyone. Gloria and Esther said if he didn't mind. Cynthia lived in Kennington, a mile further on. Roland said he was prepared to go out of his way just this once.

Then he asked Lorna if anyone were meeting her. When she said no, she too set off to join the squeeze into his car. 'Don't you envy me?' Roland called to Rob as the carloads departed in opposite directions. Rob thought the remark contradicted ILEA's anti-sexist guidelines, but as he was quite jealous of the attention the women were giving Roland, and had been having doubts about Shakespeare's soundness all evening, and it was half past eleven, he let it pass.

Cynthia was squashed into the back between Gloria and Esther. From the front seat Lorna could see in Roland's mirror that Cynthia looked less than cheerful. Could Lorna help it if her right heel had become stuck in the pavement and she was the last to climb in the car?

Roland let Gloria and Esther out at his estate. 'Put some lager on ice,' he said. 'I'll check you later!' They shrieked.

Then he drove Cynthia home, passing at the Oval that evening's crop of buses halted by their conductors because of squabbles, arguments and fights. To free Cynthia, Lorna had to get out of her seat again. Cynthia gave Roland a curt thank you but blanked Lorna entirely.

So at last Roland was driving her home. She had not been driven alone by a man she liked for so long that her mind was a maze of possibilities.

'Pretty neat, this evening, wasn't it?' he said, switching on a jazz station. The speaker on Lorna's side was working.

To give precise directions, Lorna had to concentrate,

but it seemed Roland knew her street, and had been there to buy spares for the Escort.

Lorna was longing to test if her interest, desire, was reciprocated, to say something like, 'Next time you need a spare part, drop in,' but she didn't want to speak to Roland as she had the blokes in Benidorm. She didn't want the evening to end with a fumbled question or a misfired remark.

Instead she said, 'It's very good of you to put yourself out,' opening the door on her side and scraping it on the camber as she got out. Standing on the pavement, pulling her clutch bag closer to her, she added, 'See you at the class on Wednesday.'

'See me?' Roland answered. 'You sure will.'

He hooted and waved as he drove away.

As Roland drew up to the traffic lights of Camberwell New Road, a policeman on the pavement stuck out his arm in front of the car, and indicated that he should pull in. The policeman strolled round to his quarter-open window. 'Mr Stephens,' he told him. 'Out of the car, please.'

Roland climbed out, dazed. Why had they stopped him? At the Barbican prices, he had only had one rum and blackcurrant. Hardly enough to make his driving erratic. His tax wasn't out of date. Had thinking about Lorna made him go through a red light? They must have radioed their computer to trace him from the number plate. Knowing his name gave them power over him which he resented.

The policeman escorted Roland to the pavement, where they joined another officer who was standing by a motor cycle. In a West Country accent (they were never Londoners) the first policeman demanded, 'Your driving licence, Mr Stephens?'

Surprise turned to anger. As he searched in his jacket, Roland asked, 'What's all this? You can't make random stops.'

'Who says this is random, Mr Stephens?' Noting its two endorsements for parking on chevrons, the policeman fingered Roland's licence with distaste. 'It is Mr Stephens, isn't it?' Roland nodded. Their computer was infallible. 'Mr Stephens, approximately a quarter of an hour ago this evening, did you carry four women in your car?'

Roland was startled again. 'Yes,' he said defensively. 'It's my car. I carry who I like.'

'And where did these four women board your car, sir?'

'Brixton.'

'Could you be more precise, sir?'

'The car was parked in Popes Road.'

'Were all these women known to you before this evening?'

'Yes.'

'Could you tell me their names?'

'What's all this about?'

'Just answer the question, sir.'

'Lorna. Cynthia. Gloria and Esther.'

'No surnames to the ladies, sir?'

'What?!'

'Unfortunate, sir.' The policeman stopped scribbling on his notepad. 'And you agree that you met these women in the market and took them to your car?'

Roland could not believe this. Was it a candid hoax for a television programme? 'I didn't meet them in the market. My car was parked there. We'd been to the theatre.'

'The theatre, sir?' The policeman threw his colleague a sceptical look. After three months on the beat he was growing familiar with wild invention. The bike, though, was receiving information about more urgent situations on its radio receiver, and raring to move off.

'Yes,' said Roland. 'The theatre. To see Shakespeare.'

'Shakespeare, sir? I hope it was enjoyable. I have to ask you, sir, if, after your visit to Shakespeare, in your car, was any money exchanged between you and these four women?'

Roland's fury exploded. 'No, it wasn't. Look, what are you saying? What is this all about? You don't have the right just to stop and question people's movements.'

The word 'right' riled the policeman, but he had spent two days of his Hendon training course learning how to deflate Afro-Caribbean anger, so Roland received an explanation. 'A number of vehicles have been plying for hire in the Brixton area as illegal mini-cabs. Women have been placed in difficult situations, and worse. Earlier this evening, Mr Stephens, you were observed in your car picking up and setting down four women in three different situations. Remember, your MOT has not been asked for, but strictly off the record, sir, your car doesn't look fit enough to carry you, let alone a full party of theatre-goers. But, be that as it may, you may recommence your journey. Your registration number has been noted. Let's just hope we don't meet again after your next visit to the theatre.'

* * *

At seven in the morning Weston rang Roland to demand the removal of the annuals. Roland gave him an earful of abuse. When they discovered they both had the day off, Roland agreed to call at his mother's at six o'clock that evening, because neither wanted to waste any of their free time bickering.

As it was, Roland wallowed in his unmade bed until eleven, then spent the rest of the morning tidying his bedroom. Last week a pigeon had flown in the open window, and it had shat upon the dressing table as he tried to guide the bird back to freedom. He fetched a bowl and brush and scrubbed the surface vigorously.

The more he reflected on being pulled in, the angrier he grew. It wasn't the stopping. It was the assumption that he couldn't have been going to the theatre, that he couldn't just have been doing people favours. He had been so stunned that he hadn't tried to force the truth on the policeman. He walked around the flat cussing and slamming doors and cupboards.

At the launderette he poured Persil with such aggression that most of his dosage was spilt. When the machine rested too long within its programme he kicked it, and, drying his sheets, he occupied more than his fair share of tumblers. When he came to wash his clothes, he bundled them together. The new crisp white shirt Lorna had admired became tinged with the grey of his market socks.

After fantasies of tracing the home of the arrogant young officer and pulping him against a wall with his own line of sarcasm and karate, he decided to write letters to the police, the papers, the London Programme, Margaret Thatcher, Bernie Grant and other as yet unfocused authorities. He would put his newly honed written fluency to use. Rob would be proud of him.

Despite his rancour, his mind also ran on the evening out, and a gentler, more optimistic passion possessed him. Lorna was definitely, definitely interested. She had made that obvious through her eyes, her non-accidental nudges, her attention to any stupidity he might say, her wish to boost his opinions. He had to hand it to her, her flirting was blatant, but successful.

The idea of her between his sheets was attractive. This had made him wish to stand up for himself, and prompted the overdue trip to the launderette. Last night, he had imagined Lorna's body in bed: her breasts, tanned legs, and auburn hair in his face. He would ask her out. She would be the first white girl he had gone with. Though he had often had dreams about them, he had never slept with a white girl.

In the days when they talked about such things, he and Weston had of course discussed the idea. Weston now had definite views. Roland knew that if – she should be so lucky – he took up with Lorna, the difference in colour would be significant to Weston, his mother, and himself. But he would worry about that after Lorna was actually underneath the duvet. Why was he already thinking long-term? He hardly knew the girl.

Why was she interested? What did she want? She might be one of those women who sleep with black men to complete some sexual shopping list, or adopt you as a fashion accessory in West End discos, for your bare chest, bandana and ripped jeans. After all, she had mentioned Benidorm, and he knew from the posse at the bank the kind of thing that went on there. But though she was eager, he didn't think Lorna was so crass or shallow. When that girl in the play's love problems had been sorted out last night, there had been tears on her cheeks. Someone who wept like that wasn't just after him to copy the latest Kylie Minogue videos.

Should he have brought her home? He had considered it throughout the play, but the evening had hardly been a date, and the bedroom had been a tip. Would she think him lukewarm because he hadn't been more forceful when they said goodbye? These questions as well as the police's arrogance had kept him awake all night.

At his mother's, Weston was sitting in the kitchen using a portable phone lent him by Charlie during his Jamaican holiday. As Roland waited, Weston made several 'business' calls which he extended un-necessarily.

When Weston had finished a last call to the African designers, Roland told him about the police. Weston was the first person he had spoken to face to face all day. For once, Weston listened, but showed no expression. When he had told his tale, Weston commented, 'I'm not surprised. You drive around in that beat-up Dagenham dustbin – what do you expect the police to think?'

'I don't expect to be disbelieved when I'm innocent.'

'Look where you were driving. I'm not surprised. And were you wearing those trampy clothes?'

'No, as it happens, I was dressed up smart. So what

you saying? That the police never stop flash blacks in fast cars? Get real!'

'No, I'm saying you should expect to be stopped. Be ready for them. But if you match their aggro with yours, you'll get nowhere. You know the police always distress it too much. You can't complain when they're just doing their business. And even if you wasn't, why let four women use your car like a taxi? You're soft.'

Mrs Stephens had been to the market. When she came in, Roland had to hear how she and Weston had that day received registration forms for the poll tax, which rumour had set at over five hundred pounds. Mrs Stephens seemed to think that the government had designed the tax as a punitive measure for blacks. 'Black people have no life,' she gasped, catching her breath after her walk up the stairs, as if she might expire and prove her theory. 'When we came to this mother country dem tell us Englan' was a land of Paradise.'

Roland supplied the response: 'But now the mother is getting wicked and want to flag her children.'

Taken aback by her own words, she began to unpack her shopping. 'Back home food grew on trees,'

'And here you gotta buy your food,' Roland intoned.

Weston began to explain that the poll tax was designed to make people realise the cost of services they took for granted, when his phone rang. His mother screamed, 'Lord, not a cent has that bwoy paid me for a month and him have a phone in him pocket!'

'I'll reach you later,' said Weston, to the phone. 'I have a window at, say, six-thirty.' He placed the machine on the table. 'I pay you monthly, Mother.'

'Yes, but can she cope with that?' asked Roland. 'She gets her other money weekly.'

Weston told his mother that Roland had been pulled in by the police. The telling pained and surprised Roland, for he would not have told her. The news wounded his mother, too. Her elder son, Roland, the market inspector everybody looked up to, in trouble. It wasn't possible. So far, for all their talk, her sons had kept themselves righteous. She needed to sit down again. Weston had not mentioned the details, nor would she have taken them in if he had. Holding her head, she asked, 'Is it serious?'

Weston replied, 'It's not serious. He's making a noise about nothing.'

'You're the one who told her,' said Roland. 'Mum, he's right. It's not serious. Nothing to worry about. A routine check.'

Mrs Stephens needed a pill, so she went to the bathroom. As she shuffled out, she muttered, 'Lord Jesus.'

When she could be heard at the bathroom cabinet, Weston looked at Roland. 'So it's not serious now?'

'Of course it's serious,' Roland replied. 'I'm innocent.'

'So what you going to do about it? Bomb the base?'

'I've got the chief's number. I'm going to write letters.'

'With your job, is that wise?'

'You think the council will object if I complain of police harassment? I'll be a hero. They'll name a street after me.'

'I don't want my brother identified as some agitator,' said Weston. 'It wouldn't help me. You weren't charged with anything – forget it.'

'I'm not forgetting it. And who's going to connect you with me?'

'We share a surname. We are in the public eye. People talk.' He stretched back in his chair. 'But you won't write no letters.'

'I'll phone, then,' said Roland, picking up Charlie's phone.

Weston snatched the instrument back and placed it inside his leather jacket. 'Sorry. Business calls only.'

Mrs Stephens had returned to the kitchen and seen the scramble. 'Your brother,' she told Roland, 'is stubborn. He get vexed when people mess with him tings.' She was interrupted by the doorbell.

'That'll be the doorbell,' said Roland, a childhood joke he and Weston had shared.

'More likely the police.'

'Weston,' said Mrs Stephens, addressing him to his face as Roland went to the door, 'what to do about Roland? You tink it's serious?'

'There's no problem,' said Weston. 'Just the police not showing enough respect.'

'Mum, it's Sherene,' Roland yelled along the corridor. 'With her gran's new catalogue. Do you want to see it?'

'When I was small,' mused Mrs Stephens, not hearing Roland, 'one policeman follow us just to look at our backside, not for riot.'

'Who's rioting?' asked Roland, returning.

'Who's rioting?' echoed Sherene, following. 'Not in this flat?'

''Ello, darlin',' said Mrs Stephens.

'Evenin', Mrs Stephens. What's up?'

'The police. They blast Roland last night and now Weston blast him.'

Her sons looked angrily at her and each other. 'Well,' said Sherene, removing her red coat, 'the last scene of *The Cosby Show*. All harmony and hugs, and have I told you in the last five minutes how much I love you?'

'Brother should be good to one another,' sulked Mrs Stephens.

'In trouble with the police, then, Roland?' Sherene asked. 'Rather a black mark for the Stephens family, isn't it, if we can use that expression? And moaning about it? It's funny, you know, I always thought you two were such coconuts, too squeaky clean, that you didn't believe in the oppression of Babylon?'

'Sherene,' said Weston, 'Mother will give me the catalogue when she's looked through it. I'll give any orders to Marcia and she can pass them to your grandmother. There's no need to delay yourself.' He indicated the door.

'Weston,' snapped Mrs Stephens, 'you supposed to talk with you mouth, not yuh finger. Sherene, rest. Roland's in trouble.'

'I'm not,' said Roland.

'There was no charge,' said Weston. 'If he's told me everything straight.'

'This must be very worrying,' Sherene smiled, sitting down.

'I'll fetch those albums,' said Weston, getting up.

'Chill,' said Roland. 'Leave them. I don't want my bedroom cluttered just now.'

'Neither do I. If you don't take them, I'll dump them.'

'It's me and you, then.'

'Oh,' said Sherene, remembering. 'How was the Shakespeare?'

'Good.'

'Did you impress all those literature-reading girls with your knowledge?'

'I might have.'

'He gave half the class a lift home,' said Weston, 'which is why the police pulled him.'

'Lord Jesus!' said Mrs Stephens. 'Because he's so soft, everyone seem to tek hadvantage.'

'Next time,' said Roland, 'there won't be so many.'

'Tell us more,' said Sherene.

Mrs Stephens' friends told her that both her sons, in their attitudes, were 'white t'inking'. Charmaine, when she was vexed and had wanted to annoy Roland, had also called him a 'coconut' – brown outside, white inside. When Roland quoted Martin Luther King – that you should be judged by the conduct of your character and not your colour – Charmaine had snapped that that was exactly what she was doing: that Martin Luther King had never met Roland, and that if he'd been to the mountain top and found Roland and Weston there, his Dream would have been seriously troubled.

Despite such jibes, Roland tried to live by King's principle, and bearing it in mind, later that evening for his homework – postponed as usual – he tried to describe the incident with the police as objectively as possible, and to pinpoint why he still felt so angry. He also wanted to impress Lorna with his analysis.

The police, he reasoned, were probably trying to

prevent attacks on women, and to catch rogue taxis. He himself spent his days suspecting irregularities and illegalities, but he was more discriminating. Surely they could see that a potential attacker would hardly pick up *four* women in the first place?

The deepest wound, though, was that he knew, with that babyface policeman, that if he had been white, he probably would not have been stopped, or at least given the benefit of the doubt. And when he said where he had been, his story would not have been immediately disbelieved. That policeman, and as far as he could tell, his companion on the bike, hadn't considered it possible he might be telling the truth. What also grated and fired his rage was that he knew he had a wider experience of Brixton than that youngster. He was more tactful, thoughtful, and tolerant.

OK – the policeman might have been one eager new recruit, but if he had treated Roland like that – who fortunately hadn't exactly lost his cool under inquisition – how might he deal with brothers on the front line?

It was the treatment, not the inquisition, he was criticising. He had as much stake in a less criminal South London as anyone. His block of flats was visited by drug dealers who drove down in massive cars from the outer suburbs to sell their poison. His mother had been mugged and burgled three times. Try as he might, even at school, as Sherene had hinted, Roland had not seen the police as oppressors. There was no hope, no future in thinking like that. He had cousins in Canada who were policemen. London, too, he argued, as his biro sped on, needed more blacks to take the shame of being 'coconuts' and join the force, before things would improve. After filling a waste-paper bin and five sides of A4 with his arguments, he felt calmer. He would show his essay to Lorna tomorrow evening and see what she thought.

He spent the next morning at Brixton police station. As their drills had not attacked it for some time, the council was proposing to dig up Station Road. Market pitches had to be resited and arrangements made for traffic flows and parking, so a meeting had been called. The traffic wardens were represented by a Jamaican called Mr Nembhard, who had once been a Rasta in Roland's year at school. His locks were shorn, but the uniform had gone to his head and his mouth, and he drilled holes in every proposal. Roland's views were more respected. He was known by the police on the market committee as a calm and well-prepared contributor. He listened and he made his points succinctly. Although Roland was suffering from a lapse of faith, this morning he made an effort to preserve his reputation.

He supposed that when he and Weston were youngsters, they had been lucky not to have been picked on, stopped and searched and accused, before irredeemable distrust had been built.

Such heavy matters were jumbled in his mind as he cultivated his anger, but gradually he thought more of the class that evening and of Lorna, and anyone watching his expressions would have seen them change from frowning to smiles of anticipation.

Arsenal were on television tonight in a Rumbelows match, and for a moment he hesitated about the class.

But he needed to show Lorna he was receiving and responding to her signals. Football could wait.

The normal set-up at the class might be awkward. Lorna usually arrived, like him, just on time after work – and if Rob were there, the class would already be focusing on some exercise; if not, they'd be discussing last week's homework. The only people who disappeared at the break were the smokers, so he could hardly draw her apart then, and she usually moved off swiftly at nine.

He decided to look in at Marks & Spencers when the meeting ended. The traffic warden was becoming heated about item 12. Roland had long realised that if you spent all day finding fault you could become carping about everything. Fortunately his benevolent nature had prevented too much critical development in his case. 'I think Mr Nembhard's made his point very strongly,' he said, indicating his wish to move on by shifting his papers.

He had always seen Lorna's store as too shiny, too harsh, too satisfied with itself, but today it gleamed invitingly. He did not know in what part she worked. He couldn't see her near the Christmas gifts, the potted plants, nor attending to a queue demanding refunds. He did not wish to stray through the rows of bras, slips, panties, tights and stockings, so he wandered idly past the food cabinets. Eventually he saw her, wearing a duvet waistcoat, standing by a till with a clipboard, supervising a trainee. When she looked up and noticed him, she blushed, and stopped in mid-sentence. He approached, and read her label. 'Hallo, Miss Duggan.'

'Hallo, Mr Stephens.' It was like her to have caught his surname too. With the trainee panting for further instruction, and a row of customers regretting they had chosen the slowest till, when it came to it, Roland could not think what to say in a few words.

Lorna pressed a bell, set a light flashing, and another supervisor appeared from the store's endless supply of helpful clones. 'Mrs Khan,' Lorna said, her voice wavering, 'can you keep an eye on Kelly for a moment? Watch her finger work and check the change. I have to talk to this gentleman.' Giving Roland her full attention at last, she smiled, and asked, 'Is this an official visit?'

'My brief doesn't extend this far,' Roland replied, 'but I'm glad to hear I'm a gentleman.'

'As long,' she replied, 'as you don't prefer blondes.'

Her repartee was second-hand, but it did not matter. For once Roland was at a loss for words, so he said, rather lamely, 'Have you done the homework?'

Lorna smiled. She must know he hadn't sought her out just to ask about homework. 'Yes,' she said.

'What's yours about?'

'Oh. Children. Shopping.'

Trying to sound sincere, he said, 'Sounds interesting.'

Lorna looked over to Kelly and Mrs Khan. They seemed to mirror her anxious glance. 'Thanks for the lift on Monday,' she said. 'You got caught, didn't you, acting as a taxi service?'

'I wouldn't say that,' said Roland, gritting his teeth. 'But,' he hesitated, 'I'll have the car again tonight. Give you another lift, if you like.'

He saw Lorna breathe in. Mrs Khan was gesturing

for her to return to the puzzled trainee. It appeared there was some problem over faulty bar codes. 'Well,' she said, moving back to the till, 'who could refuse an offer like that?'

'If the police haven't pulled in the car,' added Roland.

Lorna laughed.

That evening there was a division between those who had been to *Twelfth Night* and those who hadn't. Even Rob noticed the sour faces of the others as the lucky nine spilled over with anecdotes. They talked more about the prices of drinks and the confusing layers of the Barbican than Shakespeare's layers of meaning, but Rob supposed this was inevitable. To mould the class together again, he explained that the exam had marks for speaking and listening as well as reading and writing, and he hoped the homework had focused their thoughts on one subject. Though it was scary, would anybody like to present their argument and lead a discussion?

Never one to be held back, Albert volunteered to speak about meditation. The class learnt that he had adopted the word 'chrysanthemum' as a mantra. Some, embarrassed by the exotic, shifted uneasily. Fortunately Esther talked next about clothes and how expensive they had become. This created a consensus. To raise the discussion from anecdotes, Rob tried to argue that fashion was an artificial capitalist device to draw money from gullible customers, but Claudette said: 'You could do with some new clothes.' She was scolded publicly by her mother. Most of the class wondered why Rob tolerated the rudeness.

Next, Lorna took up Esther's theme and spoke about how children's television programmes promoted toys so that children became obsessed with owning them. She had confirmed this the Saturday previously when, to avoid thinking about her father signing the contract, she had taken Jason and Natasha shopping in Oxford Street.

Because she understood the allure of shops, her talk was passionate. 'Kids are just as happy with cardboard boxes and saucepan lids.' She concluded, 'The thing is, kids and adults, we always think the next thing we're going to buy is what will make us happy. We shouldn't let kids start thinking that too early. It never is. It never does.'

Roland was admiring Lorna's eloquence. Could she make him happy?

Rob warmed to Lorna's theme. 'Yes, yes, yes, you're right. Surface glamour is just an illusion. We must teach people that.'

'Roland, you're quiet tonight,' said Esther, interrupting as the argument soared. 'What did you write about?'

'Police harassment.' Roland wondered if Rob would treat this topic as respectfully as the liberal teachers at school. A history teacher had once responded to the demands of the young Rastas – 'Don't tell us about Lambeth cholera in the 1840s, teach us the oppression of Babylon' – and taken them to the British Museum to see the solid winged horses which had once stood sentinel outside Nebuchadnezzar's palace. Roland remembered them to this day. They were bigger than the man-size speakers at Fresh's nightclub.

Rob looked at his watch suddenly and said, 'Perhaps

we could leave that topic until after the break.'

Roland smiled.

During the break several men decided in favour of Arsenal rather than a lot more chat, and afterwards, Rob allowed an inaudible newcomer from Malta to talk about his island for so long that there was no time left for any more exposition. All in all, Roland was relieved. First he wanted to talk to Lorna on her own about the police. Her reaction would tell him a lot.

At the end of the lesson Lorna stayed in the classroom studying the remedial reading posters. Roland found it necessary to ask Rob about the agreement of pronouns and verbs which he was finding troublesome in his written work. 'It's the African influence on West Indian speech', Rob said earnestly.

'The buggers get everywhere,' said Roland.

Startled, Rob gathered his plastic bags and ushered Roland and Lorna through the door. Saying 'See you next week', he left them.

The corridor was deserted. Roland looked across at Lorna.

'Is your offer still on?' she asked.

'Buy now, while stocks last.'

'Or the car,' said Lorna.

Roland was almost entirely happy to let her cuss the car. After all, he had set the example, and she had been in the vehicle.

He had not, though, noticed the state of the inside for a long time. Along the handbrake and gear lever there were traces of sweet and sour sauce from a leaking takeaway beaker. As on Monday, Lorna had difficulty with the grudging mechanism of her seat belt. Both speakers had now ceased working. Roland thought that a second ride really must show her what a garbage hole the car was. He'd kept it because he couldn't afford anything better, and because he knew it annoyed Weston. It might do for him on his own, but Lorna deserved something better. Surface glamour may be an illusion, but it can create a good impression with a woman you have the hots for.

'Have you got time for a drink?' he said, as he drove along South Lambeth Road.

'All that talking makes you thirsty,' Lorna said. 'At least, it does me.'

Roland hoped it was not the car's smell. He had thought of taking Lorna to the new rum bar. Weston and Sherene had agreed last night that it had style, but that made Roland suspicious. It might seem too classy for a first drink. And besides, he only had a fiver, and he knew the prices of the drinks at the bars Weston frequented; they conspired to make you think you were somewhere important.

'Fancy anywhere in particular?' he asked.

'Not the Old Kent Road,' said Lorna.

'The cheapest street in Monopoly? No way.'

Roland didn't want to go somewhere he was known. Although he had rejected the rum bar, he wanted somewhere a bit special. And there were some areas he wouldn't go, areas heavy with white drinkers, or posher areas where one black face still made white people edgy.

He remembered how his history teacher had also once led them on a trail down Borough High Street past some pub Shakespeare was supposed to have frequented. Shakespeare was one thing that he and Lorna had in common. He liked the notion of going there: after Monday evening, it seemed a neat touch, a dream topping. 'The Borough all right?' he asked.

It was fine.

As he drew into the market by the Cathedral, he said, 'It's a bit olde worlde, but they have a proper market here.'

He led Lorna across the road, re-experiencing the sensation of escorting someone you fancy. 'All right?' he checked. 'Your talk tonight was good. You really let rip.'

'It seems funny they give you marks for gabbling,' said Lorna. 'Just up my street. You were quiet, but then it's often the quiet ones who have the most to say.'

She was being as generous to him as he was to her. It was a delicate balance.

At first he could not find the alleyway, but after walking up and down the High Street they stumbled into a courtyard where they came across the old galleried inn. As they paused near the outside Gents, Roland explained, 'This is where Shakespeare used to drink, or something.'

Lorna indicated the toilet. 'And that's where he used to, you know?'

'Probably.'

'They've found one of his theatres near here, haven't they? It was on Thames News.'

'I'd like a Time Machine,' said Roland. 'To go back to one of those theatres. Like in *Doctor Who*.'

'I could never bear that programme,' said Lorna.

Roland told her it had always been a favourite. Lorna said she had noticed he had a thing about space and science from the bits of his work that Rob read out. Roland was flattered. What else had she noticed? He knew little about her, really.

The pub was crowded with office workers who should have caught trains from London Bridge hours ago, and the dregs of the summer's tourists. The only black person Roland could see (a medical student from Guy's?) nodded to him as he carried the drinks from the bar. He and Lorna squeezed on to a trestle bench between an American coach party and a lone drunk, slumped muttering over his beer.

'You didn't get to do your talk,' Lorna repeated, smiling as she sipped her gin and tonic.

Roland had changed his mind about discussing the police tonight. It would leaden things. He did want to know what she thought – it would be a test before greater involvement – but it could wait. He felt Lorna would be on the side of fairness, but she might also think that on this occasion he was making a fuss about nothing much.

Instead, over his lager, he found himself telling her about his meeting that morning. To his relief and surprise, he could tell that she was fascinated. 'There's so much to think about,' she said, her eyes wide open, 'but then, everything has to be planned really, doesn't it?'

Lorna insisted on paying for the second round, but he ordered the drinks. Lorna seemed not to want to go to the bar, but slipped him a fiver across the table. He had another half and Lorna a mineral water. He said that she certainly rang the changes with her drinks.

Lorna replied, 'Most of the time what I'd really like in a pub is a cup of tea, but it wouldn't do really, would it?' He smiled. Sometimes she seemed so adventurous, sometimes like a *Carry On* film.

As they walked back to the car at closing time, Roland realised that she had not asked the questions other women demanded immediately: what were his salary and prospects, how many brothers and sisters did he have, were his parents over here, was he Church or not? She had also not trapped him into revealing his romantic history. All she really knew was what estate he lived on and what his car was like.

He drove her home and stopped the car in her road in the same place as on Monday night. He switched off the engine, and it juddered to a halt.

'That was a nice idea,' Lorna said. 'A Shakespeare play on Monday, and a Shakespeare pub on Wednesday!'

'Where to next, then?'

Lorna studied his face for a moment. 'Well,' she said, 'I don't think Shakespeare went to Catford Dogs or we could go there.'

Roland noticed the nervous 'we'. 'Catford Dogs?' he repeated. Was she serious?

'I've never been there,' Lorna said, 'but my dad says it's a right laugh.'

'Friday?' Roland asked.

'Fine by me,' Lorna nodded eagerly.

'Seven o'clock? Pick you up?'

As she went to open the door, Roland leant over, put his face down and kissed her on the cheek. Then he moved his lips to hers, and rested them there.

For a minute he looked into her eyes, and then he

said, 'If you want to open the door, you need to pull up the button.'

'I don't want to open the door, but I suppose I'd better.'

Lorna got out slowly and, looking back all the time, walked across the road to her house.

6

Going to the Dogs

Lorna lay spread on her floral duvet. She stretched
her arms and legs, and flapped her feet up and down.
As on the rubber castle at Jason's school fête, she
bounced on the bed. Then she pogo-ed past the
dressing table, and pushed up the sash window. She
wanted to shout 'Yes!' to the whole street. She wanted
the multiplying satellite dishes to receive the message
of joy and transmit it, first to Roland's estate, and
then to the stars. But her science was faulty, and
apart from the drunks and the rogue taxi drivers,
there was no one in tune with her exhilaration. The
snores of her father showed that for once he was
sleeping soundly, and her mother, now that she had
registered that Lorna was in, would soon be dreaming
of removal lorries being overturned on the road to
Lydd.

No such concern weighed or checked Lorna. She
wanted to yell. She wanted to cheer and whoop and
all the other expressions of delight in that sub-section
of Yvonne's Thesaurus. All evening she had tried to
achieve a balance between appearing delighted and
suffocating Roland with her enthusiasm. Roland
himself had set the time and place for the next meeting.
He had made the booking. As on Sundays when she

mixed a successful Yorkshire pudding, she had got the measure right.

She was purring like next door's cats. Her heart was pounding. Waves of delight washed over her. It was not – what did Rob call it? – a cliché. She felt the warmth spread from head to toe like the flushes which not long ago had been her mother's constant companions. She tried the breathing exercises she had practised on the deep-pile shag carpet with her sister when Diane had been carrying. But neither her mother's climacteric pills nor ante-natal respiration could have calmed her.

She reached for her diary. Sitting on her bed, she hastily wrote a few words, then let the book and biro drop. She wanted to savour her feelings – of hope, of being special and valued – not have them evaporate while she tried description. There was too much to write. Her diary served times when she needed to create excitement. Now she did not need to. She thought of the kiss. There had been the slightest touch of his white teeth. Such beautiful lips.

Now he was going to take her to the Dogs. She had only suggested the place as a joke, but Roland, though he could make and taste jokes, had a seriousness which made him pursue ideas once he had a notion. First, the tropical drinks. Then, the Shakespeare pub. Now the Dogs. Did he think she went there often?

Until his illness her dad had gone most Fridays, but not any more. She longed to introduce Roland to her father. She wondered if she should make him come in when he called to pick her up, get things over with, from the start. At first her mum and dad would be shocked, but when they saw what a nice bloke he was, they'd be pleased she had someone like him taking her out. She remembered some old film on the television one Sunday about a white girl who'd taken a black doctor home for dinner. Her mother had said then, 'Now, if they was all like that, you wouldn't mind.' They'd moan, and there would be sticky patches, but when they got to know him, they wouldn't mind.

There had never been anyone like him before. So calm, so smart. Such a straight back. Tomorrow she would tell Tracey and Louise.

Benidorm had nothing on Brixton. She wouldn't phone Diane and Barry yet. Diane might be awkward, as she always found some objection with any of the blokes her sister fancied. Jason and Natasha would love him. He'd be good with kids.

She would tell them all at work. For weeks all their chat had been of bottom drawers, trousseaux, weddings and honeymoons. They'd looked at her strangely if she'd started talking about the classes. Now she would make them listen.

She closed her eyes and recalled Roland's face. She would not let it fade, the brown eyes and long eyelashes. She fell asleep conjuring them, his ears, his hair, his neck, his long fingers, his pale nails, the back of his hands . . . all the parts she had studied so far.

Though she did not imagine she would, she slept. The alarm, with its two elves see-sawing on a spotted toadstool, rang piercingly at seven. She groaned for a moment, at being conscious again, but then the evening before came into focus, and she snuggled back under the covers with delicious content. Seven-thirty on Friday, he had said. Thirty-six hours. Could she wait?

She could search him out today across the road at work, but that would be pushing it. He might say he'd only been joking, or that something or someone else had turned up. She wouldn't risk that.

Now it was morning, as she washed and checked her features in the bathroom mirror, she knew that she would not make any calls or say anything at work or arrange an introduction with her parents just yet. If this were to last, she had to get it right from the start.

Though the focus of her desire in her dreams, Roland's colour was a big visible difference. Her mum and dad wouldn't know what to say, but they'd soon start talking. They wouldn't know what they thought either, but it wouldn't stop them mouthing off. It would have been bad enough if she'd taken up with a man from North London, or the wrong part of Northern Ireland, but their protests wouldn't be as noisy as the instant alarm Roland would cause. She couldn't ignore it. She didn't know if they'd ever considered this a possibility. (She herself had often considered it.) She would need to think about how she could bring up the subject. She couldn't hurt Roland. She thought back to six weeks ago when all that concerned her was announcing that she was staying on in London. She had imagined then that that would be the most difficult thing to tell.

In the kitchen her mother was pushing her All-Bran around the bowl. She laid down her spoon. 'Well, that's that.'

'What's what?'

'The move. Your father's booked a date.'

'When?'

'November the tenth.'

'November the tenth!'

'It's earlier than we thought.'

'It's three weeks away!'

'I know it's three weeks.'

'Doesn't Dad need two months' notice?'

'What about my notice? He says his don't matter. If you ask me, they only kept him on because they felt sorry for him. He can't be much use. He dithers.'

'He does what he can.'

'I'll miss a fortnight's wages. But it's done now.'

'Will they give him a big send-off?'

'There's not many of the old ones left. There'll be a bit of a do.'

'It's all very quick.' Lorna poured herself a cup of tea. What would Roland be having for breakfast? Would he have an appetite? Would she still be seeing him in three weeks' time? She tried to concentrate on what her mother was saying.

'And that's another thing – Barry can't do the moving. Can't or won't, more like. He's off abroad somewhere. Work, Diane says.'

'So who's doing it?'

'Who do you think? Usual story. Somebody at his work knows somebody.'

Lorna was pleased with this distraction. Her mother had not noticed she could not eat anything. She tried to make her more positive. 'At least it's settled now.'

'I'm glad you think it's settled,' said Rose, lighting a cigarette. 'All this happened last night while you was out. We could have done with you here. You,

you've got to sort something out quick. At this rate you'll be kipping on the streets.'

'No,' said Lorna decisively. 'I won't.' Her eyes avoided her mother's. 'That room you were going on about – with Trixie. Is it still going?'

Rose looked irritated. 'Trixie offered it weeks ago, but you didn't want to know. She'll be a bit miffed now if I say you've suddenly changed your mind. She don't like to be messed about. Probably let it by now. You'll have to phone her yourself.'

All day Lorna found it difficult to concentrate. Two boys on work experience set off the hose in the staff toilet, and flooded the back stairs and the stationery stock. The fire brigade, the phone calls to the schools, and the reprimands and dismissals occupied her, but could not oust Roland from the central position in her mind.

Several times she almost decided to dash across the road in a break, but always checked herself. Once she thought she glimpsed Roland near the pre-cooked Italian selection with a basket, but it was a man of similar build and height.

As she misted the hibiscus and jasmine in the houseplant corner, she asked herself, would he expect sex on the first night? Who might he talk to afterwards? His brother? His mates? Was he the kind of man who would tell people her secrets? She didn't think so.

In the afternoon Miss Robinson called in and seemed surprised to hear that Lorna had acted on her suggestion about qualifications. Lorna knew that in their brief conversation once again she appeared distracted. Why did the woman always turn up when she had something else on her mind?

When she arrived home, Diane was there with the children. Natasha was combing the acrylic hair of a blue plastic pony, while Jason was pressing an electronic game. A gorilla had to swing across the screen on a rope to catch a banana. The bananas were fading and Jason was grizzling. Rose had popped out to the shops for cup cakes and Kia-ora.

'How's Barry?' asked Lorna.

'Busy. Off to Spain next week.'

'Taking holidays on his own now?'

'If you must know,' said Diane, 'he's wiring some time shares near Malaga.'

'It's OK for some.'

'It's work. When you've a home to keep up, you need every penny. You'll find things a lot less easy when you move in with this Trixie.'

'Who says I am?'

'It's fixed,' said Diane. 'Mum saw her at work. You're to be shown the room tomorrow evening.'

'We'll see about that.'

'You can't afford to be picky now. Sometimes you have to make the best of a bad deal. At least this Trixie's place is nearer us. It won't be such a journey back at nights.'

Lorna could guess what was coming.

Diane continued, 'I've a few evenings fixed up in the next weeks.'

'While the old man's away?'

Diana gave her a withering look. 'Next Tuesday,' she said, in a hushed voice, 'if you must know, I'm running an Ann Summers party, for some friends. I certainly don't want these two around then. Can you take them off my hands?'

Lorna's nighties, she realised, were all frayed at the edges. She needed some new ones. Perhaps she would gate-crash. 'And what else?' she asked.

'Susie's having a hen night.'

'With male strippers?' Lorna mouthed the words in a whisper. Jason looked up from his game. Diane put a finger to her lips. 'Well,' said Lorna, 'I'll have to see. There might be one or two nights I can't oblige.'

'Why not?'

'With Christmas coming on, we have to work more lates.'

'This isn't Christmas. This is the next few weeks. You won't want to be here every evening once they start packing. You know what they'll be like. And when they've gone you'll feel at a loose end. Can you do Tuesday for starters?'

'I'll let you know.'

'You're edgy tonight. You're not P-R-E-M-E-N-S-T-R-U-A-L?'

Diane allowed Jason to get down from the table before Rose had finished her tea. This provoked comment. Natasha covered herself and her little pony with chocolate icing. Toys should not have been brought to the table. Shortly afterwards, Diane left. Lorna had given no promise to babysit next Tuesday or any other evening. As Diane went out, Jason wanted to know who Ann Summers was and why was she having her party at their house and not McDonald's.

Fred came in half an hour later. If Rose suspected he had been saying farewell to one of his floozies, she did not say. She moaned instead about the tea-chests he had found at work, transported in the Cortina, and was now lugging in during *EastEnders*. Spiders were soon crawling across the carpet which was too good to leave to the council but would not fit in the bungalow. At eight o'clock Rose went into the front room and began wrapping the best dinner service with pages from the pile of free newspapers she had been saving since the move was mooted.

Lorna thought that her parents should work out a system, but did not want to interfere. She sensed that for them it would be strange and sad to be packing away so many memories. She wondered if, like her, they intended to clear some of the clutter in their heads at the same time as they cleared the house. Her mother, she admitted reluctantly, sometimes had so much of a struggle just getting through life, that Lorna doubted she would be very successful.

She walked into an argument about the Spanish porcelain figures of cats, dogs and women praying. Her father said they were bloody soppy, he'd never liked them, and now was a good time to get rid of them. He didn't want them in the bungalow. Her mother said could he leave her to wrap them on her own, then if they got smashed, she'd know whose fault it was. Muttering, her father went into the back yard to sort out his tools.

Biting her lip, Lorna said to her mother, 'So you've fixed it with Trixie? Thanks.'

'You're lucky. She had let it to some nurse, but she left after three days.'

Lorna wouldn't ask why.

'She wants to see you there tomorrow night, at

eight. We're to come with you, me and your father.'

'I can't tomorrow night.'

'You're not working. I checked on your list.'

'No, I'm not working.'

'Then what you playing at?'

Lorna hesitated. 'It's to do with the evening class.'

'That class has gone to your head. Not more Shakespeare.' She picked up a straw donkey carrying red plastic wine jars.

'No, not more Shakespeare.'

Fortunately her mother seemed too preoccupied to interrogate her further. 'Well, it's awkward. Trixie's expecting you.'

'You should have let me phone her.'

'I know you. I want something settled.'

'I'll phone her now.'

'You'll be lucky to catch her in.'

Lorna caught her. Trixie sounded as if she liked to control events, but passion making her determined, Lorna arranged to call round on Saturday morning.

'But,' Trixie shouted, 'tell your mum and dad they're expected on Friday anyway.' Lorna held the phone from her ear. 'Might as well get a few g and t's from the old man before he buggers off to God knows where.'

Her mother wasn't too pleased. 'I was only going because of you. I haven't got the time now to stop out drinking with your father. He's got enough to do here. But we'll have to go now after what you've done, or she'll be even more put out. Can't you skip this nightschool thing? What's more important, after all?'

Her father also seemed annoyed when Lorna rushed to tell him where he was spending Friday evening.

'That bloody woman,' Fred puffed. 'What your mother sees in her, I don't know.'

'Everybody needs a friend,' said Lorna.

Her father ignored this. 'Why you want to go and live with her beats me.'

'Hadn't you better go now she's invited you?' Lorna asked, as casually as possible. She did not want to appear too keen, or rouse suspicion. 'For Mum's sake.'

'Anyone would think you was having half a dozen blokes back while we're out.'

'I'm going out myself.'

'Oh?' Her father stopped rummaging among broken tools. As far as Lorna could tell he was shifting everything from one box to another. 'Who's this with?'

'Some bloke from the evening class.'

'Is he a swot?'

'You could say that.'

'Where's he taking you?'

'Not sure yet.'

'Somewhere posh? Shakespeare?'

'Not Shakespeare.'

'Well, you be careful.'

'And Dad, Mum doesn't know it's a bloke.'

Friday passed as slowly. The desire to see Roland at work increased hourly, but as the damp afternoon dragged on, Lorna knew, like the well-packed digestives she was shelving, that she would not crumble. Occasionally she wondered what she would do if Roland stood her up. She dispelled this demon by thinking about possible clothes for the evening, and how she might arrange her hair.

In Benidorm a beach towel had been enough to

stake her place by the pool. Once home she laid claim to the bathroom by spreading the same towel on the radiator, running the hot water, and placing her transistor on the windowsill. She turned up the volume. She had yet to decide if there was a current song which described her and Roland.

After the bath, she studied her face in the misting mirror tiles, and as much of her body as she could see. She met her features with some approval. On holiday, the annual opportunity for long reflection in mirrors, she had reminded herself of her good points. Her tan had now faded but on Wednesday evening her ego had received a boost which had done more than hours of sunlight.

When she unbolted the door in answer to complaints about time and water, as a penance she had to admire a top embroidered with glittering butterflies which her mother had bought that day from an East Street stall.

She could hear her father muttering downstairs. He too would have been ordered to change.

When her father had taken her mother to the Dogs, Rose had worn her best frocks, jewellery and fake fur. When Diane used to go out with Barry before they married, she had left the house in jeans, heels and ankle bracelet. Not too tarty, not too demure was Lorna's aim. After much pulling out of hangers and drawers, she chose a blouse, baggy trousers and flat shoes. Then she remembered how smart the black girls at work looked when they had dates, and though she had decided that Roland did not judge by appearances, she applied some eyeliner and lipstick.

'Those bloody clodhoppers,' said her father, looking at her shoes as she came into the living room. 'Real passion-killers. Wearing *them* you won't need to be careful.'

'I'll be off, then.'

'Isn't he picking you up?'

'No. Yes. Not here.'

'Right sort of date you've got.'

Lorna cautioned her father to lower his voice. 'I'm meeting him at the end of the street.'

'Ashamed of this place, now?'

'He wasn't sure of the road, Dad.'

'Where's he live, then?'

'Stockwell.'

'Blimey. A dodgy area. Should be able to stand up for himself, then.' He looked at her blouse. 'It's nippy out there. You'll need a coat.'

Roland stared in the mirror as he lathered his face. He scrutinised his nose and bloodshot eyes. His hair was receding slowly, forming, Weston said, the peaks of the McDonald's sign. Could Lorna possibly find him attractive? He had always been surprised by the Lonelyhearts in which men described themselves as attractive. Was it possible to view yourself with a woman's eyes?

As he shaved, he wondered if he was doing the right thing, asking Lorna out. Would he be able to sustain his chat-up lines? If she did come back and stay the night, suppose after all this time he fumbled the lovemaking? Would Lorna relate it all afterwards to her sister, mother, the girls at work? He didn't think so, but he really didn't know her. Suddenly his detached non-committed life seemed comfortable after all.

He had to remind himself he had – what was the word? – procrastinated long enough. He liked the word, but not the meaning. As he cut through the foam with his Bic disposable, he wondered why he always felt the need to sabotage himself. This was one night. If things went wrong, he had enough nous to let himself (and Lorna) out gently.

He thought of one of Weston's texts: *Rise above the sense of fault and failure. Use the errors of the past as wisdom.* One of the errors of Roland's present was not to notice when disposable razors needed to be disposed of. He nicked himself on the chin, and this time only several palmfuls of aftershave would contain the blood. The scent reminded him of schoolday dates when he would cover himself in lotions. When she smelt him, Lorna would think he was unbelievably keen.

Lorna and her coat were out of the house before there could be any more questions. It was seven o'clock. She did not want to risk Roland being early, and if he had noticed the number, starting the door chimes. *Wogan* or *Family Fortunes* on the television meant that most of the curtain-twitchers would now have sat down for the evening. She had only to shift her feet for half an hour.

Her mind ran over all that Roland had said on Monday and Wednesday. As Rob had pointed out, it wasn't only in books that you had to dig beneath the surface. From little experience and much poring over magazines, she knew that at this stage in a relationship (a relationship!) each partner will say anything to please the other and not necessarily mean it. Would this relationship last? Her toes tingled at the thought. But first, would he turn up?

When Roland's car appeared at the corner, ten minutes early, she ran down the road, her heart beating. The car gave a hoarse hoot as it pulled up. Were Mum and Dad behind the nets? Did he understand why she was waiting in the road?

She saw him smile. She relaxed, ran round the front, and jumped in.

He looked her up and down. 'Detrimental, Miss Duggan. Ready for your big night out?'

'Are you sure you want to, Mr Stephens?' Lorna asked, fastening her seat belt.

'It's something new.'

To herself, Lorna added the rest of the rhyme, *something borrowed* . . . She wouldn't chant it aloud there and then. You didn't mention weddings on a first real date!

'I'm ready to go to the dogs,' she said. 'I'm game if you are.'

'I'm glad to hear it,' said Roland.

As they passed Camberwell Green, with its sad crew of meths drinkers, Lorna began to panic that they had not said anything else. She shifted in her seat. The springs creaked.

'Do you want that back a bit?' Roland asked.

Lorna was relieved. 'No, thanks, I'm fine. It's funny, you know, where we're going. I don't usually gamble. Just a bet in the sweepstakes at work. The Derby and the Grand National, you know.'

'In our house,' said Roland, taking his eyes off the road as he drew up to a red light, 'gambling was the

Devil's work.' The light reflected in his eyes.

With the springs sticking in her back, Lorna settled into her seat as comfortably as she could. The interior had been cleaned since Wednesday. The plastic fittings smelt of Mr Sheen and by the mirror a card hung with traffic-light globes of air freshener. Roland smelt good too. It was a heady mixture.

With him driving, as the car kangarooed through Peckham, Lorna felt as if she was gliding in a Rolls. She knew the warmth was not from any heater. It was Roland's thighs, squeezed into those tight blue jeans. Whenever he changed gear, his left hand brushed her. She let her right hand dangle near the lever, as on Monday judging how much contact might not be irritating but enjoyable.

Not commenting on her flirtatious conduct, Roland asked her what kind of a day she'd had. Eager to get the conversation flowing, she told him about last night's arguments with her parents and the future moves. Though he was concentrating on following the road to Catford, he seemed interested in her problems. Yet she still knew little about his circumstances. She did some mental collating. She knew how old his brother was. And his mum seemed to be churchy. Was his dad around? She would like to know all about his family. She wondered if he would open up tonight.

The stadium car park could have catered for several supermarkets. Ahead, arc lights loomed like a neighbourhood concentration camp. A railway track ran along the perimeter. Looking at the semi-detached houses beyond the fences, Lorna said, 'It's dreary round here.'

'They've got gardens, though.'

'How long have you been in your flat, then?'
'Three years.'
'Council?'
'Yes.'
'Is it just you?'
'For the last year, yes.'
Who had been there before? Why didn't he supply the information? Why couldn't you have a CV when you started going out with someone?

The stadium entrance had a neon sign above it with red and yellow hounds fruitlessly chasing a winking electronic hare. In the distance they could hear real barking. Despite Lorna's protests, Roland paid.

Between the stands, a scoreboard of electric lights flashed continually changing information. It didn't make much sense, but, fascinated, they watched touts chalking odds and ticktack men in sheepskin coats relaying messages through hand signals and mobile phones to the opposite enclosure.

They climbed the terrace, bought coffee (in polystyrene cups) and cheese sandwiches (in triangles of stale white bread), then sat down at a table to study the programme. Above them, revolving fans extracted some of the smell of chips and cigarettes and Roland's aftershave.

Looking at the discarded cups, Lorna said, 'It's not the Barbican, is it?'

'You can't make money at Shakespeare, can you?' laughed Roland.

Some people were staring at them. For a moment Roland's was the only black face Lorna could see. She felt less uncomfortable when a black couple settled at a table near them (though the woman gave her a dirty look) and she spotted a young black man in a tracksuit reading the *Sporting Life*. She did not know yet whether to voice these thoughts to Roland. Then she realised that again, unusually, she had been silent for half a minute, so she asked instead, 'Have you any idea what you do?'

Roland raised his eyes from the print and shook his head.

She liked that. A less modest or confident man would have blustered. 'It's like the teacher would say,' she said, 'we might have landed here from space. An alien would be puzzled.'

'This alien is puzzled,' said Roland.

Why had he said that? thought Lorna. Was he just echoing her words? Did he really feel out of place? Was he joking? Usually there was a hint of laughter about most things he said, but she wasn't sure. She noticed that a group of four or five older black men had congregated by the bar.

'An alien,' Roland continued, 'might think this is a religious ceremony, or a sacrifice.'

'Well, it is a sacrifice as far as I'm concerned,' said Lorna. 'I'm missing *Coronation Street*.'

She saw Roland check to see if she were serious, before he asked excitedly, 'What makes people come to a joint like this? Why do people gamble? They must know the odds are stacked against them. Is this their only excitement?'

'You've put your finger on it. It's something to do. It fills in the time.' Though she did not believe it, she added, 'No different to going to Shakespeare, really.'

'But Shakespeare,' said Roland, 'feeds your mind. What does this feed?'

'It's exciting,' said Lorna. 'You don't know what's going to happen.'

'But can't they see it's a huge cheat?'

His tone was critical, but not of her. His words, as well as his brown eyes, wooed her. She loved him because he asked questions. Other people must have asked them before, and found answers, but that was irrelevant. He stood apart from the everyday world which threatened to flood over her. Like Jason's favourite squawking plastic bird in the bubblegum dispenser outside the sweetshop at Camberwell Green, her heart was fluttering.

A fanfare of recorded trumpets announced the first race. Six muzzled dogs were paraded on to the golden sand. Each had a different racing jacket to correspond with the colour on the scoreboard. The kennelmaids in their white coats who led the dogs to the starting traps reminded Lorna of schoolmates who, she remembered, had been attracted to the stadiums: Catford, Wimbledon, Harringay. She had wondered then how they could like sleek dogs and pot-bellied men. Tracey's first blokes had all been that type, though she had since shifted her hunting-ground to motorbike cafés and car auctions. She and Louise had always teased Lorna for wanting a bit of smooth, a touch of class. Lorna didn't know how they would react to Roland – and she didn't much care. She was growing out of worrying about other people's opinions. Roland was smooth, and had class.

The lights dimmed on the enclosure and the betting booths closed automatically. 'We didn't bet,' said Lorna.

'There's enough races.'

Seconds after the hare wobbled zippily past, as on a giant Fisher-Price track, the dogs were off. There was much shouting and banging on tables.

'Come on, number two!'

'Move your fucking arse!'

It was all over in less than a minute.

'Is that it?' asked Roland.

"Fraid so.'

'I've seen better races round our market.'

'What d'you mean?'

'The other day a stallholder's Rottweiler slipped his leash. He demolished four stalls and almost ate some stray mongrel. It was all hell let loose while it lasted. Here it's all over on the first bend. The dog who gets possession is bound to win.'

Lorna looked at his animated face. 'You don't want to leave?'

'No way. This is an education.'

'My dad says you can tell which dog is healthy by looking at them in their pens.'

'Is he an expert?'

'He likes to think he is. On everything.'

'Well, perhaps we should take his advice. On this point.'

After they had watched the video re-runs they left their seats and went into the damp air to the pens. The grooms were stroking and patting the elegant creatures. Lorna wondered if she and Roland would be stroking and patting before the evening was over. Had it been a mistake, coming to the stadium? He seemed to be enjoying it, but it wasn't exactly a glamorous setting.

'They're all bone and muscle,' said Roland.

'The owners have to walk miles to keep them fit. My dad says all kinds of fiddles go on. Sometimes they bring a winner over from Ireland that no one has heard of. They feed it up and don't exercise it, let it race and get it a bad name. Then they train it again and when it's fit they enter it. They back it themselves, tell their mates, and all make a killing.'

'Good luck to them.'

'But you spend all day sorting out fiddles.'

'If everybody was honest, I wouldn't have a job, would I? Mind you, I knew a girl once who was so straight she wouldn't even pick a pound off the pavement.'

Lorna's eyes dilated. Had this been the one who shared the flat? She was slowly collecting enough to make the edges of his jigsaw, but the pieces wouldn't all come at once.

They studied the dogs as they emerged from their chalets. 'It's like people,' Lorna said. 'You go for the healthiest.'

'That counts me out.' Roland took her arm. He looked at her, burst out laughing, gazed over at the greyhounds, then down at his programme. 'No contest,' he said. 'That's our dog. Number three.'

Lorna leant against him to see the programme. 'What's his name?'

'Opportunity Knocks.'

Between them, in the rush of last-minute betting, they placed five pounds to win with one of the touts. They surprised themselves by how much they cheered and how disappointed they were when the loud-speaker and the re-runs revealed that their dog had

177

come second in a photofinish.

Their luck was not in. They tried predicting winners, combinations, reverse forecasts, and any other ways of placing money they could understand. Freddie Kruger was badly crowded in the 8.30 385 metres, Ebony Return finished cramped in the 9 o'clock, Miss Dynamite in the 9.15 baulked one, and Funny Fluff in the 9.30 hurdles was slow away.

After the ninth race, they moved to the bar for a drink. 'Roland,' said Lorna, 'when you were little, did you have a dog?'

'No,' said Roland, 'with always living in flats. And it's what your parents say. In Jamaica, man is man, and dog is dog. You don't waste money buying food for dogs. Back home dogs eat what they can. Anyway, me and my brother ate so much there was none left for pets.'

Lorna shifted uncomfortably in the bucket seat. 'Don't look now,' she said, 'but I think there's a man staring at us.'

Roland looked at her seriously. 'Miss Duggan, if you're going to meet me in an unprofessional capacity, you're going to have to get used to that.'

'No, I mean,' said Lorna, 'really staring, not just being out of order. Have a look. By the bar. Do you know him?'

Ronald turned round. His eyebrows rose. A man with salt and pepper hair and beard was supping a pint of lager and, between sips, waving and shouting in his direction.

Lorna could tell that Roland was watching her closely. 'Well, do you know him?'

'Easy.'

'Who is it?'

'My brother's dad.'

Lorna was glad she had not looked disapproving. Becoming agitated, she asked, 'Is your mum here, too?'

'No,' said Roland, smiling again. 'No way. He's not . . . on the scene much, so to speak. Not at the moment. He must have found some new mates. Catford's not his usual patch.'

He excused himself for a moment, and went over to Mr Langley and bought him another Carlsberg.

Roland knew Mr Langley spent what money he had on drink, gambling and spliffs. For weeks at a time he would not surface and then every day would be outside the betting shop in Electric Avenue, waiting for a result and a win until his money run out. When he was sober, Mr Langley looked distinguished in the grey suits he tailored himself, and Roland could glimpse, as Weston never did, what his mother had seen in him, and why at whatever age he was, he still had supporting admirers.

There were half-brothers in SW2, but though his mother could have told him Weston never chose to make enquiries, and Roland never raised the topic.

Previously Mr Langley had only bet in shops, and on horses, and in Brixton, so his appearance at Catford must mean he had met more adventurous Friday-night companions. When Roland had bought him the drink, Lorna had not looked down her nose at the man, and afterwards, there had not been too many questions. Whatever she did ask, though, he generally found easy to talk about. For months he had been tongue-tied. Now there were so many things he wanted to say. Lorna made him articulate. She made him clever.

For the last year he had been in a chrysalis. Gone were the days when he buzzed in vain against a window like a frustrated bee. Tonight he would be crowned Mr Superfresh. He would fly like a butterfly.

Nothing Roland had said so far that evening had excluded Lorna. She had not been baulked, cramped or crowded. She felt that, on the contrary, she was gaining possession, and Roland was willing to grant it.

Though for most punters the romance of the dog track lay in accumulating money, or at least leaving with as much as you went in with, for Lorna it was the chance to share decisions with Roland. She felt as if she had been given a reviving tonic, or breathed deeply of Lydd's Channel ozone. With him the most ordinary things, like buying tickets, eating cheese sandwiches, looking at dogs, talking about your family, seemed interesting and funny. Now she was on edge to know how the evening would continue.

They stayed for the presentation of a trophy by an actor from *EastEnders*. Roland could not remember whether the man played a lost Australian relative, a disputed father, or was merely a stallholder. He thought the market in the programme was a joke. It was run without control or direction.

Lorna did not want to join the queue for signed photographs. He thought she was being polite, but as they walked towards the exit, she said, 'I've got to get rid of bits. Not collect more.'

Thinking of his paperbacks, Roland said, 'I'd like my place free of clutter. Nothing but what's necessary – like the Japanese.' He wondered if Lorna really agreed. Women liked collecting things. Charmaine had been miserable on a Saturday if she had not bought something new. But tonight he was not concerned with Lorna's attitude to frittering. Could he control circumstances the way he wanted?

After ten minutes, he had to admit that the car wouldn't start. It was no use turning the ignition key ever more savagely, pumping the accelerator, or fiddling with wires under the bonnet. Whole cans of WD40 could have been sprayed or coils of jumpleads connected without making a difference. The car had run out of petrol. Roland had known all week that the pointer on the fuel had moved into the dangerous orange zone where a breakdown might occur at any time, but with his other preparations for this evening, he had forgotten.

He knew that Lorna was watching his every action, and could sense that frustration was slowly mingling with her fascination. They were entering their own dangerous zone. Eventually he said, 'The tank needs topping.'

'You haven't run out of petrol?' she asked. So far it had been smooth running. She had read him perfectly all evening. But had she read the fuel gauge too? In his experience, women only noticed these things if they drove themselves.

'The petrol's a bit low,' he admitted. 'It gets sluggish if you're drawing up dregs.'

'So you haven't run out?'

'We got here, didn't we?' So far she had accepted what he said, or challenged things with a joke. Now she had suddenly stopped being flirtatious. Was it because he had not been concentrating on her? Why, now things had got difficult, would she not stop questioning? And why, all of a sudden, could he not tell her the truth?

'The car was jumping,' Lorna continued. 'You never know, Roland, you might have run out. My dad says it takes a lot of petrol to get started, and you were trying for some time. Perhaps you've flooded it?'

So she knew about flooding. He did not answer.

'When did you fill it up?'

'Some time last week.'

'Should you let the tank get low?'

'I don't know. What does your dad say?' This was not the time for sparring. Why had he said that? Even in the darkness, the arc lights allowed him to see her bite her lip. She would not forget the remark or the tone. Was it all over?

Though the car was dead, his mind was racing. It had been a long time since he had had to take criticism or account for his actions to a girlfriend. And this one did go on about her dad! If he was going to be compared with some know-it-all old John Crow every time things went wrong, perhaps he should ditch her now. Charmaine had been like this in the last days, always complaining and running him down. With a dispirited feeling that despite all his intentions he would never change, Roland climbed out of the car again.

Lorna joined him at the boot. This time she did not lean on him. Nor did he take her arm. 'What are we going to do?' she asked blankly.

He rummaged among his unwashed football kit and the boxes of undelivered vegetables for Mrs Stephens. 'There's a petrol can in here somewhere.'

Lorna looked sceptical. 'Can't you call the AA?'

'I'd have to join first.'

'Can't you join when they arrive?'

'It doesn't work like that.'

'I've got some money.'

Why couldn't she just be quiet? Roland remembered he had lent the can to a neighbour on the estate. Slamming the boot, he said, 'Fancy a walk?'

'Home?'

'To a garage.'

'Oh. Where's the nearest?'

'I don't know this area.'

'Neither do I.'

'I thought you came here a lot.'

'No.' Lorna suddenly brightened. 'What about your dad – Weston's dad?'

'What about him?'

'How did he get here?'

'Probably with his mates.'

'They must have come by car.'

'What you saying?'

'They could drive us to a garage.'

'No.'

'It would save a walk.'

'No.'

'Let's try.'

'I'm not going back.'

'I kept the tickets. They'll let us in.'

'I'm not involving him.' He could imagine Mr

Langley's reaction if he turned up with Lorna and asked for a lift.

'But he's family. Surely he'd help?'

'It's not like that.'

On their walk, they were scrupulously polite, but soon exhausted their observations about the local shops.

At the garage, Roland disturbed a sleepy African who overcharged him for a gallon of petrol and a can.

On the way back, Lorna tried to make a joke about the dogs, but Roland did not respond.

Twenty minutes later, Roland stopped at the garage again to fill up properly. He spilt petrol on his jeans, slammed down the pump, screwed the petrol cap savagely, and banged angrily on the grille to distract the African from his portable television.

On the drive home, he had never wished more for a radio which worked. Lorna sat stiffly in silence, gazing straight ahead. He pulled up jerkily at the end of her road just before the railway arches.

'Thanks,' Lorna croaked as she got out.

In the corner of his eye he caught her confused and miserable face. He hesitated, mumbled 'Laters,' and sped off.

Trixie opened her door. 'You look like you've had a rough night. Who's the lucky bloke?'

Lorna said nothing.

'Oh, secret, is it?'

Had Dad said something? She didn't care now.

'Your mum thought you was off somewhere special. Where was it?'

What did it matter who knew what? 'Catford Dogs.'

'Last of the big spenders, eh?' Trixie cackled. 'What's the matter? Did he ditch you?'

'Can I see the room, please?'

It was a small box, with a built-in wardrobe and a single bed. It would do for someone who would stay in alone night after night. She said flatly, 'It's fine.'

'I thought you might be picky,' said Trixie, 'like your father. When you want to move in?'

'November the tenth. That's the date at present.' Her mind was miles, two miles away.

'Fine. Your mum knows what I'll charge. Have you got much stuff?'

'This and that.'

'I bet you have. I bet you fetch home lots of Marks' nick-nacks. They do lovely pillboxes.'

'Ours is a food store.' Why was she bothering to correct her?

'Any chance of a discount on booze?'

Trixie led her back to the front door. She looked at Lorna's face. 'Cheer up, love,' she said, her varnished nails on the latch. 'It's not the end of the world, whatever it is.'

Was there hope? Lorna thought as she threaded her way back to Camberwell New Road. Trixie was right – it couldn't be the end. Roland's last words had been Laters. But why had he gone so cold? Why had she been so moany about the petrol? But at the time she had been shocked. She had wondered if she could go with someone who was so disorganised. But now she would put up with anything to be close to him. Would he listen if she told him it didn't matter? Did he have her phone number? She didn't have his. She didn't know where he lived exactly, only the estate. Should she visit him at work? Could she wait until Wednesday and the evening class? She didn't sleep, debating.

In the market, two Rastas were waiting for a pitch. They had been regulars, but had missed the last few Saturdays. One had boxes of whistles, leather pendants, bum bags, belts and thongs, all with cut-out maps of Africa. Another had a stock of shrivelled coconuts, peanuts, aloes, teas and potions. These included an extract of a Bajan bark which would be boosted later as an '*Afro*-disiac for the eleventh finger'.

Usually Roland smiled at such claims. Today he counted the would-be traders grimly.

'I and I is weary,' the leatherman moaned.

'Wait your turn,' Roland growled, then plodded to the Portakabin which served market inspectors as an office.

Jimmy was reading the *Sun*. 'Did you sort out the queue?'

'It's your turn.'

'I did the eight o'clockers. Many turn up late?'

'The Rastamen.'

'Nobody buys their rubbish.'

'That's where you're wrong.'

'Says you.'

'Where's the seniority list?'

'You had it yesterday.'

'I put it back where it belong.'

'Did it hurt?'

'What?'

'The wall when it hit you getting out of bed.'

Roland returned to the queue and allocated the Rastas positions he knew Jimmy would not approve of.

Another latecomer, a stationer, had acquired a stock of outmoded black annive:sary cards. The couples displayed wide collars and the greasy ringlets of the Hollywood curl and looked at each other adoringly. Roland glanced at the sample. Who would be stupid enough to buy these? He gave the cards a pitch in the shadows of the railway.

The last person in the queue, a bookseller, was offering a range of illustrated children's stories from the Caribbean. She could show Anansi the spiderman stalking through mangrove swamps and lurking behind banana trees. She also had autobiographies of black women ill treated by men more fearful than spiders. Roland had flicked through the books on previous Saturdays. Since Charmaine he had felt unsympathetic to female cries of anguish. He had thought Lorna might make him reassess the troubles they'd seen, but now it seemed doubtful. Was Lorna crying now? Her face had been before him all night. He tried to dismiss her image, and felt weary. Every time he set his heart on something, planned for it, and wanted it to happen, it backfired. Explaining to the bookseller that all the other positions were taken, he placed her next to a dub vendor who blasted rare grooves all day.

By eleven Jimmy had left to mitigate a quarrel in Streatham between rival newspaper kiosks, and Roland was compiling a council report sheet. There was a knock at the door. The public weren't supposed to enter the yard, let alone disturb the officers. Through the glass he could see a shadowy form. He jumped. Had Lorna come to see him? What would he say? He hadn't decided yet where he stood. Then he recognised the red mac. He wondered what gossip had blown Sherene's way. He pulled the door open.

'Respect,' she said.

'If you say so.'

She claimed she had come to enquire about demonstrating Marcia's haircare products in the market. Roland had supposed she thought both hairdressing and market trading degrading, but though he recognised that the sisters' rivalry and antagonism mirrored his and Weston's, he could not follow its changing details. And today he was in no mood for jibes. Suppose Lorna did turn up?

When he said that promotions were not allowed on Saturdays, Sherene did not seem downhearted. He guessed her real motivation for calling was some new source of gloating. He would give her no joy.

Settling on a seat, she said, 'I called round your mother's early. To pick up the catalogue.'

Roland continued with his form. The pencil kept breaking.

'She hadn't gone to work this morning.'

'Is she sick?'

'She was having breakfast.'

'Good. She doesn't eat enough.'

'Roland, she wasn't eating alone.'

'So? Weston has his nuts and honey most mornings.' Today his brother's pretensions irritated more than amused. In his absence, he blasted him. 'Mostly he tries to eat before she comes from cleaning, but even with his time management, he can't always do it.'

'Weston wasn't eating anything. Weston wasn't there. But his dad was.'

Roland's eyebrows rose.

'Next to your mum, buttering toast. Very cosy.'

Roland looked up. 'What you saying?'

'Seems the Sainsbury's checkout girl wants to check him no longer.'

'What you mean?'

'Mr Langley reached the girl's yard at one o'clock this evening. She had just returned too. He was living drunk. She barred the door.'

Despite his intentions, Roland had to ask more questions. 'Who told you this?'

'Mr Langley, of course. I joined them for breakfast. He told me he was drunk. He told me he'd been locked out. He's always found it easy to talk to me.'

'The old still have steam. He'll be moving in with you next.'

'The son is enough of a chief. I'm not taking on the father.'

'Who let him in?'

'Weston heard him outside. Coughing. Spitting. Woke him up. Weston give him a lecture but Mr Langley tell him to drop his Mrs Queen talking. In the end he let him in.'

'Weston?'

'Weston. Weston was vexed. The man was drunk and dribbling.' She shrieked. 'The neighbours came out to bawl. Weston told them to move away. Mr Langley tell me all. How shameful. We've never had one noise with any of our neighbours.'

'So you came to dish me the dirt?'

'No. I want to display Sporting Waves, I told you.'

'Was I born yesterday?'

'Roland, I want to branch into selling.'

'It'll give you something to do with your mout.'

Sherene looked triumphant. 'That wasn't the only thing he told.'

Roland looked cagey. He had sensed what was coming. 'What?' he asked.

'Last night. He went to Catford.'

'Yes, the Dogs. So did I. I saw him. So?'

'Did you enjoy yourself?'

'Sherene,' he said fiercely, 'don't come here pretending you want to sell when you came to crow.'

Sherene reached her point. 'He told us about your . . . date.'

'Sherene, I've work to do.'

'Some secretary? Invited home to do the washing? Some white girl looking for a piece of black? Something exotic? Roland, it's not like you.'

Roland snatched up his clipboard and keys. 'Sherene,' he said, rising from behind the desk, 'who I check is my business. And now,' he said, rattling a steel tape measure and pushing the door open, 'I have to check some pitches.'

In McDonald's, Weston tapped Roland on his left shoulder. 'I saw you on the monitor,' he said wearily, and indicated a door marked STAFF ONLY. 'Come through.'

In the Manager's office Roland ripped open the non-dairy creamer, stirred his coffee with a thin plastic spoon and, replaying all that Sherene had said, watched his brother at work. Weston was feeding that week's food sales into a computer. He had recorded thousands of Big Macs, each cooked for a hundred seconds, and millions of fries, streamlined from standard potatoes. It was emerging that during the week the demand for filets had fallen.

Tiring of this display of management, Roland said, 'I hear you had a visitor in the night.'

Weston stopped his two-finger typing, did not move his eyes from the screen, then asked, 'Roland, who's the girl?'

Roland was not going to let his baby brother manipulate him. 'News travels fast,' he said. 'Your dad told you he'd seen me?'

Weston continued staring at his spreadsheets. The store was under pressure to reduce labour costs. It had even been mooted they could no longer sustain an Assistant Manager.

'You let him in,' said Roland. 'Such generosity.'

Weston snarled, but kept his eyes on the graphs.

'Sherene came to tell me, of course. To keep me up to date.'

'She needs keeping in order,' said Weston. He repeated, 'Roland, who is this girl?'

'What's it to you?' Roland asked guardedly.

'I like to know these things.'

'Why? Who I check is my affair.' He thought of Lorna's attempted jokes on the walk from the garage. Why had he not responded?

'She's from that evening class, isn't she?'

'She could be.'

'I knew it. I told you. I know those classes. Some unemployed secretary.'

Roland got up and moved behind Weston's chair.

191

He looked at the flickering screen. 'If you must know, she's a supervisor.' Why was he bothering to tell? But he could not resist scoring a point.

'Where?'

'Marks.'

'A good firm,' said Weston. He always genuflected before quality. 'Good on staff performance. What branch?'

'Along the road.'

'Brixton?' This was not so impressive. Weston tapped in some more figures, then asked: 'What's she like?'

'What's it to you?'

Weston paused. 'I want to know what a white girl has over a sister.'

'What's it to you?' Roland repeated fiercely. 'You don't approve. I remember you once saying that black men who make it only take up with white women to show they've arrived.'

'You haven't arrived. You haven't even set out.'

Roland wanted to smash Weston and his computer, but he had finished with bust-ups years ago. 'Hush your mout,' he said.

'What's she like?' Weston repeated.

'You'll have to wonder.'

'Once in a while,' said Weston slowly, 'we all have a fling. We can all have a taste.'

Roland's anger rose. 'About a taste! What is she? Fast food?'

'You tell me,' said Weston. 'In the long run you have to decide whose side you're on. No wonder it was Catford Dogs last night. Where next? A knees-up in some Cockney tavern? Butlins?'

Roland did up his coat.

'It's not serious, is it?' asked Weston.

'You never know,' said Roland.

'Roland,' said Weston, turning at last from the screen and facing him. 'I know it's been a long time on your own now, but for God's sake, man, if you're desperate, try up West again, try down Streatham, try The Fridge. Do some market research. Decide what you want. Don't be content with some white . . .'

'Rest,' said Roland, seizing Weston's typing arm, and twisting it in a half-nelson, as he used to in bedroom squabbles. 'I don't need your advice,' he said. 'Not on this, I don't.'

'You are serious, aren't you?' said Weston, wincing.

'I might be.'

'Are you checking her again?'

Roland increased the hold, then suddenly let Weston's arm drop. 'I have to go.' He screwed up the coffee beaker, flung it into a bin, and left, slamming the Private door.

The preacher continued, 'It's another grand and glorious privilege given us this morning to be found in the House of the Lord. We commence by singing *Jesus is the Light*, number sixty-nine from the large, forty-eight from the small.'

> *There is sunshine in my soul today*
> *More glorious and bright*
> *Than flows in any earthly sky*
> *For Jesus is my light.*

Normally during the hymn Mrs Stephens would have studied her neighbours' hats, as much as she could, to judge what shops they came from, or who had a hand-made copy, but today she could not concentrate. Today her soul was troubled. Since Friday night Mr Langley had been so gracious, and he was still here on a Sunday. Usually he did not stay so long. This time she was daring herself to believe it was different.

When the hymn had ended, she opened her Bible. Even with the alternate red and black print, and the high-lighter which Weston, on a benign day, had given her to emphasise golden texts, she could hardly read the word of God.

She took comfort in the fact that the lunch-time service would be short since tonight there would be Holy Communion and foot-washing, teaching humility and service. For once she did not know if she would come. You were supposed to wash the feet of a stranger, but Mrs Stephens knew most of the congregation by sight, by name and foot disease. She was acquainted with their bunions, verrucas and athlete's foot. Today she thought instead of Mr Langley's feet, and shivered. Roland's father had been lanky and long-toed, but Mr Langley's had more flesh on them.

'We are an empty shell without Jesus,' said the preacher. Usually Mrs Stephens would agree aloud, and hold her hymnbook in the air. Today she sat quietly. Could she dare to hope for comfort on earth again as well?

Saturday and Sunday passed for Lorna somehow. On Monday she was glad to be back at work, where activity could mask her misery. How much had she offended Roland with her remarks about petrol and his car? Perhaps he was proud and ashamed he couldn't run something flashier.

Though she longed to, she could not risk meeting him in the market. She was actually fearful that they might meet in the street or by the bus-stop. Now she was pinning all her hopes on Wednesday evening. She rehearsed seeing him, talking, apologising, setting things straight.

Yet even at the evening class she would have to sit through two hours. It would only be at the end that they could really talk, that she could find out if he ever wanted to date her again. Before that she would have to appear interested and unconcerned. They couldn't slip out together in the break. And suppose he might have some reason for leaving early?

She wished she could switch off her mind, but as she slid the food and drink across the barcode reader, the bleeps recorded her worries like the beads of a rosary.

Roland debated whether he should return to night school, whether he should blank Sherene, smash Weston, ignore his family's protests, whether he could dismiss the thought of Lorna's touch, whether he should set her aside.

On the other hand, forfeiting the Wednesday evening would be a sacrifice; he knew the class made him think. He was weary and wary of analysis, particularly when it sailed close to him, but in its odd way the class offered a necessary filter to the flood of information and feeling which struck him every day. But he wondered whether, if he abandoned Lorna, he would still be able to concentrate.

For his homework, he tried to list arguments for

increasing competitive sport in schools, but stopped at number three. Would he be able to talk in front of her? Would he be able to talk to her? Could he face her again, now he had gone dark on her?

It was half-term. Apart from the English class, the scuba-divers and a short course on 'Cookery for Christmas' starting in the classroom next door, the Institute was empty. Outside, the wind was howling.

Despite the weather, most of the regulars were there when Lorna arrived. But not Roland. She assumed a brave face.

Eager to be first Sean spoke about recorded appearances of the Virgin, and Her weeping statues. Rob was supposed to be impartial in discussion, marking for concepts, interest, delivery and matching language to content, but he was moved to say it was time superstition was rooted out. This offended Sean and inflamed others. An argument began, but Lorna couldn't concentrate. She sat in despair. If she were a statue, she would have wept. Roland had given up the class and her. He wasn't coming.

Yvonne, Gloria and Esther noticed Lorna's misery, and that Roland was missing. Putting the two together was more interesting than the discussion.

Darren spoke next, about fishing. 'Fishing is an interesting hobby. I've always liked fishing.' As he tried to develop his concept, his normal jokiness disappeared. 'I first went fishing when I was nine. I went with my dad. I found it very interesting.'

Nobody spoke when he had finished. It was not a controversial topic. Their interest had not been engaged. Even Rob was at a loss for praise.

The door creaked open. Lorna checked it, as she had for every noise. This time it was not the wind. Roland walked in and nodded slightly. His greeting included Lorna but was for everyone, not particularly for her. He sat at a vacant desk near the door.

Seeing that Lorna was animated, Rob asked, 'Lorna, what did you think of Darren's talk?'

After Rob had repeated the question, she began, 'It was interesting.' She was conscious that Roland was watching and listening. But how closely? 'If you're really into fishing,' she continued, 'I should imagine there's never a dull moment. You never know, I mean, what someone else might find interesting.'

The smell of cakes seeped through the holes in the plaster. As she spoke encouragingly of Darren, it was Roland she was really talking to. But was he listening? Would he understand? 'If you're interested in something,' she finished, 'you should go for it heart and soul.'

Rob added, 'I don't think many of us could get that worked up about fishing. But what matters is that we get worked up about *something*. Fishing, believing in visions – it doesn't matter what.'

'You're dead right,' said Lorna.

Sean was now concerned that Marian manifestations were being linked to fishing, so Rob suggested an early break. Roland moved out with Yvonne, Gloria and Esther, and sat with them. As Lorna left the tea counter with her shaking cup, he nodded to her. She sat with Sean, Darren and Rob. Would they talk at the end of the class? Would he hang back?

* * *

197

Rob asked Roland if he would like to give his speech on police harassment. He replied that he did not have his notes. When Rob asked her, Lorna in turn said she was sorry but she had not had time to do her homework. Rob reprimanded them gently and said it was easy to lose momentum. Sean agreed eagerly and Yvonne looked up the meaning of the word. As no one else was ready to talk, Rob gave out a comprehension exercise instead and all the students' momentum declined there and then.

Lorna dropped her paper, and bending to pick it up, looked back at Roland, taking in again his serious face and heavy-lidded eyes.

At the end of the class the others hurried away, fearful of the increasing wind. Lorna helped Rob clear his scattered papers, shut the windows against the blast, and wiped the blackboard. Roland sat engrossed in his work. Rob was ready to turn out the lights and lock up. He looked at his two remaining students.

'You two all right?' he asked. 'You haven't stayed behind to tell me you're giving up?'

Lorna blushed. Roland stood up without saying anything, put his pen in his pocket, mumbled his customary 'Laters' and walked out. Lorna left Rob searching for his keys, and grabbing her clutch bag and folder, she dashed into the corridor. 'Roland,' she croaked.

He had not got far. He stopped, turned, and looked. His face was still serious. 'It was good at the Dogs,' Lorna gasped.

He still did not smile, but he did not scowl. She continued in a rush, 'And it didn't matter about your car.'

'You could have fooled me,' he mumbled, seemingly studying a photo display of divers in wet suits.

'What do you mean?' Lorna asked.

'I ran out of petrol,' Roland replied bluntly. 'That's all.'

'The petrol doesn't matter now,' Lorna assured him.

'It didn't matter then.'

Lorna wondered if she were being reprimanded. 'Of course it didn't matter then. Not really. I shouldn't have gone on about it.'

Roland turned to face her completely, then said gently, 'It wasn't only petrol we ran out of, was it?'

'What do you mean?'

'We ran out of words as well, didn't we?'

'You could put it like that,' said Lorna, relaxing, grasping slowly that she was absolved. Only later did she wonder if he too had prepared his words. In amazement at her change in fortunes she dared to ask, 'Sean and Darren said they were going to the pub. Fancy a drink now?'

'I'm a bit busy.'

Was she pushing it too far? Would he have gone home without saying anything if she had not called him back?

Then he said, 'What about this Friday? We could do something this Friday.'

Lorna beamed.

'This time I'll have petrol.'

Lorna moved closer and touched his arm. 'I'm sorry.'

'What about the cinema?'

'Sounds all right by me.'

They walked slowly downstairs, both anxious not

199

to put a foot wrong. Roland pulled out his car keys. 'Want a lift? It's a nasty night.'

'No,' Lorna said warily. 'I'll walk. It's not your way. And you're busy.'

'Not as busy as all that.'

7

Breeze blowing hard

Roland had thought the Ritzy was showing *Nightmare on Elm Street III* but it turned out there was to be the South London première of a new film about the anguish of white Liberals in South Africa, preceded by the first short in the Lapp language.

When he saw that Lorna was turning her nose up at the clothes of the people in the queue (Doc Martens, combat jackets, jeans, bookshop badges, and drooping earrings) he decided it wasn't their scene, and they went instead to the pub on the corner of Coldharbour Lane.

A chill blast blew through the cracks in the windows and rattled the doors. They huddled together in a corner for warmth. Lorna determined to make no comment about the change of plans.

Roland surprised her. 'Why do you want to go out with me?'

'Good taste,' she replied quickly. 'Isn't that enough?' Outside a siren was wailing. It reminded her. 'What were you going to say about the police the other night?'

When Roland had finished his tale, she cried, 'How can they think you're a criminal?'

'Easy,' he warned her. 'You never know who's listening.'

'Did you get the policeman's name?'

'No.'

'It's terrible. You were only doing a favour. It's not right. I know why they stopped you.'

She sounded annoyed, as if she cared. It might seem strange, but this was the confirmation he needed. The way she had listened and her response showed that she looked at things squarely and was prepared to believe him. He hadn't been sure he'd find it so clearly in a white girl. Now he knew she wasn't just after a quick lay. Perhaps the police had done him a favour.

As they left the pub, and walked back through the deserted market, orange wrappers, crisp packets and cigarette packets hit their faces and wrapped around their legs. The wind had got up and was raring to blow. 'It's the beginning of our hurricane season,' he told her. 'It's nature's way of making Jamaicans feel at home in the English climate.'

Lorna said yes, she would like to come back for a coffee, so he drove to Stockwell and parked the car. Some years back a municipal artist in residence had painted a mural of black and white children playing ball games in harmony. The picture was crumbling now, but was still lit at night by flickering neon strips, the target for footballs and air rifles. Lorna stared at the figures and then turned to the barren land around. He took her by the hand. 'They gave us the mural, then banned the games.'

Papers swirled around them as they staggered against the wind across the concrete to the entrance hall of Roland's block. 'You see I arranged a ticker-tape welcome.'

Lorna lifted her eyes to the tower. 'It looks nice, all those lights.'

In the tiled hall, they waited five minutes for the lift. As usual the rumblings and bangings from the shaft sounded as if even at this hour someone ten storeys above was shifting three-piece suites.

They began to climb the stairs. Roland guided her past some youths smoking. They fell silent as the couple made their way through, but when he and Lorna turned the landing, he heard mutterings of, 'Chah, white pussy.'

He winced. Tonight everything had to be perfect. Fortunately, Lorna seemed not to have noticed. The climbing made her cheeks redder. The moonlight through the cracked windows shone on her hair and the wind blew it across her face. She seemed unconscious of the picture she made, more concerned with negotiating the steps where someone had been sick.

'All human life is here, isn't it?' she mumbled, holding her hand over her mouth.

'Not very human, some of it.'

He had read stories where the Adventurer leads the Maiden through Certain Trials. Like those heroines, in his eyes, Lorna did not flinch. She rose above insults, urine, broken lifts, spliffs and vomit and reached the breeze on the balcony outside his flat. He blessed her for making light of everything.

Though swept in their faces, the fresh air was welcome and necessary. He told her, 'The whole building shakes.' She looked concerned, so he quickly added, 'But it's OK. It's safe.'

He cursed the wind. Would it chill the flat? Would

it make Lorna edgy and insecure? He put his arm round her against the blast. Though she might have been wondering why he did not open the door to his flat, given the weather conditions, she allowed him to become protective. Facing the gusts they looked past the gas-holders to the building sites and illuminated cranes of central London. He apologised, 'Sorry about that on the stairs.' He knew it wasn't his fault, but after the Dogs fiasco he wanted things to be perfect.

'Do you have to put up with that all the time?'

'Some nights are worse than others.'

'You must invite me back when things really hot up.'

She certainly was keen. What should be his next move? He was out of practice. She must know that he had more on his mind than admiring the view and the furniture he and MFI had built together. 'Coffee, was it?' he asked, slowly removing his arm.

Lorna croaked, 'Yes, please.' He found her sudden uncertainty reassuring. He held open the door to the landing and his flat, fumbled to find the keyhole and pushed open his front door. On the mat were a final electricity demand and that week's envelope from the Reader's Digest. Would, he thought, MISS LORNA DUGGAN, of 13 STATION ROAD, CAMBERWELL, SE5, whose name he had printed in bold letters that morning in his address book, take up his offer, and when it came to his chief hope, tick the box marked YES?

Lorna liked looking at other people's places. When she and Diane had been taken to relations as children they had always tiptoed into spare rooms and closed bedrooms. She liked to compare differences in padded bedheads and flouncy quilts. Her only delight in helping her parents choose their bungalow had been in contrasting carpets and coffee tables. She vowed that when she was sixty she would make a hobby of wasting estate agents' time.

Roland took her coat and hung it on a peg. Her heart was beating. He must have read her mind when she lingered in the hall, as he said, 'Have a look round. I'll put the kettle on.'

She had never been in the flat of a man who did for himself. Other men she had known had relied on someone else, usually their mothers.

After noting the plate-glass windows at either end of the living room, the mock leather armchairs, the black veneer bookshelves, and the central light swinging low in the increasing draught over a round table, she caught sight of herself in a gold-framed mirror, and suddenly anxious, and hearing Roland banging mugs and spoons and jars in the kitchen, went into the bathroom to comb her hair.

Roland's bathroom lacked her mother's familiar crocheted shepherdesses, the crinoline dresses hiding spare toilet rolls. However, once she had satisfied herself that her hair was under control, she did find a packet of tampons pushed to the back of a cabinet behind some cream for athlete's foot.

Re-emerging, she glanced quickly into the bedrooms. One seemed full of books, tea chests, football kit and a tailor's dummy. The other had a double bed neatly made with white sheets and a duvet whose cover she could just make out to be grey with a red stripe. It wasn't one of Marks' designs.

'Well?'

She felt a thrill of fright and turned round. Roland was behind her with two mugs. 'It's nice up here,' she said. 'You can forget what's below.'

All her senses were alert. She knew she would not be going down until morning. She followed Roland as he carried the mugs into the living room. He demonstrated the dimmer, put on one of his favourite mellow jazz records, scratching it twice before finding the starting groove, then sat down on the settee next to her. The wind circled the flat.

She shivered. 'It's getting nasty out there.'

'Like angry wolves looking for a crack to get in,' said Roland, growling.

'You are getting poetic,' she laughed nervously.

'You never know, if this continues, you might have to stay the night.'

She went quiet, then looked straight in his eyes. 'As long as you realise that's the only reason why I'm staying.'

'Of course,' he grinned. 'No question.'

'I wouldn't be staying for any other reason.'

'No way.'

Normally she would have worried about phoning home to say where she was, but at the top of the tower, nothing else mattered. She had rarely felt so snug. They were the only two people in the world, floating like those cranes above the whole of London.

The record stuck at the end of the side, and Roland had to rouse himself to prolong the music. As he took his place again on the settee, he kicked over a coffee mug. So far, apart from misreading the cinema programme, he had not put a foot wrong. 'There goes your coffee,' he said.

'Never mind. It keeps me awake.' She laughed, realising what she had said. She surely was intent on staying.

'You'd better drink it then, to be on the safe side.'

Should he wear a condom? Part of him, the lower part, disliked the idea of making love to a plastic glove, but his intellect cautioned him. How well did he know her? Below her brash exterior she was probably more naive than she pretended; that was part of her charm. But appearances could deceive. She had been on those Spanish holidays. What did women think about condoms? When she saw the packet, would she think he slept around? Chance would be a fine thing. Would she think he was over-prepared or a worrier? He didn't know her well enough yet to talk about it. There was no one else who could answer his questions. At the pub they didn't talk about things like this. And if they ever did, you wouldn't speak the truth. In these cases, you were on your own.

The record jumped again, slowed to a deeper tone, like the voice in that lager advert, became incomprehensible, then stopped entirely, the same sequence as on wind-up gramophones that surfaced occasionally in the market. In contrast Roland felt like a turntable spinning at seventy-eight revolutions.

The lights had gone out the moment the record had stopped. It wasn't his dimmer. 'The power's gone,' he told her.

'Has it?' Lorna snuggled deeper into his cuddle. 'It doesn't matter. Do you have any candles?'

'No.'

She giggled. 'You should always be prepared for emergencies.'

He could feel their hearts beating. It startled him again, after all this time, to feel another human being responding. He removed his arm and, tentatively, slowly, undid a button on her blouse. His hands slipped inside. She gasped, but did not protest. After three buttons he revealed in the moonlight her full breasts encased in lace, and gazed at them in wonder.

She felt the security of the touch of capable hands. On her body they felt strong, tender, inquisitive, electrifying. In response, she began to unbutton his denim shirt. 'I'm all fingers and thumbs.'

'It doesn't matter,' he said. 'We've got all night.'

She had undone his shirt, and removed his loafers. Even though it was October, he wasn't wearing any socks. Perhaps that stopped the athlete's foot, letting the air to your toes. He had opened her blouse and loosened her trousers. She felt, as in other things, that they were equally balanced in laying themselves open. She had never imagined that loving might start with such a bold yet gentle game. Before it had always been so rushed and urgent. Slowly she began to unbuckle the belt on his jeans. 'You'll be glad to get out of these. They look as if they're getting far too tight for you, Mr Stephens.'

'They must have shrunk, Miss Duggan,'

'You must obey the washing instructions,' she warned him, in her best shop voice.

* * *

When they were almost down to their underwear, Roland folded her again in his arms. She had never known anyone kiss so perfectly. His lips covered hers like an ample duvet. 'I'm rather tired,' she told him. 'I think I'll have to lie down.'

Roland guided her to the bedroom. With the moonlight shining on the sheets, she felt like the boy who met the Snowman, floating in the air, walking in her sleep. He pulled back the cover and helped her in. The sheets smelt of Ariel. It was the indulgence of childhood.

He slipped in beside her. The sheets emphasised his beautiful dark brown body. With the moonlight coming in through the window, he looked like a breath-taking bronze statue. Beside him her previous lovers seemed pale, insipid. The contrast made her shiver.

'Do you want a hot water bottle?'

'I think you'll do nicely.'

Suddenly she remembered the condoms. She had a packet in her clutch bag. Could she mention them now? She took a deep breath. At the same time he began his exploration. It was like that game at fêtes where you had to guide a ring around an electronic wire and a bell rang if you nudged it. The slightest touch made you tremble. She had to acknowledge parts of her body she had not considered for years.

Replying, her finger-ends dabbed at his bristles and the bumps where his curly stubble had baulked a razor. His hair was surprisingly smooth, softness where she had expected wire. His skin too was soft as silk. She drew a line down the channel to his neck, then moved suddenly to the hair under his arms. As she tickled him, he chuckled.

Even from her limited experience she knew that men did not always appreciate the joys of a route march. They usually wanted an immediate lower focus. But Roland seemed content to wait. After a while, she squeezed him too, then moved further down to his buttocks. He moved her hand around.

Roland kissed her soft lips. As he stroked her, he felt her body reciprocate affection, and respond with another nuzzle. Pushing the cover aside, he marvelled at the whiteness of her breasts. They must have been hidden from the Spanish sun. He moved his gaze and his hands to her broad hips and the gently curving belly.

'Roland, do we need a Durex?' she whispered.

'Perhaps we do.' He removed his fingers slowly, leant out of the bed, and fumbled in his bedside cabinet. Gazing at his broad back, she watched him draw out what she took to be a bottle of aspirins, newspaper cuttings, some rubber bands and phone cards, before he found the packet.

Sitting up, trembling, she helped him peel one on. As she rolled it down, she held the closed end of the rubber between her fumbling fingers and thumbs. She giggled again. 'You can't see the little safety kite in the dark.'

'Let's hope it's got one.'

Putting the thing on had separated them for a moment, made them pull apart, stand aside from loving. He did not like wearing them, but if that was how she wanted it . . . He pressed his body against her again, and felt the length of her against him. Despite the rubber, soon he once more felt comforted, excited, vulnerable, powerful.

Nothing in her magazines prepared you for how physical it was, the sweat, the movement, the fluids, the scratches. As Roland withdrew, she thought how strange it was, in the oldest of positions, to have that weight on top of you, and yet be secure. She felt sweetly trapped, ran her fingers over the bumps of his head, then guided his fingers below.

Half an hour later, Roland was sleeping beside her. She gazed at his serene face. There had not been the fireworks she had read should be a woman's goal, a woman's right, but his desire was flattering. She watched his chest rise up and fall down, and felt her breathing, pulse, and heartbeat synchronise. Outside the wind was still roaring, and above that she could hear the frequent wails of fire engines, ambulances, and police cars. For once they did not make her tense. They were distant monsters whose terrors could not harm her.

By seven o'clock it was becoming light. Roland studied Lorna. Though the lids were shut on those green eyes, was she lying awake? He slid out of bed, pulled on his boxer shorts, and went to the kitchen to see if the electricity had been restored. He jiggled the light switch. It was still off. He filled a pan with water, and lit the gas.

He would have liked to breakfast at leisure, watching the cartoons together in bed, or talking round the table. Today of all days would have to be a Saturday on. Could he phone and say he was sick? It was tempting, but not fair on Jimmy. Saturdays were always the busiest days; it needed two. And if earlier storms were anything to judge by, the market would be in a state, with scaffolding across the road, loosened slates, shattered windows.

While he watched the bubbles rise slowly to the surface, he switched on his radio. The battery was working. It crackled. The pirates were not up yet. He twiddled the dial and found a pop station, one he usually avoided. It had not been silenced.

The presenter chirped: 'They're calling it the biggest hurricane to hit these shores since the last time. It's only ten past seven on a Saturday morning, so now's the time to snuggle back under those covers for a long lazy lie-in.'

'Please,' said Roland.

The presenter relented. 'The police have warned everybody not to travel unless it's absolutely necessary but for those of you who think you have to, we'll be bringing an update on the situation out there as and when it happens. For now, let's just say it's still very milky. So don't touch that dial. Coming up now is Nick with our "Sing that Song" competition. You could be the one who wins a fabulous trip to Florida for two on Concorde.'

Roland touched the dial again. The water was boiling. He made two mugs of tea, and placed one on the bedside cabinet. Then, leaning over, he stroked Lorna's cheek and arranged her hair behind her ears.

He wanted to return to bed, to cuddle all morning, but work was calling. She opened her eyes and smiled.

'Don't let the tea get cold,' he told her.

In her dreams Lorna had seen again the sweep of the bay at Benidorm, where she had sunned herself by the oleander and hibiscus. She had seen again the gleaming towers, ethereal in the sun's haze. But this time Roland had been beside her.

She had lain with him on the twentieth floor, surveying the swimmers, the pleasure boats, the raked artificial sand, and municipal palm trees, listening to the Iberian beat of a hundred discos. Later they had danced the Birdie Song together.

She roused herself, pulled herself up, picked up the mug, took a sip, and noted its gold and black design (commemorating the Pope's visit to London). 'Are you Catholic?'

'No!' He was surprised at her question. Was it some comment on the condoms? Then he realised. 'No. Job lot in the market. Are you, then?'

'No,' said Lorna. 'My dad's family were, but he never really bothered.' Then she noted his clothes. 'Have you got to work today?'

''Fraid so.'

She sighed. 'What time?'

He looked at his watch. 'Soon.' He saw her face drop. 'What about you?'

'No, but I'll get up. I've got to go somewhere.'

Roland wondered where and why. 'The wind's dropped. I hope it hasn't done much damage. Didn't it disturb you?'

'No, I slept all through it.'

'I know you did. Like a child. Like a log.' He kissed her forehead, then went to the bathroom.

As she finished her tea, Lorna felt a sudden shuddering guilt. She had not phoned her parents: they would be worried sick. When she was a teenager, she had often stayed out all night. There had been many arguments. Should she still be having them at twenty-seven? In the last few years, she had been more scrupulous about informing them about most things. She must end their worry and hers.

She did not want Roland to glimpse her agitation, to see how little independence she really had. She thought of phoning while he was washing but it would be underhand, and he might reappear in the middle of an explanation.

She got out of the bed, went to the bathroom door, and called: 'Do you mind if I use your phone?'

'Of course not,' he replied. 'On the floor by the bed – if it's working. Last year they went dead.'

Her pulse racing, she picked up the receiver, only to hear a crackling line. She tapped anxiously. At first she was connected to a wrong number, who told her to be more fucking careful, but she was relieved that the lines were at least working. She tapped again. This time she was rewarded with the right change of tone. She hoped her mother would answer. After a minute, she heard her father. She swallowed and spoke. 'Dad, it's me.'

There was a pause. Then he replied. 'You're bloody alive, then.'

Lorna felt choked. 'Dad, I'm sorry.'

'Where the hell are you?'

'Stockwell.'

'What's up?'

'Nothing.'

'What happened? Your mother's in a state.'

'I'm in Roland's flat.'

'Who?'

'The bloke who took me out last night.'

'We had you wrapped up in some morgue.'

'I should have phoned. I know.'

'You're damn right. Your mother's been bawling all night. We phoned the police – not that we could get through. I got in the car to drive round looking but it was too dicey to go far. We had you in some gutter.'

'I'm sorry.'

'Don't bother bloody apologising. You get home.'

Despite his bluster, Lorna could tell anger was abating and tenderness welling up. His worst fears had been ungrounded.

Rose had been hanging on Fred's every word. She tried to grab the phone from him, but he kept his grip. She had to gauge what Lorna said by his responses. When he replaced the receiver, he would not look her in the eyes. She had to pin him down. 'Where is she?' she screamed.

'You heard.'

'What's she up to?'

'She stayed over somewhere.'

'Where?'

'You heard.'

'She doesn't think.'

'She's all right. She ain't been mugged.'

'How do you know? You wait till she gets home.'

'What you going to do? Belt her?'

'She'll do right by us while she's under our roof.'

'Well, she won't be for much longer.'

Rose was loading the information she had been fed. Suddenly she said, 'She's been staying with some bloke, hasn't she? You know all about it, don't you? She has, hasn't she?'

'Ask her yourself. When she gets in.'

'You know what's up, don't you?'

'No more than you,' he lied.

'I give up,' said Rose. 'I'll give her blokes. She's supposed to be at Trixie's again at ten. I bet she's forgotten.'

Fred showed signs of irritation and exhaustion. He knew he should comfort his wife, but when they were in this groove they could only be stubborn with one another. 'You still want her living with that lush?' he asked.

'Trixie'll keep an eye on her. It looks as if someone's going to have to.'

'Well, she'll have to stay sober to do it.'

'You knew she was going with some bloke, didn't you?' Rose screamed again. 'You two are always sticking up for one another. It all fits in. She's been mopey lately. She was in the bathroom again for ages.'

'When she gets in, let her be. It's been a rough night.'

'I nearly died worrying.'

'But you didn't, did you?'

'I don't know how I'm going to get through these next few weeks.'

'You'll have to.'

'All this upset. It's not good for your heart.'

Fred applied a counter irritant. 'I'll have to phone Kent.'

'What do you mean?'

'They took it bad down Kent last time. On that corner.'

'So?'

'The roof may have blown off.'

Rose looked aghast. 'I was never happy with that bungalow.'

'Well, if there's no roof, you'll have good reason, won't you?'

Rose sobbed again.

'Don't worry,' said Fred. 'I'm not buying no bungalow with no roof, contract or no bloody contract.'

'Oh no, I'm not having this,' said Rose. 'All this stopping and starting. I can't stand it. I'll end up in the Maudsley. We're moving. Even if you have to put the roof back on yourself.'

While Rose worried about the ravages of Nature, Fred wondered if Lorna had really taken up with a man again at last, or if the bloke had just not wanted to chance driving her home.

Normally he would have wanted to know everything about any developing relationship of his favourite daughter, but since the move had been fixed he had felt increasingly under an anaesthetic. He must let things run their course.

Roland wanted to give Lorna a lift home, but as he was late, she declined. She walked from Stockwell to Camberwell, crossing the strangely silent Clapham and Brixton Roads, tracing her way by back streets.

She saw that the radio had overreacted and the results of the storm were less spectacular than in the previous October. She saw two plane trees down in Myatt's Fields by the bandstand, their roots exposed above damp earth, and an oak, familiar from schooldays, had smashed the roof of a rusty Citroën in Knatchbull Road. But apart from tiles on the pavement, the only other effects were piles of twigs, leaves and wandering dustbin lids. Nevertheless, she felt delighted that this had happened while she was safe with Roland.

When Lorna walked in, her father put his arm around her shoulder. 'Go and get changed,' he said heavily. 'You'd better go and see the silly cow. I'll drop you round there.'

'Where was you? Where was you?' her mother demanded, blowing her nose.

'With a friend,' said Lorna, not wishing to lie.

'Some bloke?'

'Yes.'

'Who is he, then? I like the way I get told what you're doing.'

'Not now,' said her father.

'I'm the last to know anything. You're off to God knows where with God knows who.' Her tears welled up again. 'And now I'm expected to go and live somewhere with no roof.'

'You just said you wanted to,' said Fred.

'What's this?' asked Lorna.

'She's been up all night,' said Fred. 'We both have.'

Later that morning, Rose tried to calm herself by sorting out her wardrobes, but pushed to the back of one she found a box of old photographs which caused more tears – this time of nostalgia and regret. There were snaps of her schooldays, with her wearing a serge gymslip, wartime holidays at Clacton, where the beaches were cut off with barbed wire, and her first trips on her own to the West End, at the end of the war. In one, a smiling black GI had his arm round her in Trafalgar Square. She had been sixteen, and had met the soldier during a matinée at the Empire, Leicester Square. He had promised to write, but she had never heard.

She moved on to her wedding, years later, her hair in a beehive, then Lorna and Diane bouncing to Beatles songs, coloured school portraits, showing missing teeth or braces, and family holidays at the caravan. They had been happy then, she convinced herself. What had gone wrong? Was it just that she was getting too old? She, who had grown from a girl to a woman during the war, who had seen so many changes since, felt she could take no more. Why couldn't things stop still? Normally she would have been excited by a possible love affair of Lorna's which might result in another wedding and more loving grandchildren, but her present worries prevented this.

When Fred returned from the allotment he was surprised to see the disorder she had created in the bedroom with his clothes. She explained, however, that she had been making three piles: best, those fit for mucking about, and those he never wore or was now too fat to get into. These last she would ditch.

'Diane says we should try a boot fair,' said Fred.

'If she can be bothered, let her come and fetch this lot,' said Rose, yawning. 'Though I don't see why she should make money out of our cast-offs. No, the rag and bone man can have them.'

Despite her tiredness, Rose now felt strong enough to probe Fred about what he knew. 'Who is this bloke,' she demanded, 'this bloke she stayed with? Is he at this night school?'

'Yes.'

'What's he call himself?'

'Roland.'

'That's a wet name.'

'No, it sounds posh. He's from Stockwell. He's probably a yuppie. He could be loaded.'

'I've never liked yuppies. And there are some funny types in Stockwell.'

'There are funny types in Lydd.'

'Yes, but that's different.'

'If she's keen,' said Fred, 'I'll tell her to get him to pick her up here next time. You can have a nose at the door.'

'You can, you mean. I could have done without all this just now. She would have to pick now to be awkward.'

'Don't be daft.'

Jimmy had already made a tour of the market. The damage was surprisingly minimal. Only three pitches needed to be relocated. And, despite the winds in the night, there were still people awaiting pitches.

A couple hoping to sell Bibles and evangelical literature, sensing an audience, were preaching God's word. Last night's storm, they declared, was His displeasure in these last days before Judgement. There would be no escape unless youth renounced alcohol and sex in dark places. Roland wasn't renouncing either just yet. It wasn't his fault the lights had blown. Neither did he think it was God's. It had been sweet, though!

Today the task of checking merchandise and allocating spaces seemed light. For once he allowed the Bibles and tracts a favourable position, and with a spring in his step, moved to his Portakabin.

He was meeting Lorna at one. He had pressed for this, before they parted, and confirmed it with a last kiss. Despite his euphoria, it seemed a long morning.

He met her outside Marks. She had been shopping for comforting food for her father. Though they had only been parted for five hours, they regarded each other shyly in the bright daylight. 'Well, Miss Duggan,' said Roland, wondering if he should take her hand publicly, 'let's rock down to Electric Avenue.'

'And then you'll take me higher?'

He led her kamikaze fashion across the road, through the regurgitated bus and tube passengers, the dogged and persistent Marxists, the Pentecostal choir singing in the shadows of the railway arches, to the curving avenue, once the first in the capital to have outside electric lighting.

Lorna said her gran had talked of the famous illumination. 'Makes you wonder why they chose to light up Brixton.'

'Trying to stop the muggers?'

'These days they wouldn't bother.'

'I don't know,' said Roland. 'My brother says Brixton is going up in the world. But he says that because he thinks he is.'

'It seems less tense than it was.'

Roland's destination was the pizzeria off Market Row. They squeezed on to a bench at a table outside, under the arched skylights, opposite a ladies' outsize outfitters. In the twenty minutes while their pizzas cooked, he spoke about Mr Langley's flight in the night. Editing deftly, he also told her a little more about Weston. Lorna thought, however, that he demonstrated more love for Weston than she did for Diane. The brothers did not seem in competition. She was at the stage where she found almost anything Roland did admirable.

After a coffee, she stuttered that she needed to stay in that night. Even though Saturday evenings had been the most painful to be on her own, or to babysit, there were things, she said, that she had to sort out with her parents about the move, and so on.

As he was still keen to please her in every respect, Roland hid his disappointment and made no protest. He was relieved when she agreed to go out on Sunday afternoon.

That evening, Roland attempted Rob's latest assignment but words would not flow. He tried to read but could not concentrate as a world of possibilities flowed before him, so he returned to the Leisure Centre. Twenty lengths in the pool calmed him slightly. Afterwards he stopped his car at his mother's estate.

For once, Weston was out with Marcia. There was no sign of Mr Langley, but a pile of crumpled washing sat in a plastic bucket. He asked, 'Are they his clothes?'

Mrs Stephens stood the iron upright. 'Me just tank

de Lord 'Im gi' me strength to raise me children.'

Roland sighed. What answer was this? He filled the kettle for a cup of tea. 'Is he gone?'

''Im and Weston cuss some bad words, you know,' replied Mrs Stephens, more to the point. 'Shameful.'

Roland was encouraged by receiving information, and helped himself to a dumpling. 'Is he coming back?'

'Yuh hungry, Roland?' his mother demanded.

'I've been swimming.'

'Hungry better than sickness,' she added, adjusting the heat level of her iron. 'You going out wid a white girl, Roland?'

His mouth full of dumpling, Roland gulped. 'What have you heard?'

'Somet'ing.'

'What has Weston been saying?'

Mrs Stephens looked blank and said no more.

Uncertain of how to continue, he left her to the ironing, and went into the living room to watch the Saturday evening vet. His mind raced.

Five minutes later Mrs Stephens shuffled in and sat in an armchair.

'What about Sherene?' she shouted. 'A pretty brown-skin girl. Why you no take up wi' she?'

'I don't want Weston's cast-offs.'

'You could settle down and have nice pickney dem. You're twenty-five years old. Why don't you sort your life out and settle down?'

'Why don't you sort *your* life out?'

'Sherene's a good girl. She won't go behind your back and do dirtiness.'

'Who you talking about?' For a moment, Roland

continued watching the television. A spoilt Pekinese was being sick on the vet's Harris Tweed. Then he spoke again. 'Mum, her name's Lorna. She's a good girl, too. You'll like her.'

'Don't bring her ina me house. She na fe come 'ere.'

Roland had anticipated this. 'Rubbish. That's not Christian.'

Mrs Stephens needed to believe that coming to England had not been in vain, that her daily struggle had been worthwhile. 'I want grandpickney before I dead. I feel sorry for half-caste pickney. I feel sorry for the child. Dem stuck in between. They don't know which way fe turn.'

'Mum, stop living in some nightmare. I'm not looking to have children. I'm going to bring Lorna to meet you. You'll like her.'

'Look how Weston get on with Marcia. They never argue. They never quarrel. They's always peaceful.'

'That's because they never show up round here.' He continued quietly, 'Lorna's peaceful too. You'll see.'

'Lord have mercy,' said Mrs Stephens, her finger on the zapper to increase the volume on the television and silence Roland for the evening. 'A white girl. There'll be heartache and sufferation. Hear me. You will see, bwoy, you will see.'

Back home, Roland was saddened by his mother's negativity. She must have been brooding during the day, and Weston had obviously been stirring. Albeit for different reasons, for once his mother and his brother shared a viewpoint, and they were not alone in their opinion. In *The Voice* that Tuesday there had been an uncomfortable feature about black men turning to white women, with interviews from the streets. Daultan of Crouch End, a trainee barrister, had said that black women were confused, irresponsible and vain. Certainly Charmaine had been aggressive and argumentative, cursing and fighting back, but now Roland was beginning to see she might have been driven to that by his wish to analyse everything.

The article had also described why Bill Cosby would not let his television daughters date white men. They had, it said, different body language and different ways of treating people. It also quoted Mike Tyson, who had said that as long as white men still called black men niggers he would not date a white girl.

Roland had found the arguments confusing. As with him and Lorna, too much emotion was involved. He told himself that his mother and Weston were protesting without knowing Lorna. His mother at least would change her mind when she met her. It was always individual people who blasted theories.

His throat felt sore. Was love making him sick? Searching in his bedside drawer for a pastille, he drew out the cuttings from the Lonelyhearts columns. He hoped Lorna had not realised what they were last night. He had kept one, from the men's column, for its display of vocabulary which would have overworked Yvonne's reference books. A 'sporty, contemplative twenty-four-year-old' said he could 'accommodate' and that he was 'seeking a warm, caring, sharing, mutually respecting, understanding, considerate, cerebral, witty, felicitous, sanguine, sociable, communicative, sensual, affectionate, amorous, loving, amatory relationship.'

Roland had considered placing something similar, but now he no longer needed the yellowing paper. But then, he had learnt the adjectives like a mantra. He fell asleep repeating these honeyed words and deciding in what ways they applied to Lorna.

8

Meeting the folks

When she returned home, Lorna told her mother she had given Trixie the deposit. A fortnight ago this would have been a triumph, but now her mother just said coldly, 'Well, that's that.' After two paracetamols, she retired upstairs to lie down with a hot water bottle.

Lorna stayed in the kitchenette, staring at a late edition of the *Express*. For an hour she turned the pages, looked at photographs of distressed ferries, uprooted trees and wrecked cars, but registered not an image or a word. Possible futures with Roland were all she could contemplate. She imagined evenings in, snuggled together on his settee watching *The Bill*. She redecorated his kitchen, and shifted his living room furniture. She was starting on his bedroom when her father returned.

He went to the sink in silence. He used a tea towel to dry his hands, then asked, 'What's for tea?'

Lorna stirred herself and closed the paper. 'I got two of those stew and dumpling things,' she said. 'In the fridge.'

'Your mother can't cook,' said her father, sitting down. 'Not in her present state.'

'She won't have to,' she replied, rising to fill and

switch on the kettle. 'I'll open the packets.'

'Don't be lippy.' Her father untied his laces, pulled off his boots, and wriggled his toes in their woollen socks. He began to flip through the paper. His eyes rested on the gardening notes, with new ways of making a spring show. It seemed funny at this time of the year not to be planting daffs in their back garden.

Lorna poured the boiling water into the teapot, and covered it with a cosy in the colours of Chelsea. 'It's all settled with Trixie,' she said.

'I hope you realise what you're letting yourself in for.'

She sighed, 'I do, Dad.'

'Well, you've got your own life to lead.'

Lorna placed his tea on the fridge.

He took a sip, then, tiring of the bulbs beyond his pocket with Latin names, asked bluntly, 'Was you seeing this bloke again?'

'Who? Roland?'

'That's his name, isn't it?'

'Yes. And yes, I am.'

He smiled. 'That's nice.'

She felt a rush of affection and trust. Her dad had always been on her side. She didn't like keeping things from him. Suppressing her excitement, she said, 'He's picking me up tomorrow. In the afternoon. Here.'

He winked. 'So we'll get to see him.'

'Yes, Dad.'

'We'll have an early dinner, then,' he said, flicking through the paper. 'Have you told your mother?'

'Not yet.'

'Well, see that you do. You know what she's like.

You're in enough trouble after last night.' He turned
to the sports section. In next Wednesday's friendly
against Turkey, England were adopting a new sweeper
system.

Sitting down again, tapping her fingers on the
work surface, Lorna plunged in. 'Dad, there is
something.'

Her father was mouthing the words of John Barnes
as written by the *Express* journalist. What was Bobby
Robson playing at now? Not looking up, he said,
'What's that?'

'Just . . .'

'Just what?'

'About Roland.'

'What about Roland?'

'Just . . .'

Her father laid his paper aside. 'Don't beat about
the bush, love. He's not married, is he?'

'No,' she said, blushing.

'How old is he?'

'Twenty-five.'

'Oh,' he smiled, 'a toy boy.' The phrase seemed false
on his lips.

'Dad, there's nothing wrong.' Her courage nearly
failed her. She needed more time to prepare herself.
She stuttered, 'He's a market inspector.'

'So what's the problem?'

'It's . . .'

'It's a good job. Secure, good money. And I bet
there's perks.'

'But . . .'

'You're not going snobby, are you, Lorn? I didn't
think you was like that. You shouldn't worry about

what people do. You've always said it's what they're like. Which market – East Street?'

'No, Brixton.'

'Well, someone has to work there. You've never moaned about it.'

Lorna breathed deeply. 'Dad, Roland's black.'

Her father picked up his cup and slurped heavily. Lorna knew he had heard. His increasing deafness was real but selective. Now he was trapped by his own words, her words repeated back. He replaced the cup carefully in the saucer, examining the harvest motif as if for the first time, then drew a cigarette from a packet. He lit it, inhaled, and blew out the smoke. 'Do what?'

'He's black.'

'What d'you mean, black?'

'His mum's from Jamaica.'

Her father inhaled again. 'Jamaica,' he repeated. His brow furrowed. 'Black? You're not kidding?'

'I'm not kidding.'

'Blimey, Lorna.'

'What?'

'What's your mother going to say?'

'What d'you mean?'

'She nearly pegged out last night when we thought you'd had it. What's she going to say now if you tell her this?'

'I'll tell Mum later. I'm telling you now, Dad. What are you saying?'

'Bloody hell, Lorn.'

'Is that all?'

'I don't know.' He picked his teeth with a matchstick. 'Does it worry you?'

He considered. 'I don't know, Lorn. I haven't met the bloke yet, have I? I'll tell you then.'

There was some hope. Lorna could have hugged him.

'Is it serious?' he added.

'How do I know?' she smiled.

'What you think?' he asked, anxiously.

'I've only known Roland for a month. I've only been out with him three times. But you never know.'

Her father lit another cigarette. 'It's not what I would have wanted.'

'Oh, don't say that.' Lorna did not want him to withdraw the first spark of generosity. 'You just said you haven't met Roland. Wait till you do. He's a lovely bloke, Dad. Kind, sensible, funny . . . reliable.'

'You want to be careful, Lorn. You know what some of those black blokes are like.'

'I know what some white blokes are like, too.'

'Well, I don't know. This takes some swallowing.'

'Nobody really plans these things. It might be a one-night stand. It might be a flash in the pan.' She did not believe this.

'Well, you'd better tell your mum yourself, you know. It won't sound good if she hears it from me. God knows how she'll take it. She's hardly at her best.'

Lorna made a fresh pot of tea, then spilt a cup all the way to her parents' bedroom. She cared less what her mother thought, but flinched more at what she predicted she would say.

Her mother was asleep. Tears had run down her face. Lorna knew she would cause more but they could not be avoided. Her feelings for Roland made her impatient with a problem that was not a problem.

Her parents' protests were irrelevant, insulting.

She shook her mother gently. Rose stirred on her pillows and opened her eyes. Sad reality did not come flooding back with a jolt, but spread slowly like a tea-stain on a freshly laundered tablecloth. 'What's up now?'

'Nothing,' said Lorna, sitting on the floral duvet. 'Mum, I'm sorry that . . .'

'So you should be,' said her mother, blinking to check if this unfamiliar closeness with her elder daughter were not the last stage of a mocking dream.

Lorna had never found it easy to apologise to her mother. Now to start with, she let her think she had intended an apology. She continued, 'Roland's coming round tomorrow.'

'This new bloke?' Her mother wiped the crust from her eyes.

'Yes.'

'Not to eat he isn't.' She became more animated. 'I don't know if your dad's got any meat out the freezer yet. We'll have to run that freezer down, you know. God knows what he's still got in there. He's still stuffing fruit into it every week. And that woman along the road keeps baking him apple pies.'

'Roland's coming to pick me up tomorrow,' repeated Lorna. 'After dinner.'

'All right for some. Nothing but outings.'

'Mum, when you see him, don't be shocked.'

'Why, has he got something wrong with him?'

'No.'

'He's not handicapped, is he? I know what you're like with blokes in wheelchairs. I've seen you in that shop.'

'No, Mum. He's black.'

'Black?'

'Yes, you know, coloured.'

Her mother lost most of her own colour. 'You're having me on.'

'No, I'm not.'

'I don't believe you.' She looked as if this were a hoax, and expected to find a camera and a television presenter hidden in the fitted wardrobes.

'It's true.'

'You're not serious?'

'Yes, I am.'

Wearily her mother propped herself against the pillows. 'What! You stayed the night with some coloured you hardly know.'

'Mum, for God's sake.'

'I don't believe it. It's that holiday, isn't it? Those two you went with. They've got some funny ideas.'

'Mum, listen to me.'

'No, I don't believe it.'

Nevertheless, Lorna could tell her mother realised she was in earnest. She saw the confusion in Rose's face. Though she was sitting closer to her than she had for ages, Lorna felt the lack of trust which had grown between them. 'Mum, don't you want to know what he's like? You usually do.'

'Have you told your dad? I bet you have.'

'I did say something.'

'I bet you did. He's known about this all along. And what did he say?'

Lorna edited for the sake of effect. 'He said it's what you're like that matters.'

'He would.' She pulled her cardigan around her

shoulders, clutching the lukewarm hot water bottle. 'I don't get you any more, Lorn. First you say you're not coming to Lydd. That was news to me. Then you go all stroppy when I try to fix you up somewhere decent, and now you say you're walking out with some . . .'

'Man,' supplied Lorna.

'How old is he?'

'Twenty-five.'

'Does he have a job?'

'He works in Brixton market.'

'What's he sell? That funny veg they all eat?'

'No, he's an inspector.'

'Did he chat you up? I never liked that market. I've told you before to mind who you talk to. You never think. Or was he in your shop? You get all types since you stay open late.'

'I told you. I met him at the evening class.'

'Well, I never thought much of that idea.'

'You can meet him for yourself, tomorrow. Whatever you say, he's coming to pick me up.'

Her mother sat upright. In the pillows, she looked like a sick patient losing control of events. 'No, not tomorrow. I've got enough on my plate. You've not invited him to dinner, have you?'

'No.'

'Well, let's be grateful for that. Di and Barry was coming, but now they're dropping round tonight. I don't know what they'll say.'

Lorna rose from the bed. 'It's none of their business. They can like it or lump it.'

She went downstairs. Her father said he was out of cigarettes. Lorna said she would pop down the Green. She needed some time on her own.

* * *

Rose was too tired and drained to be as shocked by Lorna's news as she might have been in calmer times. Then she would have given it her full attention, and stormed her brain for all the problems. Now it was just another body blow.

Fred meant what he said. He would wait until he met Roland before passing judgement. He acknowledged he would be jealous of any man who laid claim to Lorna. He knew it was right to judge the man for himself, not the colour of his skin. The colour made things more awkward, less comfortable, but then, nothing was comfortable just now, so he might as well accept it. If it made Lorna happy, perhaps it was worth the trouble. He knew Rose would be hostile. Her world was narrower. She had always been more scared of the unknown.

He was about to take his wife another cup of tea, when she appeared with the one Lorna had made. There had not been much tea left in the cup by the time it had arrived in the bedroom. It had then gone cold, and a scum had settled on the surface.

Rose poured the liquid down the sink, then picking up the soiled tea-towel with disgust, said, 'She's told you, then?'

'Yes.'

'I suppose you told her it's no problem?'

'Don't start creating. We haven't met the bloke yet.'

'She needn't think she can invite who she likes round here.'

'You'll have to meet him,' Fred said sternly. 'Can't you see she's interested?'

'You're not saying it's a good idea, are you?'

'Well, no, but we don't know the bloke. You'll have to meet him sooner or later. She says he's decent. Lots of them are, you know.' He searched for an example. 'He could be like Lenny Henry.'

Rose stared blankly at the fridge. 'I've never found him funny.'

'Or John Barnes.' Fred had exhausted his list of famous black Englishmen. 'They've all got white wives, you know, those footballers.'

'He works in Brixton market,' said Rose. 'He's not a footballer. It's all right for that sort. They don't live round here.'

'We won't much longer.'

'It'll take off, then, won't it? Left to herself. She'll be expecting before we know where we are.'

'Hold your horses. She's not that daft.'

Rose took the packets of stew from the fridge. 'She wastes money on these things. Anyway, it's the kiddies I feel sorry for. They're neither one thing nor the other. How does a kiddie like that know where to turn?'

'They get by,' said Fred, touching Rose's hands. 'People have to. And she's not expecting.'

'Yet.'

'It's a different world to when we was young. You can't bury your head in the sand. Though, come to think of it, you can once you're at Lydd.'

Rose found his joke infuriating. 'Well, I'm glad you think it's a laugh. Where is she now? She hasn't gone out again, has she?'

'Only to fetch some fags.'

'She encourages you to smoke.'

'And you drive me to it.'

* * *

Fred buttered some bread, inspired by the 'serving suggestion' on the stew packets. Rose said, 'I'm not up to eating much,' but was silenced.

During tea the three showed unaccustomed interest in the television programme where an ageing disc jockey in a purple tracksuit was realising children's dreams. Roland was not mentioned, nor the move.

Barry was off to Spain on Monday. Some time ago, Fred had borrowed a power drill and a paint stripper from him, and Diane was anxious that these items should be reclaimed. 'I don't know why it's so urgent all of a sudden,' said Rose. 'Beats me why they can't pick them up when they come down.'

Diane and Barry arrived at nine, two hours later than expected. Barry carried cans of lager; Diane a litre of Asti Spumante. 'What's that for?' asked Rose.

'Drinking to your move,' said Barry. 'To wish you luck.'

'You chuck money away,' said Rose.

'We've always got drink in,' said Fred, indicating the globe which sheltered under its surface gin, whisky, sherry, Malibu and a bottle of Irish cream slowly turning to curd.

'I'm not drinking,' said Rose. 'Not after the day I've had.'

'What's up?' said Diane.

'Ask your sister.'

'Your mother had a rough night,' Fred interrupted.

'They say it sounded worse than it was,' said Diane. 'Not that we was bothered with our triple glazing.'

'What have you got where you're going?' asked Barry.

'He says we'll be lucky to have a roof left.'

Diplomatically, Barry asked, 'Was you kept awake, Lorn?'

'I should think she was,' said Rose.

'Leave it out,' said Fred.

'Your sister didn't stop here last night,' continued Rose.

'What's this, Lorn?' asked Barry. 'A night on the tiles?'

'We need glasses,' said Lorna, getting up. She removed five beakers from a chrome band which ran around the world. 'These are dusty,' she said. 'They could do with a wash.'

'Don't get so high and mighty,' said Rose. 'I spend all day cleaning as it is.'

'Don't stand on ceremony,' said Fred, picking up a can. He opened one, and threw another at Barry. Barry opened it, and it spurted over his trousers.

'New on tonight,' said Diane. Barry sucked in the remains of the drink.

After listening for two minutes on the best way to wash corduroy, Fred said, 'I'll go and see what's she's up to.'

'Probably on the phone,' said Rose. 'Never asks, these days.'

While Fred was out, Rose relayed Lorna's news. She could not tell what Diane and Barry thought. Neither seemed particularly shocked or interested. Neither seemed immediately eager to condemn. Diane shrugged her shoulders and said, 'So that's why she's so busy all of a sudden.' Barry pulled open another can.

'But suppose she sticks with this bloke,' said Rose,

gulping, 'and has . . . kiddies. What would your two think?'

'Don't worry, Mum,' said Diane. 'It won't last. Does anything ever last with Lorna? She's too set in her ways. She'll fuss too much. Don't get all het up. Now, has Dad sorted out Barry's tools?'

When Lorna returned with her father and the clean glasses, Diane looked at her with increased jealousy and a little more respect.

'So who's a dark horse?' asked Barry.

'Who's this bloke?' asked Diane.

'Can't you keep your mouth shut?' Fred snapped at Rose.

'It's early days,' Lorna blushed.

'You have your fling while you can,' said Barry, denting a polystyrene ceiling tile with the Spumante cork. He poured out three glasses of wine, handed them round, then proposed a toast to which they responded limply. When they had downed three cans, he was told enough was enough. Tonight he obeyed, but smirked. The day after tomorrow he would be free of such restrictions.

Diane was looking forward to the next weeks to enjoy again the freedom Lorna took for granted. If her sister was too busy now, she could always find other baby-sitters.

Drink always went to Rose's head and spark-ling warm wine to her nose. After two glasses she could just about blot out what had disturbed her and concentrate on a pretence of harmony. Though she knew it was Diane's excuse to come round for the tools, she was touched by the idea of her saying goodbye to the old house.

With his daughters around him, Fred felt he had not done so badly. He even felt some warmth for Barry. Though it was a bit dodgy going off and leaving Diane, these days you had to go where the work was. He looked next at Lorna. Despite all the criticism, she looked glowing.

Once again Lorna was relieved she had spoken. Nothing now would be as difficult. She glanced at her watch. Another hour less until Sunday. She poured herself a bubbling glass.

Knocked out by exhaustion, Spumante and love, Lorna slept. In the morning when her eyes were focused on the clock she felt again as excited and lightheaded as the mischievous elves.

How had Roland spent last night . . . on his own? She hoped so. Reading of some distant planet, or remembering the night before? Or had he gone out – to a pub, perhaps, or a club? She hoped not. Visions of other women he might attract bounced in her brain. It was bad to have such thoughts, but inevitable, since she could not understand why all heads did not turn immediately when they saw him.

Once she was up, after the stimulated breeziness of last night, her parents seemed equally grumpy, as if she had placed an unnecessary burden on their day. Her father was scraping the potatoes savagely, while her mother, prodding the joint, was complaining that it was only half-thawed. To avoid their unwelcome comments she took a walk to East Street.

The bustle cheered her. In the crush she nodded to schoolfriends, some with children, some, against the odds, still with husbands seven or eight years on. She wanted to boast that she had a new bloke at last, but word would soon spread. 'Saw Lorna Duggan with some black bloke,' or 'That Lorna's checking some brother.' She would be a minor curiosity for a while, one who had done something a bit out of the ordinary, like the girl who married the Moroccan plumber and emigrated to Australia, or that one who joined the Wrens, then set up home with a woman police officer.

Lorna looked at the streamers of tinsel and sheets of flimsy wrapping paper, and dared to imagine a Christmas with Roland. For years her most important shopping concern from October to December had been choosing a present for her father. This year it would be different. She would have to go to Lydd, of course, but not for all the time. This year she had another claim! What should she buy Roland? A denim shirt? She liked him in denim. A dressing gown? He seemed to need one. She would listen for clues and do some more detective work in his flat. In the meantime she would buy him something small.

Halfway along the lane she spotted some blue and white cuff links with Shakespeare's head on them. The stallholder swore they were Wedgwood. Willing to believe him, Lorna gladly paid the ten pounds.

Yesterday afternoon, Arsenal had beaten Liverpool 4–0. The highlights, the goals at least, were to be shown on television that afternoon after a live match. Roland calculated that would be about half past four. What time would Lorna be expecting him? His own mother prepared her dinner before church, and cooked it after the morning service, with barely enough time to eat before returning to praise. Lorna's family, he reckoned, would eat about one. Where could he go with her, just for the sake of driving about? And would he bring her back here?

At ten the phone rang. Sherene wanted to know if she could cut his hair. He marvelled. Criticism seemed only to encourage her. Caught pulling his socks on – it seemed chillier today – he muttered perhaps one evening next week. Immediately afterwards Charlie rang from the changing rooms on Clapham Common. The team was short of a player.

Though cold, it was bright, so at ten-thirty Roland was in the red, gold and green strip ready to play against a team from a City bank. The Ragamuffin Posse was a loose association of men who had been at school or work together. The bank's team was flabby. After conceding three goals, they tried to cheer themselves by mouthing, 'Yo, yo, yo!' and shouting, 'Yeh, man!' at their more skilful opponents. There was also a number of fouls. Minutes before the half-time whistle, Roland was brought down in a vicious tackle by a foreign currency dealer.

Rubbing his ankle, sucking a quarter of sour orange, not knowing which was more painful, he said of the bankers, 'I know why dem chiefs are making a little hassle. Can't take the pressure.'

'All this "yo" business is insulting,' said Charlie.

'White people can't do *patois*.'

'Since when you talk so heritage?' laughed Charlie. 'I didn't check you as being so street.'

'Since their midfield mashed my ankle.'

'Remember they're merchant bankers,' said Charlie, 'trying to prove something. It's their problem.'

'Respect,' said a serious trainee solicitor, 'is straightforward. For the player. For the game. They're showing neither.'

Roland limped through the second half, but played no more part in sustaining the victory. After the shower he joined the flow to the Windmill where, for medicinal purposes, he downed two ice-cold Super T's.

Charlie warned him: 'Don't forget *The Big Match* this afternoon.'

'Would I miss it?'

Only Fred had finished everything on his plate. 'I sometimes wonder why I bother,' said Rose. 'Sunday dinners are more trouble than they're worth.'

'When I said we should have a change, you were the one who was against it,' said Fred. 'No, you said, we've always had a roast Sundays, and as long as we can manage, we'll do it.'

'You won't feel like eating much just now,' said Lorna, who had left half her dinner. 'Not till you're settled.'

'You're doing a lot to help, aren't you?' Rose snapped.

Fred laid down his spoon. 'That's enough. What time's he coming, love?'

'They eat at odd times,' said Rose.

'Mum, he lives on his own.'

'How's he feed himself, then?'

'Men can cook.'

'Wants a housekeeper, does he?'

'Did you tell him what time we eat?'

'No. He'll be here before three, you'll see.'

'That's rushing things. I won't be changed.'

Lorna was pleased that her mother's determination to resist any contact had been supplanted by a worry that she might be seen in her overall.

These words over, they carried the plates and bowls to the kitchen, where they washed and dried them meticulously. Fred switched on *Gardeners' Question Time* on his third-best transistor. It was being broadcast from Deal in Kent. The apprehensions of all three mingled with enquiries about what plants were best suited to chalky soil and sea spray.

'Barry said it'll eat away at the car,' said Fred.

'What?'

'The sea air.'

'I don't know why we're bothering.'

They were on their second cup of tea when the doorbell began *Danny Boy*. Lorna coloured. 'Well,' said Fred, 'let him in.'

Lorna sped to the door. Fred looked at Rose. As the chimes rang out, her face remained immobile. When the echoes had faded, they could hear laughter and muttering in the hall.

Following Lorna's lead, Roland limped to the kitchen. He stood in the doorway and took a breath. He looked at Lorna's parents and smiled bravely. Then he held out his hand, which Mr Duggan grasped. In her turn, Mrs Duggan barely touched it.

Fred had noticed his limp as Roland stepped forward. 'Now then, son,' he said. 'What you been up to?'

Shifting the pressure to his left foot, Roland answered, 'Playing football.'

'What happened?'

'I got kicked.'

'And the foot?'

'I think it's swollen.'

'Sit down then, son, sit down,' said Fred, indicating a chair. 'Take the weight off. Move out the way, Lorna. Let Roland sit down. When was this, son?'

'This morning.'

Once Roland was settled, Fred continued to talk. Lorna knew that when her father was ill at ease he could chatter incessantly. To Roland, however, it seemed that Mr Duggan was trying hard to be welcoming.

Roland learnt that Chelsea's prospects were hopeful and that Arsenal's run of success would soon finish. Criticism of Bobby Robson's changes led somehow to descriptions of Fred's boyhood kickabouts in the alleys of Bermondsey.

How was it possible, Lorna thought, for men to become so agitated about goals? But at the same time she raised a mental glass to football. Roland could not have fed her father a safer or more suitable topic. She relaxed slightly. Roland could make anyone talking to him feel they were interesting. Her father would be flattered.

Meanwhile Rose sat stiffly in her chair, like a bored apprentice on the reserve bench, unneeded for the game. Lorna noted her glazed face. All the time her mother was twisting her wedding ring. Roland must take some notice of her mother soon, or his cause, however favourably begun, would be lost.

She was relieved when her father took a breath at last, and Roland turned to her mother and asked, 'Do you work, Mrs Duggan?'

Rose looked uncertain. Her fingers stroking her neck, she mumbled, 'Yes. Yes. I go out to work.'

'Where's your job?' Roland asked pleasantly.

'The council. I work for the council.' She enunciated slowly, as if he were deaf or understood little English.

'Yes,' Fred interrupted, 'but that's nearly done with.'

'You must be looking forward to your move,' said Roland. 'Lorna says it's soon.'

Rose thought he seemed to know too much of their business already. Unwilling to explain otherwise, she said, 'Yes.'

She was hard work. Further questions were answered in monosyllables, as if on a quiz show where to say more would cost the contest.

Fred filled the silence by inviting Roland to watch *The Big Match*. Rose glared and turned to Lorna. 'Didn't you say you was going out?'

'To do what?' asked Fred. 'It's getting dark.'

'That's putting the clocks back,' Rose said to him, her eyes avoiding Roland. 'I don't know why they bother. In the long run it makes no difference.'

'It does,' said Fred. 'That's why they do it.'

'It makes a difference in the market,' said Roland, trying hard. Rose chose not to hear.

'It must affect your trade,' said Fred.

'We'd best be going.' Lorna was impatient. Before they went, Fred wanted to examine Roland's ankle, but by standing up and putting on her coat Lorna prevented the nursing and another ten-minute dialogue from which she and her mother might be excluded.

* * *

In the car she wanted to ask how he had felt and what he had thought of her parents, but his mind was apparently elsewhere. His foot must be hurting; he seemed to have it stuck on the accelerator. Couldn't he feel the pedal properly?

'Where we going?' she asked.

'I don't know, really.'

'I did fancy a walk by the river, but I think we should drop in at your place first and bandage that foot.'

'That's fine by me.'

When he had kissed her in the hall, she'd noticed he'd been drinking. She didn't know if her parents had smelt anything. If they had, depending on what they'd decided to think, they would either dismiss it as something men did, or store it as ammunition. She wouldn't let it worry her now. But did he often drink and drive?

Roland felt annoyed with himself that he was on the borderline of being too drunk to drive. Where was his self-control? Where was his sense? Why did Lorna's parents have to see him first like this?

As neither lift was working, he had to rely on Lorna and the handrail to help him and his sore foot up the stairs. He consulted his watch at the bottom, and near the top.

Was he timing his climb? Lorna thought. Testing his heartbeat? Her heart was surely beating fast as they approached his front door a second time.

Inside, she noted the pile of dirty plates. After opening all the kitchen cupboards she finally amassed a bowl, soap, antiseptic and a bandage. Roland sat in an armchair in the lounge. She knelt, removed his shoes and socks, and washed his feet. They were beautiful: long-toed, with paler skin on the soles.

Sunday afternoon in bed seemed an erotic luxury. With the clocks going backwards and forwards or whatever they did, it grew darker. The massage and her tenderness had displaced the siren call of Arsenal. As he slid into her, Lorna said, 'I'm glad, Mr Stephens, that it's only the ankle that's sprained.'

Afterwards, they snuggled under the duvet. Although she did not want to break the enchantment, Lorna wanted them to talk before Roland fell asleep. She pulled herself up slightly. 'Roland,' she began.

'What?'

'What did you think?'

Roland was surprised. He didn't think Lorna was one of those women who required marks for lovemaking. Tentatively he asked, 'Of what?'

'Mum and Dad.'

'Oh.'

'Well?'

'They're nice.'

'You mean my dad is. You two got on fine.'

'It's football,' said Roland, suddenly consulting his watch again. 'It unites people.'

'It unites men, you mean.'

'You wait till the World Cup. You'll see.'

'Remind me to go out.' Whenever that was, would they still be together? Was he hoping they would be? She broached a more difficult question. 'What about Mum?'

'What about her?'

'What did you think?'

'She's shy.'

'That's one way of putting it.'

She could tell that something was on Roland's mind, even though he was being kind and gentle. What was it? Was he brooding? Her mother must have offended him. Had he sensed her worries about his drinking? She was irritated but relieved when he leant out of bed and switched on his portable television. It answered her question. His unease wasn't personal. It was football. She remembered that Tracey had finally chucked one of her lovers, when, in the act of making love, she discovered him turning the football pages of the *Sun* over her shoulder.

As the goals were shown during the next five minutes, Roland continued to stroke her arms, but his eyes were following the ball. For the time being, she would let it rest.

Despite Mr Duggan's kindness, the lovemaking, and Arsenal's goals, all afternoon a slight sense of depression had been hovering over them. The week had been exhausting. Despair, relief, having fun, having sex, and at the same time being on their best behaviour. They did not yet know each other's routines. That afternoon their doubts and irritations had again reminded them that even with a new passion, they remained the same people they had been before.

Action calmed them. While Lorna washed up, Roland perched on a stool and cooked spaghetti bolognese. Lorna resisted making a collection of jars which had passed their sell-by date. She also thought Roland's mince had been at its best some days ago, but kept silent. She must not criticise his domestic arrangements. She must be prepared to risk her stomach.

While the spaghetti was sticking to the pan, Roland lugged the television back to the living room. They ate on the couch and spilt tomato sauce on their clothes while they watched a spy film. Roland had seen it before, and enjoyed telling Lorna what would happen. Safe in his arms from the chases and explosions, Lorna preferred his commentary to the screen. Afterwards he switched to *That's Life*, where performing dogs appeared between investigations into rogue scaffolders and child abusers.

When the news came on, Lorna phoned home. She had no doubt she wanted to stay with Roland, but wished she could beam herself back for five minutes to learn what her father thought. She could not talk properly with Roland listening, but as he sounded reasonably content, this made her feel more settled.

Before they went to bed she gave Roland the cufflinks. He said they were nice but seemed puzzled. It wasn't his birthday, and all his shirts had buttons.

In the morning, Roland's ankle was still swollen. Lorna traced the bruise shading the skin and re-bandaged the foot. He would not stay off work. That Monday he had to visit the market at Lower Marsh, to check whether trade was still falling following the closure of County Hall.

First he drove Lorna to her house. He waited in the car while she collected her work clothes. 'Have to maintain the corporate image,' she said, as she leapt back into the car in her uniform.

'You sound like Weston,' said Roland.

'Will you phone me tonight?' she gasped as he dropped her outside Marks & Spencer. She had written her number on the pad by his phone, and on his bathroom mirror with his shaving foam.

'Every hour, on the hour.'

Even after the weekend, Lorna needed the assurance of a definite next meeting. All morning, as she arranged a consignment of men's pullovers (94% acrylic, 6% polyester), she rehearsed what she had learnt of his family. When would she meet them? Men were always so secretive about their mothers. She had heard more about his brother.

She was not yet ready to tell the others at work about the weekend. She was also tired of the bland food in the canteen. Giving herself these excuses then, at lunchtime, after she had bought a toothbrush from Boots to keep at Roland's flat, she walked to McDonald's.

Jason and Natasha thought the stores were a branch of heaven, but Lorna only saw them as magical when they were with her. Today, as she queued, she gazed around for Weston. The only superior on view was a burly white man in a dark suit who kept clapping at the counter-hands and barking, 'Keep it snappy. They're hungry out there.'

She took her order and sat down next to a plastic weeping fig. As she stirred her coffee, a youth was sweeping around her. Normally Lorna squirmed at boldness, but today she asked impetuously: 'Excuse me, is Mr Stephens here?'

'Mr Stephens?' repeated the youth. 'He's in the office.'

Lorna blushed. What was she doing? 'No, on second thoughts, it's OK. I just wondered.'

'No problem,' said the youth. 'I can call him.'

'It's not important.' But the eager sweeper had pressed a buzzer by the door marked Private. In a few moments Weston was out and asking why he had been summoned. Trembling at his resemblance to Roland, Lorna took in that he was shorter, lighter-skinned, as handsome (more handsome?), but had a hard expression.

'What is this, Gary?' he demanded.

'Lady asked if you was here, Mr Stephens.'

'Did you ask if this is a point-of-sale complaint?'

Lorna wished she could disappear. Whatever had possessed her? However, she could not vanish, so she had better be bold. Interrupting from the table, she called, with forced brightness, 'It's not important.'

Weston looked at her. He showed no trace of warmth. She tried to keep smiling. She wanted him to like her. Although her staff brooch and name tag were hidden by her coat, he must have registered what showed of her uniform. Roland would have told him where she worked. Surely he must recognise who she was.

'Leave this to me, Gary.' He moved beside her and looked at her tray. 'Did you have a complaint, madam?'

'No, not at all.'

'Are you sure? The food – the service?'

'No, no, it's all OK.'

'You asked for me by name? Is this a company matter?'

'No.'

'I'm busy. Are you some kind of rep?'

'No.'

He stared at her coldly. 'Have we met? At the rum bar?'

'No.'

He paused. As in a cartoon, Lorna saw understanding flash as he recognised her dress. He said slowly, 'This is Roland, isn't it?'

'I suppose it is.'

'Has he ditched you?'

'No.'

'That kind of thing happens on one-night stands.'

Lorna breathed deeply. 'No. I just called in.'

'You just called in. To check out the brother? Well, now you've seen what you came for.'

'I'm sorry you were troubled.'

'Did I say I was troubled?'

'I'll be getting back.'

'Before you go,' said Weston, 'a word. About Roland. Don't get too excited. Don't raise your hopes. There are other fish, you know, in the sea.'

As the customer looked distressed, the Manager came over. Were the human resources of his store being properly employed? 'Mr Stephens, is this something I can help with?'

'No,' said Lorna fiercely. She rose and buttoned her coat. 'No, I'm leaving. This is what you might call a domestic dispute.'

Weston gave her a look of rooting dislike.

Back at Marks, Lorna shut herself in a cubicle in the staff toilet. No longer having to preserve appearances, her tears flowed. Despair flooded over her. Since Wednesday, everything had been so perfect!

And now she had been so stupid, to go and spy on his brother! Why had she been so nosey? From what Roland had told her she might have known Weston would be annoyed. Would she like being summoned because someone wanted to look at her? And now Weston would complain to Roland, who would wonder why she had been snooping!

But it was Weston's final words that had chilled her heart. *'Don't get excited. Don't raise your hopes.'* Surely she was not being used. Surely this was more than that. Surely it was just the football which had subdued him yesterday afternoon. She could not believe in these 'other fish in the sea'. Who were they? From all she had observed of Roland, how could that be true? Roland, a two- or three-timer? Could he cheat like that? She couldn't believe it.

Tracey and Louise had always said she was naive, though. Was it possible that Roland could juggle his life in that way? Could he cope with more than one woman at a time? It didn't seem possible. Then with a shudder she remembered how even her father had not been faithful all the time. But that was after years of marriage, not at the start of a romance.

That afternoon she had to substitute at a checkout desk. Sliding food and drink over the scanner, operating the chargecard machine, giving change, shaking out plastic bags, and ringing the bell kept her occupied physically, but her mind remained feverish.

On a round of the employees, Miss Robinson saw that she looked flushed. 'Feeling unwell again, Lorna?' she asked.

Lorna cursed the woman. She could do nothing right in her eyes.

* * *

At home that evening, her mother and father were arguing over the arrangements to switch off the electricity, gas, water, and the phone. 'If you don't stop going on,' said Lorna's father, 'I'll get you switched off too.'

He saw that Lorna seemed miserable. 'Not having second thoughts are you, love?' he asked tenderly.

'Best thing she could do,' snapped her mother.

There was no discussion of yesterday. Lorna gathered that her father more or less approved of Roland, and she did not want to hear anything negative from her mother. Today it might resemble what she was telling herself.

Longing for the phone to ring, she went upstairs to sort through her bedroom drawers. Diane rang, then one of her father's workmates, then Trixie. Her mother spent half an hour chatting to her. Lorna sat on her bed, drumming her fingers, growing more agitated, willing her mother to finish. What if Roland thought they had taken the phone off the hook?

When her mother had finished repeating, 'I must get on,' Lorna ran downstairs and, in desperation, grabbed the phone. She had never rung Roland before but of course had memorised the number.

She heard him say breathlessly that he had just got in. Was this the truth? He explained that since there was a shortage of inspectors his supervisor at the Cut had been concerned and had taken him off to St Thomas' Hospital to have the ankle X-rayed. No, he hadn't broken anything. No, he hadn't tried to phone earlier. Though he sounded tired, his warm voice cleared her surface worries. She must trust him. In a rush she told him she had gone to see Weston.

He sounded at a loss to understand why. Lorna
wanted to confess everything, to hear what he had to
say about Weston's remarks, but her mother and
father, unable these days to sit still, kept going up
and down the stairs transporting boxes and carrier
bags. Frustrated, she had to ring off, but not before
she had gained a promise to be picked up tomorrow.

During his second visit the next evening, Roland
advised Mr Duggan to check that all the council
paperwork was completed or, he warned, they might
still be charged rent for the London house once they
had moved. He knew a girl in the Southwark Housing
Department whose number he would let him have. At
the mention of a girl, Lorna's ears pricked up. Fred
decided that Roland was well informed and to be
trusted.

Once Roland and Lorna had gone out, Rose
complained, 'You listen to some bloke you hardly
know, but whenever I say anything, oh no, I'm wrong.'

'That's right,' said Fred.

'That sort always know how to cheat the council.'

'Good. We might pick up some tips, then.'

Lorna wondered where they would go that evening.
All day she had wanted to talk about Weston, but
reflection had made her accept that she had been
foolish and it would be best to make light of it. She
couldn't dismiss what she had heard, but was her
faith in her own judgement, her own instincts, so
weak? You couldn't know everything about everyone.
You just had to trust and hope.

Looking around as Roland parked, she said, 'This isn't your estate.' The wasteground, the graffiti, the litter, the concrete ramps were the same . . . but not the mural. This one showed children of different races playing together in a nursery – another council vision of a harmonious Britain.

'This,' said Roland, 'is where the man spent his childhood, thought his first thoughts, played his first games of football, and set his small feet on the path to greatness.'

'So what went wrong?'

'He grew up,' said Roland, squeezing her arm, 'and sprained his ankle.'

Lorna smiled.

'Come on,' he urged. 'It's *Guess Who's Coming To Dinner*, part two.'

His jokes only partly dispelled Lorna's anxiety. She was scared of seeing Weston again. She could not know that Roland too was now feeling anxious. He particularly did not want a scene with Mr Langley or his brother.

When Mrs Stephens finally unbolted the locks, and opened the door, she sounded astonished. 'Roland, you long streak of misery! What's bothering you? Why you never tell me you were coming? Come in before I catch a cold.' Walking back down the hall, she called, 'You hungry, Roland?'

'I've eaten, Mum.'

As they followed her into the kitchen, there was no word to Lorna. Was his mother blanking her? Was Weston waiting in the living room?

In the kitchen Mrs Stephens turned and looked at Lorna guardedly. 'Since when you don't have no manners?' she said to Roland. 'Who's this young lady?'

'This is Lorna. Lorna, this is my mother.'

'Give me your coat. Have a seat. Roland, get Lorna a drink now. You like some juice, Lorna?'

'That would be nice.' She looked at Mrs Stephens. Roland had said his mother was about forty-five. She looked older. Behind her pebble glasses, she had an honest, kind, weary face. She seemed reserved but if she resented her, she kept it to herself.

Shaking, Lorna took the juice. Mrs Stephens sat with her hands on her lap, and as Lorna sipped, watched her closely. The unnerving silence was broken only by the loud tick of a pine wall-clock. Lorna admired it.

'Harding and Obbs,' said Mrs Stephens. 'In de sale. I sent another one to mi sister back home.'

'Mum had us ship an iron bedstead back home last year,' said Roland. 'All the furniture in my aunt's house is from South London department stores.'

Lorna smiled. It was a small world.

'Mum, Lorna works in Marks and Spencers.'

Mrs Stephens gave her a look of respect. Then she declared, 'Marks' food is too dear.'

'It's convenience,' said Lorna.

'Convenience cost money,' said Mrs Stephens.

Lorna sensed she was not trying to score a point, but spoke as someone for whom there had been few luxuries.

Mrs Stephens continued: 'You never know what life will bring you. But the Lord provides. The Lord's ways are the best.'

Lorna couldn't quite see what this had to do with shopping, but smiled pleasantly.

Unless the Lord had directed, Roland could not believe his mother had changed her views on white girlfriends overnight. She had always made him understand that white people were fine as long as you didn't step into their territory. He didn't think she'd ever envisaged him having a white girlfriend.

Given what she had said yesterday, he was surprised that she was behaving with such dignity. After half an hour he engineered they should leave before the welcome chilled, or Mr Langley turned up, or Weston came home.

'She's nice,' said Lorna, back in the car. 'You said she was moany.'

'She was, to us.'

'Well, I can imagine what you two were like.'

'How?' Roland suddenly sounded prickly.

Lorna was flustered. 'I just can.'

Roland demanded, 'Was this yesterday with Weston?'

Lorna stuttered, 'I was in McDonald's, so I introduced myself.'

Roland kept his eyes straight ahead. 'Was that necessary?'

'Roland, don't have a go at me. I wasn't thinking.'

'No, you wasn't.'

'He wasn't very friendly.'

'He wouldn't be.'

Tomorrow was Wednesday. They had neglected their homework. Just when Lorna was feeling despondent again, Roland said they should return to his flat for some 'serious' studying. Feeling she wanted to spite Miss Robinson, Lorna was all for leaving the class, but Roland would not hear of it. 'No question. We're going. We're staying. We're getting qualified.'

After his severity, the plural pronoun and the vision of a shared future comforted her so she did not protest.

9

What insults your soul

Roland came back with Lorna after the class. Rose was ironing in the kitchen. Until the move Fred had been ordered to wear his oldest clothes which had survived the clearout.

Roland thought hard but found it impossible to say anything encouraging about ironing. Mrs Duggan looked as sour as ever. Lorna directed him into the front room where Fred had fallen asleep, and the television was entertaining the chests and cardboard boxes.

Five minutes later Lorna woke her father with a cup of tea. He became animated when he saw the digestive biscuits and Roland, and told them about that day's phone calls. 'They say they're trying to connect you and they play bloody silly music. Then you get the wrong extension. It's bloody stupid.'

Roland drew a scrap of paper from his pocket. Scribbled on it was the number at Southwark Town Hall he'd said he could provide.

He made Fred feel assured that moving was a good idea after all. For months it had seemed like too much hard work. Now he was excited again. Through Roland's eyes he saw that he and Rose were brave, to make such a leap at their time of life. 'So, son,' he asked, 'is your dad still working? On the buses, is he?'

Lorna winced. 'Roland's dad's in Jamaica.'

'Good for him,' said Fred. 'I'd like to leave her mother in London.'

'He doesn't mean it,' said Lorna. Roland and her father were getting on so well, but she was worried her mother was being left out. The last few weeks had made her able to stand apart from her parents. She saw that now, of all times, they needed not to be pushed further apart. She returned to the kitchen and promised her mother she would help with the ironing tomorrow.

'It's all right,' said Rose. 'Diane's popping round.'

'Why don't you come and drink your tea in the front room?'

'I want to finish your father's shirts.'

Lorna invented rapidly. 'Roland's got a problem with his nets. He wants your advice on where to buy curtains.'

'Can't he ask his mother?'

'He doesn't live with his mother. I told you that. You know more about bargains.'

'Doesn't she go shopping, then?' said Rose, spreading out another shirt. Another question struck her. 'Who does his ironing?'

'He does.'

Though she had seen a man ironing on *EastEnders*, it was still a novelty. 'It beats me how some people live these days,' she said. 'Like your dad says, it's a different world.'

Next evening, Roland sat in his mother's kitchen with a towel draped around his shoulders. Sherene was shaving his head. Mrs Stephens was at a church meeting and Mr Langley had appeared for ten minutes, sneered at the hairdressing, and gone elsewhere to eat. Weston stayed at the table tapping notes into his organiser.

It was not only laziness and convenience which had made Roland accept the offer of a haircut after all. If Weston stayed with Marcia, Sherene might become family, so it was best to humour her. And he had always been more attracted by her vivacious spite than he cared to admit. It was Weston he was thinking of renouncing.

Submitting to her razor, he knew he was a sitting target for her sarcasm or worse. He was in a vulnerable position. One critical comment and his lobes might turn bloody.

Sherene pressed near his right ear and whispered, 'Perhaps Lorna would prefer you to grow it? I can see you with an Afro. And I can see her running her hands through your curls.' She picked up a strand critically. 'For her sake, Roland, you should moisturise more often. Out in the wind and rain all the time, you're losing the shine. Weston never forgets to condition. He even used to condition his Filofax.'

'Finish what you came for,' snapped Weston.

Sherene continued, 'What's Lorna's hair like then, Roland?'

He wished Weston would go to his bedroom. 'Sort of red.'

'Red? I went red once – for a week. But Weston didn't approve. Sisters should have black hair.'

Weston sighed.

'I'm surprised,' Roland told her, 'you haven't found

it necessary to go shopping in Marks yet.'

'Would I go poking my nose into other people's business?'

When Sherene had finished trimming, and gone to the toilet, Roland asked Weston, 'So Lorna came to see you, then?'

'It was out of order.'

'What did you think?'

'Pushy.'

'I thought you liked that.'

'Roland, can't she find a white man?'

'Don't talk crap.'

'You know how white women stay. Some like a touch of mystery.'

'There's no mystery about me.'

Sherene returned. 'Would Lorna like me to do her hair in dreadlocks? With some little plastic beads? Like those white women back from two weeks in Barbados? Then she'd really look the part, pouring her hot pepper sauce over her rice and peas, with jangly locks.'

At least Sherene's jibes meant she accepted his affair might be serious. Roland had decided he would not waste any energy despairing over Weston. It would need a shift in his nature to shift his attitude. If things really progressed with Lorna, perhaps he really would stop seeing Weston. For the meantime, though, he dropped Sherene at her house, then drove to Lorna's as arranged.

That Thursday evening, Diane was missing Barry more than she had anticipated and felt hurt because he had not phoned. He had also taken the keys to his

GTi, so while he was away she had to use the Fiesta. Her sadness made her more ready to listen to her mother. She was always willing to agree that Lorna was an oddball. By the way her mother condemned Lorna's new romance, she could sense she thought it was serious.

But although Diane normally had little difficulty in being mean-minded and censorious, she could not agree that Roland's being black was a stumbling block. She told her mother that of course you had to cross barriers if you went with a black bloke, but plenty of girls did it these days.

'Why's it such a big deal?' she asked. 'Lots of Barry's mates are black. They like the same things – football, music, cars. What's the problem?'

'I never thought you'd side with your sister. I thought you'd be sensible.'

'What does Dad say?'

'This moving's made him very odd. He can't think straight. He thinks this Roland is the bees-knees. Thinks he knows everything. Can't put a foot wrong.'

'It'll blow over once you've moved.' Diane did not necessarily believe this but wished to calm her mother.

'You might be right. She's only done it now for attention.'

When Lorna came in from working late, she offered to iron again, but was told it was finished, so went to wash her hair. Fred had gone to deliver an unwanted washing machine to Frank and Myra. While Lorna was on her second rinse, they phoned to invite Rose along as well for a parting drink.

Roland and his haircut arrived at half past nine.

With her dryer in one hand, Lorna shyly introduced him to Diane.

'So Thursday night is our hair night, is it?' Diane asked.

Roland smiled. 'Something like that.'

Lorna put the dryer down, and ran her hand across Roland's crop. 'It suits you short. It's nice.'

'Well, Lorn, you needn't have bothered washing yours,' said Diane, 'For all the notice it's getting. What do you think, Roland? It's had the best Body Shop treatment. Crushed wheatgerm and brazil nuts.'

Was Diane flirting? She was not usually this pleasant to her friends. Lorna winced as she continued, 'A barber did yours, was it?'

'No, Sherene.'

'And who's Sherene? You can't keep secrets from us.'

'A friend of Roland's brother,' Lorna explained quickly. 'She's a hairdresser.'

'Thinks she is.'

'Where was this?' asked Lorna.

'At home.'

She felt a pang of worry.

Diane followed her sister into the kitchen where the kettle was once more pressed into service. 'You'd better buy a razor, and learn about black hairdressing.'

'Really?' Lorna felt closer to her sister than she had for years, valuing her opinion. 'Well, what do you think of him?'

'He's only been here five minutes.'

'Yes, but first impressions.'

'Talk about sex on legs.'

Lorna blushed. 'Do you think so?'

'Blimey, Lorna. Are you blind?'

When he had drunk his tea, Roland announced that he had to leave to write some reports. Lorna had reckoned he would stay until eleven at least. Why was he going?

In the hall, once again she wanted to ask questions, but pride prevented her. Why show him how worked up she could become? He would learn soon enough. Why let him think she had doubts? She must trust him.

He put his arm round her, squashing her father's ship's barometer and Spanish swords. As they leant against the wall, she pressed for a reply. 'Where did you have your hair cut?'

'I told you. At home.'

'Your flat?'

'No, Mum's.'

This was reassuring. Why had she worried? After a moment, she asked, 'Was Weston there?'

'You're always going on about Weston. Is it him you fancy, or something?'

'Of course not.'

He stroked her hair.

'Did he say any more about Monday?'

He squeezed her. 'That's history. Anyway, he's a skanker.'

Lorna relaxed. Her fingers traced his haircut again. 'This Sherene did a good job.'

He kissed her. 'I've got to go.'

She released him. 'Go and do your work.'

'Tomorrow night. Stay over.'

These were the parting words she had longed to hear, but why did work have to get in the way? Why couldn't she go with him now? Why couldn't they spend all their time together?

Fred had annoyed Rose by talking to Myra and Frank about Roland. Rose could see they were dribbling at this gossip, and could hardly wait for their visitors to leave so that they could gloat. Fancy having to move away and leave your unmarried daughter with some black sniffing around.

Next morning, Fred and Lorna were starting work late. Rose was back from her morning shift before they had left. As Lorna put on her coat, her father said, 'I don't want you turning up tonight in trousers. You've got to wear a frock.'

'What's this?'

'Now don't go all funny,' said her mother.

'What are you on about?'

'You dad's retirement do. Don't make out you've forgotten.'

'When was this arranged?'

'Come off it, Lorn,' her father said. 'We told you last week.'

'First I've heard of it.'

'You don't listen these days.'

'What is this do?'

'Your dad's mates are standing drinks at The Clarendon. We told you.'

'Your sister's coming,' her father told her.

'It's short notice.'

'You were told,' said her mother. 'Where else d'you think you're going?'

'We haven't decided yet.'

'Bring Roland along. He'll enjoy it. It'll be a laugh. We'll learn him some songs.'

'It's just family,' said her mother, as firmly as she could. 'And people from work.'

'She can bring who she likes. We're going to get plastered.'

'You're staying sober. There's enough to do this weekend.'

Searching for her bus pass, Lorna said, 'Well, I'm late for work. I'll have to see. I'll be there if I can. I wish you'd told me.'

Once Lorna had gone, Rose declared, 'She's not bringing him.'

'Are you going to stop her?'

'What will people say?'

'No one will bat an eyelid. Half the blokes at work these days are foreign.'

'No wonder we don't get any letters these days.' Rose remembered another worry. 'Have you told the Post Office we're moving?'

'No,' said Fred. 'Where have I been working for the past forty years?'

Roland was drinking a coffee in McDonald's. He was stirring the sugar when Weston joined him with another beaker. Strangely for him, Weston noticed his hair. 'The length's uneven. Sherene doesn't know what she's doing.'

'Who says so? Marcia?'

'No. I can tell.'

Roland sipped his coffee. 'Is Sherene still with Clinton?'

'Who's Clinton?'

'The potato head.'

'How should I know?'

'They say he does the rounds.'

'Well, she'll have you at any time. She's made that clear enough.'

'I don't operate like that.'

'Not white enough for you?'

Undeterred, Roland asked, 'What did you say to Lorna?'

Weston considered. 'It was the first time I'd seen the girl.'

'Whatever you said, it upset her.'

'She disturbed me at work.'

'Like I'm doing now?'

'I've chosen to talk to you.' He smirked. 'Customer relations.'

'Seems I'm more customer than relation.'

'Stay cool, brother.'

Roland finished his coffee and fixed Weston with a stare. 'What's bugging you so much about her?'

'I've told you before.'

'We don't need your approval.'

'Think of the consequences if we all behaved like you.'

'What are the consequences?'

'Dilution.'

Roland spluttered into his beaker. 'This coffee needs diluting. These creamer things are nasty.' He compressed the beaker and threw it in a bin. 'I have a quote you should write seriously above your weights and mirrors. The night-school teacher told us it last week.'

'What is it? "The ink is black, the page is white, Together we learn to read and write"?'

'No. If I remember correctly, and I know I do, it's "Examine what you've been told. Dismiss what insults your soul." I think you should write it up. I think you should learn it by heart. I think you should do it.'

'Glad you mentioned soul,' said Weston, rising. 'Charlie's band's doing a PA at The Fridge tonight. He wants some help – he's been trying to get hold of you. See you there. Come unaccompanied.'

Sherene had been pleased: Roland had praised her restraint in not snooping. That Friday afternoon, though, curiosity got the better of her. She filled her basket with food her grandmother could freeze, then squeezed behind the checkout queues looking for a redhead at a till. Eventually she saw a woman with brownish hair, perhaps with a hint of auburn.

As she moved forward and began placing her items on the moving counter, she checked the name tag. She was right. *Lorna Duggan*. Her hair wasn't red! Men could never describe shades properly. They lumped together the subtlest differences. She looked more closely. Lorna's skin had that paleness which can be beautiful in white women but more often looks washed out.

She banged down the plastic bar to separate her items from the previous customer's, a confused old man, and stared at Lorna counting out his change.

As Lorna served her in turn, she could sense that Lorna felt she was being scrutinised. She relished the

white girl's false grin, imagined her practising it
before her mirror every morning until it was wide
enough.

'Do you want a carrier?' Lorna asked, seeing her
pile and reaching under the till.

'Well, it would be nice to have a man to carry it out,
but a bag will have to do.'

She watched as Lorna's smile grew.

Lorna told Roland about her father's celebrations as
soon as he arrived. He told her about The Fridge.
Charlie had rung asking if he could help shift
equipment from the vans. No disrespect to Lorna or
her parents, but could he show up at the pub later?
Lorna was disappointed but could see that if she went
with him she would be in the way.

As the evening wore on, Fred and Rose grew maudlin
and nostalgic. On the bar next to the ice-buckets and
the giant retirement and house-warming cards (*from
our house to yours*) a pile of unwrapped presents was
balanced. A policewoman who came to give Fred a
parking ticket stripped in front of him, to the
enjoyment of his mates and Fred's embarrassment.
As the woman unbuttoned her blouse, Trixie said to
Rose, 'She must be fifty if she's a day. And you don't
keep tits like that without plastic surgery.' Lorna
wondered if this was the kind of chat she'd soon have
to share.

At ten o'clock Trixie sat at the piano and began to
pick out *Roll Out The Barrel* and *Maybe It's Because
I'm A Londoner*. Everybody knew the words of these,
but apart from the choruses, were less certain with

Trixie's newer favourites *Viva España* and *I Just Called To Say I Love You.*

Roland arrived in the middle of a cramped conga just before last orders. Once they'd established that he wasn't a minicab driver, Fred's mates conducted him to the Duggans. When Fred saw him, he shouted to everyone that Lorna's new bloke had arrived! What time did he call this? But what could you expect from an Arsenal supporter?

The crowd sat down. Roland braved their glances and squeezed next to Lorna. Diane, merry with Malibu, patted his knee. Roland explained to Diane what he had been doing. Lorna thought this unnecessary, and slipped her arm into his. When Diane declared that she had never been to The Fridge, Lorna whispered to Roland that if the two of them didn't make a move soon, wouldn't they miss the band?

Just before midnight, Roland and Lorna joined the queue along the Town Hall parade. Vans bunched by the crash barriers were selling hamburgers to ravers who had not fitted eating into their Friday evening schedule. Later, some would regurgitate the food against the black walls and Grecian columns of the toilets.

Lorna was about to restrain Roland from buying a jumbo sausage, but reminded herself that the cautious habits of a supervisor should be kept for work. Life was not as Marks & Spencer might wish: orderly, planned, without surprises. In the last few weeks she had chanced her luck, and though it had been painful at times, she would continue. Like Roland's stomach, she might have her upsets as well as be satisfied, but it was better than never-ending sameness.

When Roland had munched the sausage, they paid their entrance money, were frisked, and moved inside. They stood by the bar under a low black ceiling, decorated with white Aboriginal squiggles. In front of them was a circle of climbing frames, supporting lights, projectors and speakers. Beyond this, on a stage at the far end, the most exhibitionistic dancers were preening individually in the pink spotlight, shadowy figures before the projections. Green and white light flickered on the dance floor. Perspex interlocking triangles revolved above, with a cartoon of a bespectacled spiky-haired man.

The drawing made Lorna relax, just as the muscular bouncers in their black T-shirts, standing by the emergency exits, seemed not disturbing, but like Roland's guiding arm, a symbol of protection.

In the past, in Benidorm and the West End, discos had always promised more than they delivered. They were usually unsettling; their glamour an illusion. But tonight as she sipped an orange juice she felt secure. She had seen Roland smile at her father's introduction in the pub, but even without that bonus, she felt powerful. These days, she realised, despite all her insecurities, she was more in charge.

She tapped her feet. The music was too fresh, too young and too black to be familiar, but she longed to move to the dance floor.

The smell of Paco Rabanne surpassed the other aftershaves hanging in the air. Lorna turned and saw Roland talking to Weston. They were having some kind of disagreement. Weston saw, but did not acknowledge her.

The bass notes from the speakers above their heads made conversation difficult, but all the same Roland ushered Weston and Marcia up to her and introduced them formally. Weston nodded, but it was clear he saw no reason to talk. Neither, in her turn, once she had looked Lorna over, did Marcia. Lorna was relieved when the couple moved away.

Roland had glimpsed Sherene among the dancers. He pointed her out. Lorna looked but did not register that she had seen her earlier in the day. She shouted, 'Why did your friend ditch her as the singer?'

'Spoke her mind,' Roland mouthed. 'Once too often.'

'Good for her.'

'I'm surprised,' bawled Roland, 'that she hasn't been down your shop sussing you out.'

'Is she after you, then?' asked Lorna, loudly speaking her mind.

'She might be.'

'If she is, I'll scratch her eyes out.'

Fear Eats the Soul was a four-piece band. Sherene's replacement spent as much energy displaying her black mini-dress as singing, and appeared to be eating the microphone. Behind her a guitarist, keyboard player and drummer, also all in black, stared through the spotlights with moody expressions. Occasionally the session percussionist shook, rattled or rolled bongos, chime bars or blocks, but try as she might Lorna found the music as monotonous as their clothes. However, from the whoops and cheers after each number she judged her reaction was not general.

The band celebrated afterwards in a backstage room. Roland and Lorna were welcomed warmly at the door. Smiling at Lorna, Charlie asked, 'Who's this, star?' and Roland made the introduction. Charlie demanded, 'Lorna, did you enjoy it?'

Lorna fumbled for praise. 'Most unusual. But nice.' She felt ill at ease and wished she could leave.

More genuine enthusiasts crammed in behind them. 'Strictly conscious lyrics, Charlie.' 'The music hit the massive.'

Weston and Marcia arrived with a jeroboam of champagne. Sherene appeared as the cork popped. Generous with success, Charlie greeted her, 'What's happenin', sister?'

'I was your cheerleader out there,' Sherene said boldly. 'So you see, I'm still doing my bit towards your success.'

For old time's sake Charlie put his arm round her. 'What you up to these days?'

'Still at the office. I'm also hairdressing.'

'Yes, we heard you attacked Roland's.'

Changing the focus, Sherene turned. 'You must be Lorna.'

Lorna smiled weakly. Sherene's face was familiar.

Sherene continued mischievously: 'Roland says you work in Marks. It's strange – I haven't seen you there.'

'Sherene, you must be that store's best customer,' said Charlie. 'I've seen you in there, ranting at Customer Service. If you could get men from that store, you would. Then when you find fault, you could return them.'

'Well, sweetheart, you've surely passed your "best-by" date.'

Feeling she should contribute, Lorna squeaked over the banter. 'There's a lot of picking up in the checkout queues. You'd be surprised.' She saw Roland stare at her nervously.

'Sainsbury's is the place for that,' said Sherene, sipping her champagne. 'Vauxhall. It's so big you can cruise all day. It shames this joint.'

'Is that where you pick up Potato Head?' asked Charlie.

Sherene ignored this. Like the dancers in the auditorium, the talk was jumping wildly. She wanted to focus on Lorna.

When the last fans had come and fawned, Roland helped Charlie load the keyboards again. Marcia went to let down her hair. Weston stayed aloof, studying posters of past acts, his hands in his camel coat.

Sherene grinned at Lorna. 'Well, is this your scene?'

Lorna was suspicious, but warming to Sherene. At least she was talking to her. 'A bit loud.'

'Roland's never been a raver. I'm sure you two prefer nice quiet evenings in with your books.'

Despite the sarcasm, Lorna understood that Sherene was acknowledging her and Roland as a couple. She asked tentatively, 'Roland said you used to be a good singer. So you don't any more?'

'Only at church. Inside every gospel lady with glasses there's a soul singer with lipstick trying to break out. But I don't really have the voice.'

'That's true,' said Weston, sneering at them both. 'Or the application.'

Roland returned and said to Lorna they should hit the dance floor. They were about to leave as Marcia emerged from the toilet and Lorna judged she needed it too. She excused herself. 'All those orange juices.'

Sherene saw the lock turn. 'So, Roland, is Lorna enjoying your guided tour of Black Brixton?'

'I think so.'

Weston kissed his teeth.

'What's up?' asked Roland, though he knew.

'I told you.'

'What's that?'

'She doesn't fit. She doesn't suit.'

'Why not?' asked Sherene.

'Too nervous. Too stiff.'

Roland replied defensively, 'About too nervous. About too stiff. Whose fault is that? You've been damn feisty all evening. You've blanked her entirely.'

'Roland, if you can't see it, you're blind. You saw her with the music. This isn't her scene.'

'Brothers, brothers,' said Sherene. 'What do scenes matter?'

'You used the word first,' said Weston.

'Well, now I'm sick of hearing it. I'm serious now. I know what you're getting at, Weston, and it's dangerous. Let the girl rest.'

'Keep your preaching for Sundays.'

Sherene faced him squarely. 'Weston, are you on some crusade? People love who they love. My God, don't you think I've had to learn that? It's a bitter pill to swallow, but life's enough of a bitch without you making things worse.'

In the toilet, breathing deeply to calm herself, trying to make no noise because of the thin walls, Lorna caught Sherene's gist. She heard her last words. Who would have thought that Sherene, of all people, would come to her defence? She certainly wasn't what Lorna had expected. At first she'd seemed catty, but what she'd just said had been thoughtful and generous.

As she pulled the chain, Lorna hoped they might become friends. Perhaps there was nothing to fear from her. Roland was not after her, and, if she stayed with him, judging from Weston, she could do with a guide to black families.

That night at Roland's they felt more comfortable, less tense. It helped that neither of them had to work the next day. Nevertheless after breakfast, as it was sunny, they walked to the market. Lorna liked the idea of being seen together where Roland worked.

Afterwards, when they reached Station Road, Fred and Rose were recovering from hangovers. Despite a throbbing head, Fred had gone across the road to the parts shop for a final scrounge. In the back yard Rose was pulling up hydrangeas. She was not going to leave them for the council. They could spend the week in pots, then take their chance in the sea air.

The countdown to the move continued. Whenever Fred complained that he couldn't find anything, Rose said it was tough, but everything was packed.

Diane had stayed overnight, her car keys wrenched from her by a sober neighbour. Rose had just uprooted her from bed to take a third phone call from Barry's mother, who had not liked sleeping over with Jason and Natasha. She had shouted that if Diane didn't get home soon she'd be late for bingo.

Lorna and Roland found Diane in the kitchen drinking black coffee. Diane resented their clear heads and day-long freedom. Sensing her mood, Roland went to say hello to Fred. As soon as he had gone, Diane muttered acidly, 'You've got a smirk on your face, Lorn. So tell me, is it true what they say about black men?'

Lorna knew what she meant. 'Don't be common,' she snapped.

Diane finished her coffee in silence, and left.

It had taken a week for Rose to tolerate Roland in the house. To Lorna's surprise, stiff politeness had quickly superseded hostility. At five, after a day's pottering, Roland even sat down to tea. Rose was using up many items which had lurked in her cupboards for years, so their meal included Spam, pease pudding, spaghetti hoops, Smash and Instant Whip. Lorna hoped Roland did not think they always ate like this.

On Sunday Roland helped Lorna transfer some belongings to Trixie's. On a second visit, the room looked smaller, and Roland went quiet when he tried to squeeze in with her boxes. Lorna told herself she would not be spending all her time there. Trixie said they'd have to come to some agreement about the television.

A local businessman who ran a hairdressing salon and a domino club picked up members of the congregation from their homes in his Shogun van. The lift was intended for the elderly and infirm, but many younger women like Mrs Stephens used it to avoid dirtying their freshly washed or dry-cleaned sparkling white outfits on public transport or the smut of the Camberwell New Road.

The women's clothes were the very best that Debenhams or C & A could provide, or had been run up by home dressmakers. The men, whom the women outnumbered ten to one, wore jazzily designed ties.

The children under ten, who had been at Sunday school for half an hour, were now penned inside rows of chairs, the boys in miniature blazers with gold buttons, and white shirts with bow ties, the girls in party dresses with ribbons in their braided hair. They were more interested in each other and the toys which their mothers hid in plastic bags than in following the service. Mrs Stephens could remember how, in her childhood, she had spent the services looking through the open doors at the John Crows gliding in the blue sky. If she was good, she was given iced lemonade at the end of the service.

As she sat down, she took in the hats of the other women in the row. One was wearing a red wide-brimmed soft felt hat, the second a black pillbox with a sprig of lace, and the third a straw creation with plastic cherries. Mrs Stephens had seen it in the milliner's in Brixton market, but had rejected it as too showy. Thinking of clothes, she didn't consider that Lorna had been particularly smart, but at least the girl had looked clean and tidy.

The visiting preacher stood in front of a banner placed over a First World War memorial; it read *He that overcometh*. He unbuttoned his waistcoat and fiddled with the gold Parker pen in his top pocket. He was renowned as a healer.

Worshippers were invited to kneel beside the rail, where he would lay his hands on their heads. 'Our Father, we present Your people kneeling at Your

altar. They have come to You with a variety of needs
– and indeed, we serve a God Who can meet all of our
needs whether they be social, religious, or personal.
We present our people kneeling before You. We present
every distress in the Name of Jesus. We command
healing in the Name of Jesus!'

'Yes! Yes! Amen! Amen!' shouted the congregation.
Old ladies and youths held up their hands in
celebration of perceived freedom. The children gazed
open-mouthed as at a conjurer. An arthritic woman
claimed to be able to walk without her frame.

The preacher continued, 'Jesus, grant Your release
to those who pray for it. Release power. Release joy.
Release knowledge.'

In her time Mrs Stephens had heard the dumb
speak and seen the lame walk, but she herself had
never needed this manifest physical contact to be
healed. It was the feeling of closeness with her
neighbours which sometimes transformed her. Could
she share this closeness with Mr Langley? She didn't
think he'd stay with her permanently after all these
years, but he'd never abandoned her entirely. And
what was Roland playing at, with this white girl? But
that was young people these days. If she made too
much fuss, he'd become as stubborn as his brother.

On Monday evening, when he called in at his mother's,
Roland discovered that although Mr Langley was out,
he had been sleeping there for a fortnight. He wasn't
sure if he'd progressed beyond the sofa, but this
prolonged stay was unprecedented.

It seemed Weston had just told his mother that
either his father went, or he would, and as he was

paying her more than the economic rent, and his father nothing, he didn't imagine her choice would be difficult.

'No respect,' grieved Mrs Stephens.

'But Mums,' said Roland, finding himself defending Weston against his will, 'you've always said his father was no good. You don't want him stopping.' His world was shifting, if his mother could accommodate a man she had dismissed for years as a godless gambler. At twenty-five he could not understand that despite her complaints and sermons she might still crave the spice which Mr Langley presented. But this might be why she had not protested more about Lorna. She was preoccupied.

When Mr Langley returned with a six-pack, he wanted to argue but his son would not talk to him. Instead, Weston resumed his attack on Lorna. 'What can she know about black culture?'

Roland had determined to say no more. 'She can read, if she wants to.'

'Not very well, or she wouldn't need evening classes. But what I really don't understand is, Roland, don't you yearn to be at one with a black woman?'

'I yearn to be at one with a woman. It's her I like, not her colour.'

'You can't escape colour.'

Oblivious of the rant, Mr Langley sat marking possible winners in the *Sporting Life* with one of Weston's high-lighters.

Weston continued, 'Isn't she just after a touch of black prick?'

'You're the prick.'

'How you know she's not sleeping around?'

'How does anyone know? In the end, you have to trust people.'

'Yes, but if a white woman does the dirty, that's the ultimate insult.'

Roland exploded. 'Crap! You're the insult. Anyway, I've told you, I'm not arguing. So why are we having this argument? What gives you the right to be Mr High and Mighty?'

'You know the song. If my brother's in trouble, so am I.'

'I'm not in trouble, but you are. They should hold a contest for warped minds. You'd win hands down.' He got up, walked over to his brother, pulled him from the chair and made him stand squarely in front of him. Mr Langley did not even blink. 'Weston,' he concluded, 'we used to deal straight. Let me tell you, I'm dealing no more. Keep your remarks to your business. Not my business. Not this girl. *Not Lorna*. Clear? If you cayn say something positive, shut yuh mout.'

Mr Langley still did not raise his eyes, but declared, 'Roley, you're right. Weston, you're a damn fool. A man should seek bups where he can.'

That week, Lorna hoped to find Wednesday evening a refuge. She felt that if she had stayed in, her mother would have somehow found a crate to pack her in, too. Rob read some poems by Wordsworth, which had jolted him when he first read them as an undergraduate on a fell-walking holiday. As the traffic snarled outside on the Stockwell Road, he hoped to stimulate similar reactions in the class. The poor standard of the photocopying and the class's inexperience of solitude worked against him.

'Wordsworth felt a sense of something almost physical stalking the hills,' he said desperately.

'It's a good job he lived in the country,' cried an old age pensioner, a newcomer with a streaming cold. 'If he'd gone out late on his own round here, he wouldn't have come home with poems.'

'He think Nature is kind and gentle,' said Laverne. 'All sheep and waterfall, but in Jamaica it's not like that. It's storm and hurricane.'

Darren looked up from his magazine. 'That last hurricane messed up the all-night fishing in the Wandle.'

'That wasn't a hurricane,' said Esther.

'Well, I couldn't sleep,' said the pensioner, sneezing.

Lorna avoided catching the glint in Roland's eye, though she was glad to glimpse it again. Since Sunday she had thought that, as with Wordsworth, something unspoken was troubling him. They had spent so much time and energy lately dealing with their families, that there hadn't been time to talk about themselves. This week everything had been a rush.

'They say we won't ever have natural weather again,' said Sean.

Uncertain of any direction he wished the discussion to take, Rob let it wander where it would, like a sheep on the fells. On her plastic seat, Lorna shifted uneasily. She tried to concentrate, but it was hard to focus.

Among the anecdotes, Albert announced that it was his birthday, and he was going for a rum afterwards and folks should join him. At nine, half the class accepted his invitation.

* * *

If the pub Albert chose had any theme, it was solitary drunken men. The publican looked hostile as the women bunched tables and chairs together and ordered Cokes individually. Roland bought a round of rums for the men.

Lorna grew discontented when Roland stayed talking with Rob, Sean and Albert, and then sat down with them. She was invited to squeeze between Cynthia and Yvonne. She had wondered what the other women thought of her affair, if they considered it at all. They had not given her a cold shoulder, not even Cynthia, whom she had considered a rival, and if there was a sense of holding back, it was probably because being in a pub in a group like this was so artificial. In a strange way it was easier to talk in the classroom.

If she had dared, Lorna would have liked to have talked about Roland, to hear what the women thought of him, but this could not be. She tried to be interested in the number of essays they had each completed and those which Rob still had to mark. Yvonne, who had lapped up all Rob's literary terms, disagreed with Cynthia about 'transactional writing'. Lorna tried to follow brightly, and keep an eye on Roland. From where she sat, she once again strained to catch his jokes. Since he had told her that before they met he found it easier to say serious things to strangers, she was tantalised now as he continued to talk, and his listeners fell quiet. What was he talking about? What did men say to other men? Surely he wasn't talking about her?

He had been on his own until now. Was he, after all, worried about commitment? She scolded herself that as usual she was panicking unnecessarily. Where was last week's newfound confidence? Where was her determination? Why was it so difficult to cast off old habits of thinking? Just once or twice this week she'd resented the fact that she needed him so much.

Albert banged his hands on the table as if he had a winning hand in dominoes. Sean shrieked his high-pitched giggle. Rob beamed. What was Roland saying that was so amusing? In an effort of will, Lorna told herself it was probably newspaper gossip about Arsenal.

The women looked on, some critically, some indulgently. Only Yvonne was concerned about why, when it had taken her ten hours, Rob had merely given her eighteen out of forty for her last essay.

10

The pursuit of happiness

Rose did not know if the council had reallocated the house to blacks, like the neighbours said, but even though in the past few years Lorna had done the cleaning at home, she would never live with herself if she didn't leave it spotless. On the night before the move she had planned to check everywhere for the last time and be finished before *Prisoner: Cell Block H* – the television would be packed last – but she was visited in turn by Diane, an insurance salesman, two Jehovah's Witnesses, and five neighbours. Through all their talk she was itching for them to go. She was sure that next door still had a key, and would be back tomorrow, snooping to see if anything was worth taking. Sometimes when she'd returned from Lydd at weekends in the summer she'd had a feeling her bits had been shifted.

Lorna had been to Trixie's for the keys, and for a drink with Roland. Her mother was grumpy that she had stopped out late. As she stepped in the hall, Rose handed her the Hoover. Lorna was peeved, but did not protest.

Normally sparing with cleaning material, Rose used so much cream on the bath it was a wonder any enamel remained; the next occupier could look forward to weeks of chalky bathing. She poured half a bottle of Domestos down the toilet and smeared the double-glazing with lashings of Windolene. Then, her bottles empty, perching on a chair, she dusted the naked lamp-bulbs and ran a damp cloth over the insides of the fitted cupboards. She even sent Lorna into the loft to check if Fred had left anything there deliberately. Finally, Fred had gone to bed to seek distraction in the radio phone-ins and dedications which would soon be beyond his reception area.

He did not sleep, but was up before dawn. He ran a bath, which caused the first row of the day. Then he cooked a fry-up with some eggs and bacon he had secreted in the shed, covering the cooker with a fresh patina of grease. When she saw the mess, Rose regretted she had been so liberal with the cleanser. She wished he would go away from under her feet.

Fred had asked for the van to be outside on the dot at nine. Rose had said all along that that was not early enough. As she washed up, she repeated several times that they should have got away before the roads got crowded. When the van had not arrived at half-past nine, they were all twitching.

Fred's particular mate had fallen sick and fielded two substitutes who arrived at a quarter to ten. Somehow within an hour everything was packed, with only one lampstand buckled. The driver had once been to Dymchurch for the day, so thought he knew the way. Fred hastily drew a map on the inside of a cigarette packet.

Once everything had been removed, Lorna had intended to walk round the house, visiting the empty rooms, stroking the doors and windowsills, like the woman in the *Imagine* video, remembering only the happy hours, but now she just wanted to go. She could imagine how her parents felt, but tried not to. Her mind was, of course, also on Roland. Last night she too had drawn a series of maps of Kent for him on various beermats.

Fortunately, some neighbours and the men from the parts shop arrived to create a noisy send-off, and between kisses and jokes, Fred locked the door for the last time, and they climbed into the Cortina. Once she was settled, Rose kept patting her handbag and the plastic bags and duvets she had arranged around her as ballast until Fred drove off to the neighbours' cheers.

They made their way in silence towards the motorways. Lorna wondered if Roland would be able to follow the route tomorrow. Would he lose the beermats? Would his car make it? As far as she could tell, he rarely went into the country.

Last night he'd been very quiet at Trixie's. Then, in the pub, just as they were leaving, he said there was something they must talk about. While she breathed deeply, he'd said it could wait though, until Saturday, as with the moving she had enough on her mind. It wasn't anything to worry about.

Why had he left it until late to say that? Had Weston been right about other women? Was he teasing her on purpose? As the car sped on and her mind raced wildly, she felt sick with motion and emotion, being squeezed into the back seat, and having eaten no breakfast.

When they arrived at the bungalow, there was no lorry parked outside. Fred told Rose not to panic. It was a good sign. You didn't pay them to speed.

They had to hand over a cheque and collect the keys from Wray & Nephew, the estate agents on the seafront. Mr Wray was showing a renovated Martello tower for a possible company let and would not be back for an hour, they were told, and the nephew was at lunch. There were no other instructions. In her calmest shop voice Lorna said this was unacceptable. She was surprised that London arrogance had spread this far. How could they treat people like this? They knew her parents were coming today; they should have made arrangements. Her complaints were met only with a professional smile and apologies.

They sat next to the scorched parlour palms drinking complimentary coffee, flicking through leaflets of recently released coastal properties. Lorna looked out to sea and wondered. She knew that today in some sense she was being released. Was it the start of her independence? When she needed real support, how much could she rely on Roland? She watched the seagulls circling.

Apart in distance for the first time, she felt suddenly that for all their talking, she and Roland hardly knew each other. So far, whenever they had met, they had been more or less on their best behaviour. Except for after the Dogs, he had not seen her grumpy and discontented, and she sensed that, like his brother, he could be sullen and moody. They had not really tested one another to see what they could get away with.

When the Duggans had been allowed the keys, they set off to the bungalow again. As they were driving along the seafront Lorna spotted a black man among the few pedestrians. Even though he was bowling against the wind, the stance and movements were familiar. Had Roland taken the day off as well? It would be like him to surprise her. So *this* was what he hadn't said in the pub! She was about to call out to her father to stop, but as they passed, she saw she was mistaken. She was glad she had kept silent and blushed unnoticed.

As they drew up outside their bungalow, the curtains twitched again in 'Quiet Mornings', 'Channel View' and 'Green Shutters'. (Her father had said that theirs should be called 'DunMoanin'.) The van still wasn't there. Lorna looked up and down the street to see if it had parked outside a wrong number.

Downhearted, they pushed the front door open, only to find sarcastic cards from the Electricity and Gas Boards saying they had called to read the meters as arranged.

They had no appetite, but Rose said they must have some food inside them. Would Lorna please fetch the plastic bag in the boot of the Cortina containing a Thermos, and some cheese and tomato sandwiches?

Lorna could only find a packet of digestives. Rose ripped this open angrily, and forced them to swallow the crumbling biscuits. She tried to smooth from her mind the missing lunch and van, and the strangeness of a kitchen she would have to make her own. She would have to do something about the windows. A miniature railway ran behind the garden fence. It didn't operate in the winter, but she'd get her nets up quickly. She didn't want anybody nosing in.

Lorna smelt the men's breath when the van arrived

half an hour later. She also saw her mother's empty bread bag and the undone Thermos. Furious, she intercepted the men as they went to speak to her parents, and ordered them to unload immediately.

When they had finished, seeing that her father was talking to a curious neighbour, she paid only what had been agreed, adding nothing 'for a drink' since, she told them, they had already eaten and drunk her mother's lunch in her father's time. As she treated them with the contempt they deserved, she trembled. It seemed easier to behave differently today, to be, as in the shop, in control – but it was still a strain, a performance.

When the van had gone, another neighbour, a retired bus conductress from Catford whom Fred had met on previous visits, delivered a casserole. After she had left Rose said to Fred suspiciously, 'It's nice of her, but I think I prefer my own cooking.'

'Don't be so bloody ungrateful.'

Lifting the lid of the stew and sniffing, Rose said, 'You don't know what she's put in it.' She poked it with a plastic knife and fished up a brown lump. 'I think that's celery. You don't put celery in casseroles. You don't even like celery.'

'Perhaps I'll start liking it.'

To Rose this seemed inconceivable.

'Well, do you like your new home anyway?' Fred asked, hugging her impetuously.

Lorna left the kitchen before she heard the answer. Her mother would find fault, she knew. It was what she enjoyed. She slipped on her coat and went outside. The converted prefabs and the railway carriages, the electricity wires and the telegraph poles sometimes made her think Lydd was like some deserted town in an American film, but she did envy her parents the sea at the end of the road.

There were three bungalows between theirs and the beach. The first had a tiny caravan in the garden, the second was ornamented with driftwood half-timbering and shells, while the third displayed a crumbling collection of colourless gnomes. She'd been right. If she'd moved here too, that's what she'd have become like.

She crossed the road, found a path through the pebbles and looked towards the power station at Dungeness. For once, its bulk and the dusk did not depress her. Her parents had made their choice. Though Lydd seemed the edge of the world, at their age its pace and wide skies were surely more pleasant than Camberwell.

But she knew that Camberwell, or more precisely, Brixton and Stockwell, were where she wanted to be. She trod the pebbles and the shingle until she realised that the foam was soaking her shoes.

'You should have heard her,' said Fred proudly the next morning as he showed Roland round the bungalow. 'She really coated that estate agent.'

'I didn't, Dad.'

'And the removal men. She didn't half give them what for.'

'She won't stand for any nonsense,' said Roland.

'You'd better watch out,' Fred smiled, looking at Lorna admiringly.

Roland had arrived, beaming, at ten o'clock. A drive along the M20 to the unclassified roads of Lydd is not an intrepid journey, but he was triumphant.

'I heard about her maps,' said Fred. 'Could you follow them?'

'They were good. I only drove round in circles once I got here. In the end I stopped and asked.'

'People friendly?' asked Fred anxiously.

'Yes,' said Roland, 'until they saw me waving beermats.'

'They have more time down here,' Fred assured himself.

Rose had gone to return next door's casserole. She didn't want that woman popping in while they were unpacking. When her mother reappeared, Lorna said to Roland it would be best if they left her parents to themselves for a while.

Roland could tell Lorna was anxious to have him to herself. He did not tantalise her long, only until the end of the road. He had been thinking of his notion for some time, and considering when to suggest it. He wondered what Lorna might think of his motives. It was obvious she couldn't stay at Trixie's. That room was too small; you might be able to sleep there, but you couldn't relax.

Whenever the jazz had faded from his transistor on the passenger seat as he had driven down, he had rehearsed his remaining doubts. If he were about to end his solitary state, he wondered if perhaps he didn't relish it after all.

It was difficult to let somebody know you, but in this respect Lorna was as reserved as he was. If they lived together, she would let him reveal as much as he wanted to, and at his own pace. It was this tact he treasured. In the past, girlfriends had tried to peel him bare, and he had always acted a part. Perhaps with Lorna he could be more himself . . .

They crossed to the beach. He could see that his plan had struck Lorna like a sudden drenching. She seemed at a loss for words. She might have hoped this would happen, he supposed, but would not have forced his hand.

They sat on a wooden bench erected in memory of a couple who had loved this seaside walk. She had gone quiet. He put his arm round her. After a moment she said, 'Isn't this rushing things a bit?'

This was a shock. Was she not as eager as he'd hoped? Had he read her wrong? He had thought she'd be delighted. 'What do you mean?'

'I don't know,' she said slowly. 'It's hard to say.'

He squeezed her hand. 'Try.'

'Yesterday I felt, I don't know, sort of free.'

'Well, my flat's not a prison.'

'Yes, but perhaps . . .' She searched for words. 'Perhaps I need a breather.'

'How, exactly?'

'I'm not sure. I don't know. Time . . . Space . . .'

'There's no space at Trixie's. That's my point.'

'No, but . . .'

'Do you want to live in that poky room?'

'No. To tell the truth, I'm dreading it.'

'But you don't want to move in with me?'

'Roland,' she said slowly, 'you must know I'd like nothing more. I can't believe you're saying it so soon. But I just wonder, I don't know, if I'm ready – if *we're* ready.'

'I'm ready. You're ready.'

'I'm not sure. Sometimes I feel as if I've never grown up. I've always lived at home. I want to know if I can be different.'

'What do you mean, different?'

'Don't I need, you know, some time on my own?'

'In that cupboard? It's not big enough for a parrot.'

'But for a while, Roland.'

'Move in tonight. What's stopping you?'

'You're not listening.'

'Have you gone off me all of a sudden?'

'No, of course not.'

'Are you sure?'

'No, I told you, I can't believe my luck.'

'So what's holding you back? Your parents? Don't you care too much what they think?'

'I'm trying not to, so much.'

'Good. So what's your problem?'

She hesitated. 'It all seems so perfect.'

'It soon won't be. A day or two with me and you'll be battering on Trixie's door.'

'Shouldn't I live there? Just for a bit?'

'Look, Lorna,' he said tenderly, 'in the long run you have to decide what you want. Not what you ought to do.' He thought of Weston. 'Not what other people tell you.'

'Does that include you, Roland?'

'Yes, it does.'

'And you're not just asking because you feel sorry for me?'

'Is my flat a refuge for homeless women? I don't think so.'

'And we'll still go out even if I don't move in?'

He bit his lip. 'Yes, of course.'
'Without a doubt?'
'Without a doubt.'

Roland decided to speak to Lorna's parents himself, on his own. After protests, Lorna agreed. Roland respected her father. Though he judged Mr Duggan would not necessarily approve, it mattered that he should also respect their decision. Roland did not want him thinking he was forcing Lorna to act against her will when her guard was down.

As Roland spoke, he could not gauge Mr Duggan's reaction. When it came to it, he did not find it easy to be forceful or persuasive, and Mr Duggan seemed taken aback. He hoped it was because fathers were always more protective of their daughters. And also, as a white man of his age, he would think you should marry before you lived together.

As his explanation tailed off, Mr Duggan kept silent. He could hear the clocks ticking in their unaccustomed positions, his wife banging cupboard doors in one of the bedrooms, and Lorna treading the gravel outside. After some time he replied, 'I'm not sure, son. You young people seem to want to rush into everything nowadays. It's not how we used to live.'

Since Roland did not know what further expression or comment might help, he shifted uncomfortably in his chair. But, though obviously vexed, Mr Duggan was not shouting. That, at least, was encouraging.

After a pause, Mr Duggan continued: 'If I'd moved in with her mother, there'd have been hell. We didn't act like that. You two want things handed on a plate.' He spoke in this vein for a while, then, after falling silent again, rose from his chair and switched on the television. A rugby match came into focus. He watched an undignified scrum, then switched it off as suddenly as he had turned it on. 'Not that I like the thought of her living with that woman.'

Roland relaxed. Was this a hint of a blessing? He sensed Mr Duggan at least appreciated being told.

'You two have got your own ideas.'

Roland smiled gratefully and hugged him.

Mr Duggan sniffed. 'You just be bloody careful.'

Roland was supposed to summon Lorna in from the garden before he spoke to Mrs Duggan, but to start with at least, he wanted to be with Rose on his own. She would be harder work. It is not easy to talk to someone who barely acknowledges your existence. But, if he wanted good, his nose would have to run.

Mrs Duggan was washing some glasses in the kitchen. He could sense she felt uneasy. As casually as he could he described his plan, but felt as if he were addressing the fridge, the cooker, and the sink.

Mrs Duggan slammed the glasses down, but did not turn her back. Finally she spoke. 'It's all the same thing, isn't it?'

Roland was not yet used to these gnomic pronouncements. He wondered what he could say that would make it easier.

She continued to stare through the net curtain at the privet. 'What does she say then?'

'It's what she wants.'

Mrs Duggan hung up the tea towel. 'Well, that's that.'

'She's happy about it.'

'She'll soon start fretting.' She was talking to the pedal bins. 'She needs her family near her. Girls do. She's a softie. She won't be able to cope without her dad.'

'She'll learn. She likes London.'

Mrs Duggan turned to face Roland for the first time, though their eyes still did not meet. 'And I suppose you think that's your doing?'

'No, I don't.'

'I'm glad to hear it.'

Roland coughed. 'You should be proud of yourself.'

'Eh?'

'You've brought her up to be happy in London. To stand on her own two feet.'

She raised her eyes. Roland recognised their sudden sparkle. He leant over. He could sense her heart beating as wildly as the pigeon which had flown unawares into his bathroom, and had panicked as he tried to free it. He dared a quick kiss. She did not flinch, but stared in amazement, then turned and twitched the hastily erected net. 'What is that girl doing out there?'

Roland and Lorna left the bungalow at seven that evening. On the doorstep Lorna promised her parents to return when she had another Saturday off, in a fortnight's time. Roland nodded enthusiastically, and said he would drive her.

'Next time,' said Fred, 'make it a long weekend. Come Friday night. Stay for Sunday dinner.'

Lorna avoided her mother's face. The spare bedroom had two single beds, but she did not know if Roland would be allowed there. Should he fetch a sleeping bag?

Her father led Roland down the path to let him admire the well-preserved Cortina. Trying to leave without bitterness, she turned to her mother again. 'A fortnight's time, then?'

'Your dad can always fetch you.'

Lorna looked at Roland and her father walking round their cars. 'Roland likes it down here,' she said. 'He gets on well with Dad.' She bit her tongue, then added hurriedly. 'He likes you too, Mum.'

'Um.'

'The tea was nice, Mum.'

'Salad? Same as normal,' her mother answered blankly.

'I'm sure you'll like it down here.'

'We'll have to see.'

Rose still looked edgy. As she gave her a kiss, Lorna was sure her mother was holding back tears.

Later that evening, Rose and Fred went out to the drinking club they had been members of since they bought their first caravan. Fred was nicer to Rose than he had been for ages. Rose listened to the complaints of some of the regulars about sons and daughters who were a disappointment and hadn't turned out as their mothers wished, but for once kept silent herself.

On the return journey, Lorna tried to entertain Roland with stories about herself and Diane in their early teens flirting with local boys on the beach. She made Roland chuckle, but sensed he too was turning things over. Falling silent, she switched on his transistor, then nearly blinded him with the aerial as she moved

302

the set searching for the best reception. She found a Kentish phone-in about DIY which she knew her father would soon discover.

On this same evening, Weston was lecturing Marcia in the rum bar. Next week they were both to be interviewed by an African-American hair care company for executive sales positions. 'It's a perfect opportunity for revenue enhancement,' he said, shifting in the wickerwork chair, stirring his non-alcoholic pina colada. 'To succeed in business, you have to read people carefully. It's an art I've acquired.'

The motorway exit signs, bridges, Little Chefs and Happy Eaters flew by. Without Roland's plan Lorna would have felt lonely and miserable travelling back. Instead she was mostly cosy and secure, except when, like the hypnotic lights from the opposite lanes, unanswered questions dazzled her brain.

Sherene had made a pattern with her crushed duck, chopped cucumber, and Soy sauce. Having sorted out Roland's life, and told off Weston, she had today ditched the potato-seller and gone for a Chinese meal with some colleagues from work to celebrate. She was still wondering why Weston resented Lorna with such passion. She outlined the problem to her companions. The thing was, she said, that this Lorna showed Weston up, and Roland to be right. The colleagues, who had heard much about the brothers, tried to stay attentive. This Lorna, Sherene continued, had shown Weston it didn't matter that his brother didn't lust after clothes, jewellery or cars.

The office junior agreed. 'Those things can't hold you while you sleep,' she said sadly, 'or whisper love when you need it.'

'Sister,' said Sherene, 'Roland is right, but you're talking sugar.'

They had left the motorway and were now on the South Circular Road. The radio was picking up dance stations baying for a Saturday night audience. Lorna felt a tingle of delight when Roland stroked her knee. 'OK?'

'Yes,' she said, switching off the radio. 'Things going through my mind.'

'I bet.'

'Sometimes,' she said, unsure if this were a good thing to say, 'when I'm happy, I feel guilty.'

'Don't be daft.'

Beside their swimming pool, Diane was sipping a large gin and tonic. An elderly Spanish gardener was removing leaves from the pool with a pointed fishing net.

'This is the life,' said Barry, stretching out on his sunbed.

'If you say so,' said Diane, pulling on a cardigan, and noting she had cracked a nail.

After another mile, Roland said, 'The Americans wrote it in their Constitution.'

'What?'

'Happiness.'

'Did they really?'

'Yes – life, liberty, and the pursuit of happiness.'

'We'll do that, won't we?'

'What's that?'

'Pursue happiness.'

'We'll try,' he said, drawing up at a red light.

'It spreads, you know, happiness.'

'Lorna, are you on something?' he joked, waiting for the lights to change.

'No, I've just been thinking.'

'Very dangerous.'

In Stockwell, Mrs Stephens was frying onions, pepper and thyme. Mr Langley had always liked her grandmother's recipe for ackee and saltfish. The pungent smell filled the house. She had stopped worrying if his stay would be permanent, but was not attending one of the church services tomorrow.

After another mile, they joined a queue of traffic before some roadworks at New Cross.

'You can't count on it all the time,' said Lorna.

'What? A clear road?'

'No, happiness.'

'I know that,' Roland said, turning to her. 'Believe me.'

Lorna believed him. Though she'd only known him six weeks and three days, she knew he was telling the truth.

In front of the television, Rob was annotating *The Life of Mary Seacole*. Cynthia had complained that his extracts in class were always white, British, and male. So far he was not convinced he would change his selections.

* * *

'Roland,' Lorna said, conscious he must be tired, 'what made you join the evening class?'

'Itchy feet,' he said. 'I was fed up. Everything seemed routine. I thought it would help. And they said at work I'd need to improve my writing if I wanted promotion.'

'That's what they told me.'

'But that's not the only reason.'

'No?'

'No, I was looking for something.'

'And you got me.'

'Weston said night schools were pick-up joints.'

'Well, he was right, wasn't he?'

'For once, yes.'

'And now we're like, together,' asked Lorna, 'we won't become fossils, will we?'

'What do you mean?'

'You know – stop asking questions.'

'Only when Arsenal's on the box.'

Roland drove up the Camberwell New Road, past the bus garage with the inspectors joyfully rescheduling the evening timetables, past the Greek Metropolitan Cathedral, where the priest was hearing confessions and learning nothing new, past the petrol station with the Astroturf, past the end of Lorna's street.

She had fallen silent again. It must be odd for her, returning to London, and not going to Station Road. But she should know that the return was strange for him as well. Though he had weighed everything as scrupulously as the best market-traders, his happiness was still in the balance, like Arsenal's prospects in the past. With his track record, he might be alone again by Christmas. But as he braked fiercely by The Clarendon, he told himself that if Lorna's parents had managed to stay together for so long, there was hope for everyone.

A posse of children had dashed across the traffic, bowling a plastic dustbin lid as a hoop. A light-skinned little girl of about eight grinned at him, inches from the bumper. Lorna sucked her teeth. It was one black habit he must cure her of.

No child of his would wander the streets like that. But he wouldn't worry about such responsibilities just yet. Now that the good times had started, they could roll a bit longer. First he'd have to get used again to a bathroom crammed with creams and soaps and shampoos before he admitted nappies and plastic ducks. And he'd change his car, take holidays – even go to Jamaica again. Perhaps he'd patronise one of those shops along Acre Lane that offered cheap flights to the Caribbean in the hurricane season.

Outside Trixie's he unlocked his seat-belt and leapt from the car, crushing a McDonald's carton with his trainers. Trixie was out, so they took Lorna's belongings, scribbled a note, and left the key.

Lorna was relieved that no more explanations were needed that evening. She would call round in the morning.

On the way to Stockwell, she became talkative again. 'Roland, will you still have itchy feet?'

'Excuse me?'

'When I move in, I mean.'

He considered for a while. 'Well, you can buy a good

cream in Boots. For itchy feet.'

Lorna looked puzzled for a moment, then beamed. He might be winding her up, but he was taking her with him. 'You're getting worse than me.'

'The thing is, Miss Duggan, you have to keep applying the treatment for some time, even though the infection seems to have cleared up.'

'We'll have to be careful, then.'

'I don't think so. I'm tired of being careful.'

The transistor was burbling on Lorna's lap. *'Listen up!'* it ordered unheeded. *'Listen up to the vibe! A big request goes out to the Camberwell massive. Also not forgetting to big up Roland and his ladyfriend cruising in the Stockwell region. That's coming from Sherene. Nuff Respect!'*

In Roland's block the youths in the stairwell disrespected them again when they entered, but for once the lift was working. It climbed slowly. Her suitcases, plastic bags and boxes were squashed between them, but Roland took the opportunity to lean over and kiss Lorna until the doors opened at the top.

TWO FOR JOY

A PERCEPTIVE NOVEL OF CONTEMPORARY FAMILY LIFE

AVRIL CAVELL

Avril Cavell casts an amused and occasionally rueful eye over the vagaries of family life in this engaging and absorbing novel.

'Twins, how lovely! Aren't you lucky?'

Delphine Dobson isn't so sure. Premature baby girls seem like double the trouble to her; and double the expense too – no joke when your husband is an actor long on charm but short of regular work.

And indeed life with identical twins proves tricky. Clover and Merrie are telepathically close and the best of friends until they are accidentally separated. When the longed-for reunion comes, the close and delicate balance of their relationship has changed. With the looks of angels and the temperaments of fiends, they chart the stormy waters of adolescence, bringing alternate despair and delight to their family. Until, eventually, they reconcile the pleasures and pains of their unique relationship in a surprising and satisfying way.

FICTION / GENERAL 0 7472 4324 7

Joanna McDonald

ISLAND GAMES

EVERYTHING YOU THINK YOU WANT IS

YOURS — AT A PRICE

Nell McLean couldn't be less like her twin brother
Tally. He is tall and slim with predatory sex appeal,
while she has put pasta before passion and
developed into dress size 'large'. He has a series of
glamorous, gossip-column girlfriends while she has
lots of good friends for platonic gossip. Neither is
content.

The twin turning point comes when Tally tires of
girls who dine on herbal tea and vitamin C and Nell
gets sick of watching other people dieting at her
dinner parties. They quit the capital and answer the
call of their Scottish roots, turning a dilapidated
castle on a beautiful Hebridean island into a low-
fat, high-luxury haven for exhausted jet-setters and
tired tycoons. An island paradise to revive the most
jaded of appetites — and not only for healthy
foods . . .

Just as the visiting guests succumb to the sensual
charm of Taliska so it works its magic on the twins,
giving each of them what they think they most
desire. Tally finds true love with an appetite and
Nell finds sex and a sylph-like figure — but at what
cost to each?

With wry humour and bittersweet accuracy,
ISLAND GAMES is for anyone who ever laughed,
loved or wanted to be someone else.

FICTION / GENERAL 0 7472 4546 0

Martina Cole

GOODNIGHT LADY

SHE KNOWS EVERYONE'S SECRETS . . .

The infamous Briony Cavanagh: quite a beauty in her day, and powerful, too. In the sixties, she ran a string of the most notorious brothels in the East End. Patronised by peers and politicians – even royalty, some said. Only Briony knew what went on behind those thick velvet curtains, those discreet closed doors, and Briony never opened her mouth – unless she stood to benefit.

Only Briony knew the hard and painful road she'd travelled to get there. From an impoverished childhood that ended abruptly with shocking betrayal, she had schemed and manipulated, determined to be mistress of her own fate.

But her flourishing business brought her into contact with the darker side of life at the violent heart of London's gangland. Along with her material success came risk and danger. And the Goodnight Lady had her own secret place, a place in her heart that was always shadowed with loss . . .

'Move over Jackie [Collins]!' *Daily Mirror*

'Sheer escapism . . . gripping . . . will definitely keep you guessing to the end' *Company*

'Graphic realism combined with dramatic flair make this a winner' Netta Martin, *Annabel*

FICTION / GENERAL 0 7472 4429 4

A Selection of bestsellers from Headline

THE CHANGING ROOM	Margaret Bond	£5.99	☐
BACKSTREET CHILD	Harry Bowling	£5.99	☐
A HIDDEN BEAUTY	Tessa Barclay	£5.99	☐
A HANDFUL OF HAPPINESS	Evelyn Hood	£5.99	☐
THE SCENT OF MAY	Sue Sully	£5.99	☐
HEARTSEASE	T R Wilson	£5.99	☐
NOBODY'S DARLING	Josephine Cox	£5.99	☐
A CHILD OF SECRETS	Mary Mackie	£5.99	☐
WHITECHAPEL GIRL	Gilda O'Neill	£5.99	☐
BID TIME RETURN	Donna Baker	£5.99	☐
THE LADIES OF BEVERLEY HILLS	Sharleen Cooper Cohen	£5.99	☐
THE OLD GIRL NETWORK	Catherine Alliott	£4.99	☐

All Headline books are available at your local bookshop or newsagent, or can be ordered direct from the publisher. Just tick the titles you want and fill in the form below. Prices and availability subject to change without notice.

Headline Book Publishing, Cash Sales Department, Bookpoint, 39 Milton Park, Abingdon, OXON, OX14 4TD, UK. If you have a credit card you may order by telephone – 01235 400400.

Please enclose a cheque or postal order made payable to Bookpoint Ltd to the value of the cover price and allow the following for postage and packing:

UK & BFPO: £1.00 for the first book, 50p for the second book and 30p for each additional book ordered up to a maximum charge of £3.00.

OVERSEAS & EIRE: £2.00 for the first book, £1.00 for the second book and 50p for each additional book.

Name ....

Address ....

....

....

If you would prefer to pay by credit card, please complete:
Please debit my Visa/Access/Diner's Card/American Express (delete as applicable) card no:

Signature .... Expiry Date ....